ERASED

Robbi McCoy

BELLA
B O O K S

2017

Bella Books, Inc.
P.O. Box 10543
Tallahassee, FL 32302

Printed in the United States of America on acid-free paper.

First Bella Books Edition 2017

Editor: Medora MacDougall
Cover Designer: Judith Fellows

ISBN: 978-1-59493-554-1

Other Bella Books by Robbi McCoy

Acknowledgments

With love and gratitude, I thank my incredible partner Dot for her enthusiastic support and continued interest in my writing. Like me, she is a great fan of science fiction, time travel in particular, and her insights into this story were invaluable. To Grace, thank you so much for giving your time and effort to improving this story, and thank you also for being a devoted reader and friend over the years. To Medora, my dogged editor, thank you for saving me from several embarrassing inconsistencies and for having the patience to delve into the brutally convoluted nature of time travel. Being an editor is hard enough work without the addition of warped space-time.

With my first effort at science fiction, I must mention that colossus of the genre, *Star Trek*. I've been there from the beginning and through all of its incarnations on television and at the movies. This series had much to do with my interest from an early age in astronomy, quantum physics and, of course, temporal mechanics. The time travel episodes were always my favorites. Just the other day I rewatched the last episode of TNG where Q takes Picard four billion years into the Earth's past to witness the first spark of life arising from the primordial ooze and "nothing happened," wiping out all life forms that would ever have evolved on the planet in that one alternate timeline moment. It gave me chills, as all time travel stories should. Time travel fiction is an opportunity to live out our most impossible dreams, allowing us to change the past and participate in the future. What could be more fascinating?

About the Author

Robbi McCoy is a native Californian who lives with her life partner and cat in the Central Valley, equidistant between the mountains and the sea. She is an avid hiker with a particular fondness for the deserts of the American Southwest. She also enjoys gardening, culinary adventures, travel and the theater.

She is recently retired from her career as a software specialist and web designer and is enjoying a life of leisure with an occasional spurt of writing.

Dedication

To my grandmothers.

CHAPTER ONE

They were rolling with lights and sirens down Interstate 101 to the Peninsula. Dani drove. Agent Bryan manned the radio, summoning the force to the headquarters of Genepac Industries, a biotechnology research lab. Dani wasn't sure what the company did. Something to do with genetics and crops. She didn't care. She only cared that there might be a bomb about to go off in the building.

The freeway was choked with vehicles moving like sludge at an average of thirty miles per hour. Most of them were unable to move out of the way of the cruiser, but she kept a rapid pace by weaving through them. She rode the left shoulder as far as she could, hugging the concrete median barrier until the shoulder ran out, then she jockeyed over to the right shoulder and used that, dodging merging vehicles while Bryan stiffened and flinched in panic.

Gee, Dani thought, *what's this dude's problem? We haven't even had a near miss.*

"Confirmed," Bryan said into the radio. Then to Dani he said, "Everybody's out of the building. Evacuation complete."

He had a nervous but reassuring smile on his pale, clean-shaven face.

In his thirties, he still had a full head of dark brown hair, parted on the left to reveal one clean white slice of scalp. His sideburns were unfashionably long and reminded Dani of the old cop shows from the eighties that she watched in reruns.

"What time is it?" he asked, glancing around the car like he'd forgotten where the computer display was.

"Is that thing on your wrist just for show?"

Bryan glanced at his wristwatch and chuckled. "Oh, right. No, it's actually not…it's not a timepiece. It's…"

"Oh, like a Fitbit or something."

Bryan vaguely smiled.

Dani pointed to the monitor to remind him that he could check the time there. Then she swerved, sending them through a narrow channel across two lanes.

"Watch it!" Bryan shouted, nearly climbing out of his seat.

"Do you want to drive?"

"Oh, no, no, no!" He looked terrified at the idea. "You're doing a great job, Officer Barsetti. There's just so much traffic. It's unnerving."

"Friday traffic is the worst! Just be damned happy it's not rush hour."

She stole a brief glance at him, at his delicate features and slightly rumpled navy blue suit. She couldn't quite figure out Frank Bryan and she wasn't ready to trust him. There was something off about him. Even his way of speaking was odd in a way she couldn't place. Nope, she definitely wasn't going to trust him if he wasn't going to trust the SFPD by sharing his intel.

"We got no call," she said, bringing up a question she'd asked earlier. "No bomb threat. You never did tell us how you know something's going down today."

He shifted uncomfortably. "No, I didn't."

So that was it, huh, thought Dani resentfully. *That's the way the FBI wants to play it. We're supposed to put everything on the line for them and they don't tell us diddly.*

"This guy doesn't know we're onto him," Bryan said, "and I want to keep it that way."

In other words, Dani inferred, the FBI doesn't trust city cops. Bryan's body tensed as Dani abruptly changed lanes.

"Who is this guy anyway?" she asked. "This Leo Darius."

Bryan relaxed into his seat. "Environmental activist gone militant. He's on a one-man crusade to save the world from all those so-called conspiracies perpetrated against the common man by corporate America and the U. S. government. He thinks everything's being poisoned—air, drinking water, food supply. And it's all being hushed up."

"What about the EPA and FDA and all the agencies working to protect people from being poisoned?"

"He thinks they're all in on it too. A huge, worldwide cover-up. He's paranoid, out of his mind." He leaned over to read the clock on the computer again.

Dani made a mental note to tell all of this to Gemma. As a former FDA employee who very conscientiously had done her best to protect the public food supply, she'd be interested.

"Demonstrating peacefully wasn't cutting it," Bryan continued. "Nobody listening, no results. At least not fast enough. So now he's taking it up a notch. He wants to get some attention. This is his coming-out party, blowing up Genepac Industries."

"Why them?"

"Genetically modified organisms. Food crops in this case. GMOs are public enemy number one in his book. At least we got the staff out of the building before it blows. Saved some lives."

"You seem sure it's going to blow."

"Unless we can get to it first."

Once they hit Burlingame, they exited onto city streets and headed east. The facility was near the bay under a steady stream of airliners arriving at San Francisco Airport. A gleaming white Lufthansa jet seemed to hang motionless over the shallow south bay before banking to the left to approach the runway. Sunlight glinted off its cockpit window like a laser beam.

Bryan checked the computer clock again.

"Why do you keep checking the time?" Dani asked.

He shook his head. "No reason. Just a nervous habit, I guess."

"Darius didn't happen to say what time this bomb was going off, did he?"

"No, no, of course not." He laughed with an undercurrent of nervousness. "I wish he had."

Yeah, Bryan was keeping his secrets, she thought bitterly. She didn't like not knowing the score. Not having all the facts put officers in danger, and one thing the SFPD sure didn't need right now was another incident. Just yesterday they had said their formal good-byes to Art Martinez in a gut-wrenching ceremony during which Dani couldn't stifle the waterworks. She wasn't the only cop there with tears running down her cheeks. Art's wife Carla and his two little boys sat front and center, all three of them looking shell-shocked. Art never knew what hit him. He was shot in the back of the head on the street by a frizzed-up junkie who couldn't tell the difference between a cop taking a lunch break and one coming after him loaded for bear. Senseless. The day before, Martinez had slapped her on the back good-naturedly and laughed his peculiar honking chortle. Everybody liked him. One day he was goofing around at the station, and the next he was just nowhere. It could happen to any of them any day. Which is why Dani never wanted to walk out of the house in the morning without making sure Gemma felt loved. This job never let you forget you were mortal.

Three other black and whites were there when they arrived, SFPD units waiting for Bryan's orders. He had the lead on this one. There were also two fire trucks on site with a full complement of firefighters and a bomb squad. A group of civilians stood together a safe distance from the building, about a half dozen button-down shirts and khakis with a couple of conservative skirts thrown in. The evacuated staff of Genepac, Dani concluded.

An industrial building of metal, glass and concrete, two stories high, utilitarian and ugly, stood before them. Puffy white clouds were reflected in the top story windows. The scene was peaceful.

While Bryan went to talk to Sergeant Tyler, Dani briefly checked her phone. There was a message from Gemma. "I'll be late tonight. It's Mom again. I'll be at Palm Terrace after work unruffling some feathers. Can you pick up something for dinner? Love, G."

Not again. Dani shook her head. Gemma's mother Harriet was becoming a pro at ruffling feathers. Most of the time she was docile, but she had episodes when she couldn't remember where she was or why she wasn't home. That's when she got frightened, angry and sometimes violent, which Dani had to admit seemed like a reasonable response to losing one's mind. Palm Terrace was the third nursing home for Harriet. She'd been kicked out of the first one for a string of nasty incidents, the last one being when she'd bitten a nursing assistant. They had moved her out of the second place, River Gardens, because Gemma was in almost constant conflict with the staff and it had worn her out. The current place was pretty good so far and Harriet seemed to be adapting better to institutionalization. Dani hoped Gemma could fix it, whatever Harriet had done this time. Otherwise, they were going to run out of places in the city to keep her.

Dani walked over to Bryan and some of the other officers, including Sergeant Rhonda Tyler, one of Dani's buddies. She was in uniform, lean, tanned and freckled from the summer sun, her eyes hidden behind mirrored sunglasses.

"No sign of anybody," reported Tyler. "The place is dead. If he's here to watch his handiwork, he's well hidden."

Dani scanned the area, taking in parking garages, warehouses, storage units, sixties-era office buildings. Lots of industrial, no residential. Darius could be tucked inside any one of those buildings with a pair of binoculars, waiting for the fireworks.

The bomb squad was suited up and ready to go in with their dog, a relaxed-looking black German shepherd. If there was a bomb, they'd find it. Everybody else was ordered to stay well away from the building, so they all moved across the street. Tyler walked over to Dani with a freshly lit cigarette, then jerked her head toward the building and said, "Do you think there's a bomb in there, Barsetti?"

Dani shrugged. "Bryan seems pretty sure of it."

She blew smoke out of the side of her mouth, deliberately aiming away from Dani. "I wish he'd share some of that intel."

"He said Darius is protesting genetically modified food. He's some kind of an environmentalist gone militant."

"Yep, that's the story. Unfortunately, we're going to have to take his word for it. We've come up with nothing on Leo Darius. And I mean *nothing*. And Bryan says his sources are classified."

"Have you ever worked with him before?"

Tyler shook her head and knocked the ash off her cigarette. "No. Never heard of him before two days ago. He's an unknown entity. When we get back to the station, I think I'll ask around."

"Why? Is there a problem?"

"No. I just like to know who I'm working with." She smiled ironically. "I know that look, Barsetti. Don't worry, I'll be tactful." She frowned. "Look, I can be tactful."

"I didn't say a word," Dani objected, but to herself she admitted her doubt that Tyler could be tactful. It just wasn't in her. She had the discretion of a wolverine going after a squirrel.

"Your wife is in the food business, right?"

"Yeah. She's a nutritionist."

"What's her take on this GMO stuff?"

"She usually tells people they've been eating it for years. Eighty-eight percent of the corn and almost all of the soybeans grown in the U.S. are genetically modified. And you know those two grains are in everything. People who think they can avoid GMOs these days are fooling themselves. They'd have to grow all their own food to escape them."

"So it's not poison like these guys say?"

Dani shrugged. "I don't know, but I'll tell you what *is* poison." She nodded toward the cigarette in Tyler's hand.

Tyler scowled. "Can it, Barsetti!" She took a drag, then rubbed the cigarette into the dirt with her boot. "Damn, this waiting makes me jumpy." She shoved her hands in her pockets as another jumbo jet roared overhead.

Dani kicked absentmindedly at the gravel, tense and nervous. Like Tyler, she didn't like waiting and doing nothing, especially when there were lives on the line.

From across the street, Bryan's frantic voice reached them. "Get out! Get out!" he shrieked at the bomb squad. "It's too late! It's going to blow! Take cover!"

Bryan and the bomb sniffers in their heavy suits and helmets streamed out of the building and bolted across the street to safety.

"How does he know?" Tyler asked, her face scrunched up in anxiety and confusion.

She and Dani ducked behind one of the patrol cars. Two other officers joined them just as a deafening explosion rang out. Dani dropped to a prone position without a second thought as all of the second-floor windows blew out, raining glass over the strip of lawn in front of the building. Shards of glass pinged against the other side of the car. Then, except for the ringing in Dani's ears, there was silence. They held their positions for a couple of minutes more.

"Are you okay?" Dani asked Tyler, who lay beside her on the grass.

Tyler nodded.

Dani peered over the hood of the car. Black smoke billowed out of the pane-less windows, and within seconds flames were visible licking at the edges of the window frames on the second floor. The fire trucks pulled into position and the firefighters went into action pouring water through the upstairs windows, dousing the flames and sending up even more black smoke.

"Looks like he had it right," Tyler said, back on her feet. She brushed down her uniform. "Right down to the minute."

"Yeah," Dani agreed. "Too bad he didn't have that all figured out in time to stop it."

CHAPTER TWO

Gemma watched as Dani ran along the surf with Tucker at her heels, her long, tanned legs carrying her easily along the shore of Aquatic Park. Tucker barked with excitement, hopping around her feet, looking comical. His snout was a little longer and his ears more floppy than a purebred Boston Terrier, but his coloring was classic black and white. Dani thought he was part beagle. Gemma had no guess, as she knew very little about dog breeds. Nor did she care. Whatever he was, he was cute, sweet and happy, and he was their baby.

She leaned back in her seat at the foot of the bleachers, enjoying the autumn sunshine on her face. The bay was calm today and dotted with white sails beneath an uncompromising blue sky. Off to the west, just beginning to embrace the orange steel girders of the Golden Gate Bridge, the fog bank inched toward them.

Predictably, Tucker dashed into the surf, anxious to play fetch. Dani obliged him by pitching a rubber bone over his head. It bobbed on the water for two seconds before he nabbed it in his mouth and swam back, dropping it at Dani's feet. She tossed it out again, then wiped her hand on her sweatshirt and laughed when Tucker's overanxious lunge at the toy popped it out of the water and on top of his head. Dani glanced toward the bleachers to see if Gemma had been watching. She waved to let her know she was.

She turned her attention to the fishermen on the pier and the sailboats further out in the bay, acknowledging that she felt blissfully happy. How else could she possibly feel? She was a lucky woman, living in this beautiful city with the love of her life and working in a rewarding career. She thought of her mother, whose mind was gradually turning to mush. *There was that*, she thought, the lone shadow over her bliss. But she wasn't the only one facing an eldercare crisis. At twenty-six, though, she was one of the younger ones. Gemma had been born long after her parents had given up trying to have children. They were told it was impossible. And then suddenly at the age of fifty-three, her mother had gotten pregnant. A miracle, they had called their little girl. It had not always been ideal having parents old enough to be grandparents, but there were advantages. They were stable, loving and patient people. But her father had died when she was eighteen and her mother was now wasting away in her last days of life. She dreaded the day that her mother would leave the world completely. It would be so lonely without her.

Thank God for Dani, she thought, searching the beach for her tousled brown hair. There she was, her sandaled feet in the lapping surf, clapping and calling to Tucker as he swam in with the toy on a more or less direct course toward her. Gemma shook away thoughts of her mother. She leapt off the bench and took off running to join her family. Today was a lovely October Saturday and they had nothing to do but love life. Maybe that was an exaggeration, but those pesky weekend chores would wait a few more hours.

Dani's naturally wavy hair was windblown and damp, sticking to her cheek. She needed a haircut. She didn't like getting haircuts, so she put it off until her bangs were hanging into her eyes and she couldn't stand it anymore. Gemma liked the messy look. It went well with Dani's playful personality and her many snarky expressions.

Gemma fished her phone out and snapped a couple of photos of Dani and Tucker playing on the sand, the towers of the Golden Gate Bridge rising out of a damp blanket of fog behind them. *What an irresistible scene*, she thought, admiring her composition.

"We should probably start back," she said, coming up beside Dani as she wrestled the bone from Tucker's mouth.

Dani nodded and smiled, then threw the bone into the bay one last time before the two of them started walking. Tucker was soon beside them, spraying them with a whirlwind of cold water drops as he shook himself off. Dani slipped her hand into Gemma's and they walked along the curving shoreline past the Maritime Museum and on to the base of the steep hill up to Fort Mason.

Looking up the hill, Dani grinned. "Ready to run?"

Gemma sighed.

"Sure you are," laughed Dani. "A month ago you wouldn't have been able to walk it without stopping to catch your breath."

It was true. She'd gotten in much better shape fast since the two of them started running together in preparation for the Bay Run for the Homeless, which was now only three weeks away. Gemma had never run a half-marathon, but each day she felt more confident that finishing was possible. After a month of training with Dani, she felt stronger than she ever had.

They started jogging up the hill at a moderate pace. Dani had been in good shape ever since Gemma had known her, but even she was more muscular now, better toned and, Gemma liked to think, healthier all around due to the not-always-welcome dietary changes Gemma had imposed on her. Gemma knew that Dani cheated on her diet, snagging chips and doughnuts during the workday, but Gemma had her for breakfast and dinner so it all evened out okay.

As they reached the top of the hill, the bridge came into view again, even less of it visible through the mist. In the distance, a foghorn sounded. They jogged through the park and over to the street, where they stopped at the traffic light, both of them breathing heavily.

"What do you want to do for dinner?" Dani asked.

Gemma shrugged. "I don't feel much like cooking. Why don't we stop at the deli and pick up something."

"Okay."

They dropped down onto Beach Street in front of the Marina Safeway where Dani attached the lead to Tucker's collar. Then they walked away from the bay toward home.

"You seem preoccupied with something today," Gemma said.

"Sorry. It's this case."

"The bombing?"

Dani jerked her chin up in affirmation. "We've got no leads. Nobody saw anything. The bomb was something anybody could put together from their local hardware store. It was in a cupboard on the second floor. Security at this place was totally lax and the cameras had been switched off at the main electrical panel, so there's no video. They said they didn't worry much about security because mostly what they've got in there are plants and seeds."

"Plants and seeds?"

"Yeah, they do something with GMO crops. So this guy, Darius, apparently comes in in the middle of the night, goes through a vent cover in the basement that's not wired, shuts off the cameras, then walks upstairs and puts his package in a cupboard. A five-year-old could have done it."

Tucker planted himself on a strip of grass alongside the sidewalk. He was worn out. Dani scooped him up and carried him in one arm against her chest, his wet fur dampening her sweatshirt. "Agent Bryan seems to think Darius is going to strike again if we can't find him. But we don't know a thing about him except his name, Leo Darius. I guess I should say his pseudonym. We don't know where he's from or where he lives or who his people are. He doesn't cast a shadow. Bryan knows more, but he isn't sharing. This isn't the way I like to do things."

"Of course not. You want to be in charge." Gemma turned and grinned at Dani. "Everywhere. Always."

Dani laughed. "True." She squeezed Gemma's hand. "So we're just blindly following Agent Bryan, trusting him. There's just something strange about that guy."

"How do you mean?"

Dani shook her head. "I don't know. But that's what's bothering me. Something's fishy, but I can't figure out what."

"Be careful."

"Always."

Their apartment was the ground floor of a two-story Victorian. The upstairs was rented out to another couple. Fortunately, the single-car garage belonged to them. Unfortunately, it was being used as storage instead of parking. It was full of stuff Dani had brought with her when she moved in and some of Gemma's mom's furniture that had been moved out of the house. Gemma knew her mother was never coming back, that she could get rid of her things, but she wasn't ready to do it yet. It would seem too much like declaring her mother already gone.

They were lucky to have a place in the city, and the quirks of this old house didn't bother Gemma much. So many of their friends commuted in from the East Bay, South Bay or even further away. Gemma's mother had lived here ever since her father had passed away, moving to San Francisco to be near her daughter. She kept saying she would come home when she was better, and Gemma let her think so. There was no reason not to.

She pushed open the door to the dim interior and switched on the entryway light, illuminating hardwood floors and the living room furniture, most of it her mother's. On the left side of the hall were the two bedrooms and one bathroom. On the right was the living room with a separate tiny room they used for a desk. At the end of the hall, at the back of the house, was the kitchen, arranged like so many of these narrow apartments carved out of Victorians.

"I forgot to tell you," Gemma said, closing the door behind them. "Your sister called earlier. She wants you to go with her to the bridal shop Monday afternoon if you can take the time off."

Dani wrinkled her nose. "Bridal shop? Those places give me the creeps. Why doesn't Mom go with her?"

"I didn't ask. You should do it."

"I guess so," Dani said reluctantly. "I should tell her to put you in the ceremony so you have to wear one of those god-awful bridesmaid dresses." Dani laughed. "I'd like to see that."

"That's not going to happen," said Gemma flatly. "The last time I wore a dress was to my senior prom." Gemma dropped her tote bag into a living room chair. "I'd say on the butch-femme scale, we're both just a little on the flat-soled shoes side of center. Well, maybe you're a little farther toward the toolbelt set, my love."

Dani put Tucker on the floor and wrapped her arms around Gemma's waist. "Gem, baby, all I know is that you're all woman and that's the way I like it."

They kissed long and slow until Dani released her, a dreamy smile on her face.

"Nice," Gemma said quietly. "Maybe we should skip dinner and go right to dessert." She nuzzled Dani's neck, then kissed her just above the collar of her sweatshirt, slipping her hands under it to feel the warm skin of Dani's back.

Dani's mouth sought hers and they kissed again until Gemma felt something wet land on her foot. She looked down to see Tucker sitting on her sandal. "You know your dog has to have a bath, right?"

"*My* dog? He's always my dog whenever he's in trouble." Dani picked him up and touched noses with him. "She loves you just as much as I do, Tuck Tuck."

"Maybe now," Gemma admitted, "but if you hadn't begged on your knees two years ago, he'd probably belong to Miko right now." Gemma shook her head, remembering how Dani had pleaded to keep the stray.

Dani held Tucker in front of her face and baby talked to him. "Miko never had a chance with you, did she, boy? You were mine the minute I saw you."

An image of Dani holding a baby flashed through Gemma's mind. She needed to tell her what she'd been thinking, that it was time to start a family. They'd talked about it vaguely in the past, so she knew Dani wanted kids at some point. Gemma hadn't been ready in the beginning, not until she could be absolutely certain that she and Dani were strong enough together, financially secure with a clear path to the future. She was ready now. With Dani's sister's surprise announcement that she would be a pregnant bride, Dani might be ready too. Her family was about to produce a new generation. She wouldn't want to be left out of that.

"Poor Miko." Dani flashed a toothy smile at Gemma and turned Tucker to face her, dark soulful eyes, moist black nose, white stripe down the center of his face. "Aren't you glad she didn't get him?"

Gemma nodded. "I'm glad because if she had, she would have named him Oreo. She told me so."

"Stupid, stupid Miko," Dani sputtered into Tucker's face. "You'd hate being named Oreo, wouldn't you, boy?"

"I'll go pick up dinner while you clean him up. How about something light like a Greek salad? I can get a couple pieces of baklava for dessert."

"Perfect."

Gemma smiled to herself, watching Dani rub noses with Tucker. As long as she loved their child as much as she loved that dog, they'd all be just fine.

CHAPTER THREE

Perkins sucked in his coffee, making that obscene noise that set Dani's teeth on edge. Nobody drank coffee noisier than this dude! He put the mug down and leaned back in his chair, rubbing his palm over his ample belly. He was like a thirty-year-old Oscar Madison. Come to think of it, he sort of looked like a young Walter Matthau—oversized nose, dark, wavy hair, thick black eyebrows and heavy in the jowls. A few more years, she realized, and she'd be sitting across the table from Max Goldman from *Grumpy Old Men*.

Dani cut her last hunk of steak into two pieces and ate one with a forkful of yolky hash browns. This diner was one of their regular spots, and the steak and eggs was one of Dani's regular orders. Not that she hadn't had breakfast. She'd had a bowl of high-fiber cereal with blueberries and almonds this morning with Gemma. But ever since then, she'd been thinking about ordering her favorite breakfast for lunch.

"You remember that fund-raising barbecue we had this summer?" Perkins asked.

"Sure." Dani mopped up the egg yolk in her plate with a half piece of toast.

"Your Gemma was working the drinks station with me."

"Yeah, I know. You mentioned it before."

"Well, I don't know if I mentioned before that she told me you two were vegetarians." He sucked his teeth before taking a swallow of coffee, then looked over the rim of his mug with a twinkle in his eyes. "That was before I got assigned to this beat, before I got to know you so well. Now I'm thinking back to that barbecue, wondering, hell, how did this woman pass on the tri-tip?"

Dani chuckled. "It was painful." She waved her fork at him. "You don't tell mine about this and I won't tell yours about the ice cream bars." She stabbed the last piece of steak and slipped it into her mouth. She felt a little guilty for the steak, but not enough to give it up. She was okay with the bulgur wheat and lentil salads for dinner, but for lunch she was on her own. There had been nothing in their wedding vows about promising not to eat meat. Gemma made healthy taste great, and Dani had to admit that under her care her body had become leaner and meaner, but she had never gotten over her craving for meat. Some people are just meant to be carnivores. She put her fork down and took a long drink from her coffee mug, making no noise. *Gemma thinks I'm a slob*, she thought. *She should have to live with Perkins for a week.*

Their waitress, Sandra, swung by with the bill. "Here's your apple, Dani," she said, placing a Red Delicious in front of her. "More coffee?"

Dani glanced at the wall clock, then shook her head. It was edging past eleven, the end of their lunch hour.

"That's it for me too, Sandy Dee," Perkins said with a grin. Sandra's last name was McCorkle. Perkins just liked the sound of his own invented name, and Dani was pretty sure he didn't realize it was because there actually was a famous Sandra Dee. Despite his resemblance to Walter Matthau, he was too young to know who she was, but names like that have a way of worming their way into your subconscious. Sandra McCorkle, on the other hand, was old enough to be well acquainted with

Sandra Dee, to whom she bore no resemblance. She gave the same little huff at Perkins that she always did, tactfully placing the bill equidistant between the two of them in the center of the table.

They paid the tab, put on their caps and walked to the corner where Old Gustav sat on a milk crate beside his pony and cart reading a newspaper through round-rimmed glasses. A sign on the sidewalk read, "Buggy rides $20." Gustav looked very Old World in dark pants, a white shirt, red suspenders and a felt hat with a feather in it. He had been at this corner for as long as Dani could remember with this same cart and same pony, Comet by name, which must have been some kind of inside joke, considering how this pony plodded along her route, especially when there were passengers in the cart. Gus and Comet were a fixture in Golden Gate Park. You could always find them right here on this corner. If not, they were off giving rides to customers.

"Hey, Gus," Dani said.

The old man raised his head and blinked at them, pulling on one end of his thick white mustache. Recognizing her, he smiled broadly and stood up. "Good morning, Dani. And you too, Officer Perkins."

"How's our little Comet today?" she said, patting the pony's forehead. Comet's eyes focused on the apple, and half of it was soon in her mouth. "You like that, girl, don't you?"

"Oh, she does!" Gus assured them. "She's always happy to see you, Dani."

Comet snorted and jerked her head up and down. Dani held out the rest of the apple on her open palm. A few more munches and it was gone. They said good-bye to Gus and returned to the patrol car.

As Perkins pulled into traffic, Dani checked her phone to find a message from Gemma. "Don't forget your sister this afternoon, bridal shop." There was no "Love, Gem" after, so chances were she was still upset.

Dani hated it when they had an argument right before it was time for her to leave for work. It hung over them all day, either getting bigger or getting smaller, she never knew which until she walked into the apartment that evening. Either way, she'd fix it tonight. It wasn't that big of a deal. Dani didn't mean to be "dismissive." Her mind had already been on work when she had failed to give Gemma the kind of attention she was after. "You always do this!" she'd said. "You trivialize things that are important to me. Whether they're important to you or not, you could at least pretend they are." In her defense, Dani had said, "Gem, I've got a lot on my mind. It's this thing with the FBI. It's really important." "Exactly!" she said. "Everything you're doing is important and everything I'm doing isn't. That was my point." So Gemma had left the house without a good-bye kiss, indicating by the stiffness of her back that she didn't want to be touched.

The truth was that Dani had forgotten what a big day this was for Gemma, and she felt bad about it. Gemma was meeting with a potential new client, a big client, big enough that getting the contract could blast her business up to the next level. So, yes, it was a big deal, and Dani had not been supportive enough, for which she was sorry.

Maybe Dani should bring home a gift tonight as a peace offering. She replied to Gemma's message, then put her phone away and observed the streets. Everything looked peaceful until they turned onto Balboa. The only vehicle in sight was a tan Toyota Camry in the lane ahead of them, creeping slowly along. The left blinker was on, but the car showed no indication of turning. It then veered over the center line, swung sharply back, then went even more slowly.

"Let's pull him over," Dani said.

She turned on the lights, and they followed the car close on the rear bumper. She could see there was an elderly man at the wheel. No passenger.

"He doesn't see us," Perkins said.

She squawked the siren briefly and saw the man look into his rearview mirror. He then pulled over to the curb and they parked behind him.

As soon as she started talking to him, Dani could tell something was wrong. "Sir, can I see your license?" she asked him.

He looked confused and worried.

"What's your name, sir?"

"Paul Cavanaugh," he answered.

"Are you feeling all right?" she asked. "Sir, are you on some kind of medication?"

"I took my blood pressure pill," he said, his voice shaky. "Did I do something wrong, Officer?"

"Do you feel light-headed, sir? Dizzy?"

He nodded.

"Okay. Sit there and relax. I'm going to call a paramedic."

She and Perkins waited with Mr. Cavanaugh until the ambulance arrived. He remained conscious but disoriented. The EMTs said his blood pressure was low and they suspected a beta blocker overdose.

"They're going to take you to the hospital, Mr. Cavanaugh," Dani said, patting his arm to keep him focused. "You'll be fine. Can we let somebody know where you are?"

"My daughter," he said. "My daughter Angela. The number's in my phone."

Dani looked up the number and wrote it down. After the EMTs took Cavanaugh away, she called his daughter to let her know what had happened and where to pick up the car.

"It's good we got him off the road," Perkins said.

Dani murmured her agreement.

* * *

Gemma glanced at her phone to read Dani's reply. "Thanks for the reminder about the bridal shop. Ugh. Good luck with your new client. Not that you need luck for that. You'll wow them! Love you."

The message bore no hint of their morning tiff. But that was typical Dani. Whenever they had an argument, it blew over her like a summer shower and left a clean blue sky and a rainbow behind. Gemma smiled to herself. It wouldn't surprise her if Dani arrived home this evening with a gift for her. But Gemma should be the one offering the apology. Dani had done nothing wrong. It was just the stress, the situation with her mother and her job. There was a lot going on and she had been nervous about today. She'd also resented it that Dani had forgotten about her interview, but Dani had a lot on her mind too. It wasn't surprising that she needed a reminder.

She rang her assistant, Shelley, who came into the office a moment later, her pale legs descending from a short, ruffled skirt, her tight-knit top revealing small breasts and the well-defined curve of her tummy. Even the indentation of her belly button was visible through the material. Basically, she seemed to be going for a ballerina look. Shelley's choice in clothing was a mystery to Gemma. *Maybe I'm getting old*, she thought, quickly calculating that she was only five years older than her ballerina.

Behind her thick-rimmed eyeglasses, Shelley's perceptive gaze locked onto Gemma, ready to serve. She was an eager and efficient assistant and, despite her outward appearance of frivolity, Gemma liked her.

"Shelley, I've got to leave for my appointment in San Raphael. Can you call the printer and make sure the meal plans for November are going out today?"

"Sure."

"And verify that they changed the side vegetable for the lemongrass chicken from carrots to green beans. I'm still trying to bump the sugar content down a little on that one."

Shelley made a note on her pad, assuring Gemma that the task would be done. "Anything else?"

"No, that'll do until I get back." Gemma took her purse from the drawer of her desk.

"By the way," Shelley said, "you asked me to remind you about the retirement party for Lois on Wednesday?"

Gemma looked up. "Oh, thanks. I'd completely forgotten." Lois was Gemma's old coworker from her days at the FDA. Her old cubicle mate, actually. They'd remained friends, though they did not see one another often with no workplace to bring them together. "Keep my schedule free for that, will you? I guess I should get her a gift."

"I can do that," Shelley offered. "Books, movies, some kind of collectible?"

Gemma racked her brain before saying, "Music. Old school."

"A gift card for digital music."

"Perfect." Gemma glanced into the wall mirror to check her hair and makeup and adjust her scarf. *Looking good*, she thought. She turned back to Shelley. "You know, Lois used to drive me nuts. She listened to her iPod all day long and hummed along with the music, very quietly so I couldn't quite make out the tune. I'd get caught up in the challenge of figuring out the song, straining to catch a familiar melody. The constant humming was like water torture. There were times I fantasized strangling her. But, you know what? I sort of miss her. Weird, isn't it? One thing I don't miss, though, is the work I used to do there. I know it was important, but it was so tedious. Spreadsheets all day long. If I never see another spreadsheet in my lifetime, I'll be a happy woman."

Shelley wrinkled up her nose.

"I can't believe Lois spent her entire career doing that, but the work seemed to suit her somehow." Gemma shoved her phone into her purse.

"By the way," Shelley asked, "how's your mother? I know you got a call about her Friday."

Gemma sighed deeply. "Yes. She yanked a handful of hair out of an aide's head when he tried to take her for her shower." Gemma could tell Shelley wanted to laugh at that, but she managed to look concerned instead.

"At least she's got spunk," Shelley remarked.

"Unfortunately, spunk is not considered an asset among the institutionalized. I just hope they don't kick her out."

Shelley's expression was sympathetic. "You'd think they'd cut you some slack for improving their food so much. I mean, that's got to reflect well on them, right?"

"I think they *are* cutting me some slack. Actually, things are going much better now with Mom since she moved into Palm Terrace. I think they might have finally gotten her meds figured out." Gemma sighed. "Anyway, I hope so."

"Maybe it's because of better nutrition," Shelley suggested with a grin.

Of course Shelley could do nothing about Gemma's problems with her mother's care, but her instinctive need to help drove her to the coatrack, where she removed Gemma's fawn-colored jacket and held it up for her to slip into. Gemma pulled it on over her shoulders and buttoned one button, then turned to face Shelley.

"How do I look?" she asked.

"Gorgeous. Confident. I'm sure you'll come back with the contract."

"Thanks."

On her way out, Gemma paused to read her name on the suite door. "Gemma A. Mettler, Nutritional Consultant." That just never got old! Just two years ago, she'd been a civil service functionary in a dead-end job for the FDA, graphing statistics, unchallenged and bored. This, her own business, had been a vague dream she had never thought would be realized. It was hard work, but so much more satisfying.

She waited for the elevator, mentally preparing for her meeting with her potential new client, North Bay Healthcare Services, the owner of half a dozen nursing and rehab hospitals in Marin and Sonoma counties. If she could land their food services contract...it made a shiver run up her spine to think of it. But after building her business for two years, she was ready for this. Reaching the ground floor, she slung the strap of her purse over her shoulder and strode purposefully out of the building, rehearsing her presentation in her mind.

CHAPTER FOUR

A call was coming in. Suspect in sight. Officer needs assistance.

"That's Agent Bryan," Dani said. "He must be after Darius."

She turned on the lights and sirens and they changed course, heading for the location just a mile away. They took the streets as fast as they could without killing anybody.

What was Bryan doing out there on his own anyway? she wondered. *And how had he found Darius?*

Their tires skidded as they stopped in front of a run-down ten-story apartment building with outside metal fire escapes. They were the first to arrive.

"I'll take the back," Perkins said.

Dani pulled her weapon and dashed toward the front doorway where an old man stood holding the door open, looking mystified.

"Get out of here!" she yelled. "Get away from this building. Get somewhere safe."

He moved aside and she entered, sweeping the entrance quickly. She spoke into her radio. "Bryan, what's your twenty?"

He immediately answered, sounding breathless. "He's heading toward the roof. I'm right behind him."

She located the stairwell and started up, taking two steps at a time. The landing of each floor was marked with a blazing red number—2…3…4…5. She could hear clattering above, footsteps, then the slamming of a metal door echoing down the stairwell. Had they reached the roof? She heard a siren die outside. Good! Another unit was here. Even more sirens sounded nearby.

She bounded up the remaining stairs. When she reached the ninth floor, a gunshot reverberated through the stairwell. It was followed closely by a second shot. She nearly flew up the last flight and burst out onto the flat roof of the building, leading with her weapon. Wind blew past and whistled through the open door behind her. Scanning the scene, she saw Bryan lying on his back nearby and another man running away from her toward the far end of the roof. Darius! Thin and lanky, he wore a gray hoodie and brown pants, and that's about all she could get from the back.

"Stop! Police!" she called, but his stride did not change.

Dani heard Bryan moan, then the moan turned into a frightening gurgle, and she feared the worst. She took a shot at the fleeing suspect as he dodged behind the HVAC units at the far end of the roof. Her bullet ricocheted off the metal.

She made her way warily toward the spot, listening for any clue to pinpoint the location of the suspect. She heard muffled footsteps far away in the stairwell below. But she heard nothing on the roof. She edged around the equipment, leading with her weapon. Nobody was behind it. It seemed Darius was no longer here. She looked over the edge at the fire escape ladders and platforms. There were three black and whites parked below and several cops surrounding the base of the building. If Darius was on his way down, somebody would intercept him. But metal fire escapes were noisy and she heard nothing between herself and the officers below.

Retreating quickly back to Bryan's position, she radioed in her location and reported a "ten double-zero," officer down.

"Ten-four on the double-zero," said the dispatcher.

Dani knelt beside Bryan. He wasn't wearing a vest and had been hit in the chest. He lay unmoving, his eyes closed, blood pooling beside him. A trickle of blood ran from the side of his mouth, ending in the thick hair of a sideburn. His weapon lay a foot from his body. Without even touching it, she could smell that it had been fired. One of the two shots she'd heard. The other one, fired by the suspect, was in his chest. His left arm was nearest to her. She lifted it to feel for a pulse, noting the object strapped to his wrist. It wasn't like any fitness monitor she'd seen before. The display showed only two small dots, one blue, one green, on a faint grid. Feeling no signs of life, she released his hand. His right arm was stretched straight out to the side, and next to his open hand was a small metal cylinder. It was silver with three translucent blue inlays equally spaced around its outer casing. The blue sections were glowing.

Dani picked it up to examine it just as Perkins burst onto the roof. She heard her name—"Barsetti"—low and rumbling, as if it were hollered into a deep canyon. That was followed by a wild ringing in her ears. Perkins disappeared in a flash of light. Everything disappeared—Bryan's body, the building, the sky. Dani felt like she was caught in a tornado, spinning wildly, surrounded by swirls of color. She couldn't distinguish up or down. Her arms and legs, flailing in all directions, contacted nothing. And then everything went dark.

* * *

On her way back to the office, Gemma realized how hungry she was. She'd been so nervous this morning she hadn't eaten much, but now, with the interview behind her, her appetite had returned with a vengeance. She stopped into the restaurant next door to her building for a salad, feeling euphoric. She hadn't gotten the contract yet, but the interview had gone so well, the final decision would be a mere formality, she was sure of it. She couldn't wait to tell Dani. She couldn't wait to tell Shelley. But she wanted to tell them in person.

When the waitress delivered her salad, a crisp bowl of lettuces, fresh vegetables and crunchy sunflower seeds, she sat with her fork poised over it, smiling to herself. There it was, right there on her plate, her entire pitch. Fresh fruits and vegetables. You can improve the morale and quality of life of long-term patients by giving them better nutrition and a sense of control over at least one aspect of their lives—what they put in their mouths. Put a salad bar in the dining room for those who are ambulatory. For those who aren't, give them a printed menu with choices. For those who are beyond choosing for themselves, at least put a piece of fresh fruit on their tray and fresh, not frozen or canned, vegetables.

Gemma put a cucumber slice in her mouth. Of course, the NBHS managers immediately objected, citing the prohibitive cost. She waved her fork over her plate like a pointer, remembering the moment. But, you see, she had told them, I've designed a system that costs no more than feeding them brown slop and canned peas...No, she hadn't said that. But she had said something along those lines, that she could put fresh food into their facilities without raising costs. That she had done it already. That's when she described where and how she had done it and how it could be done on a larger scale. If they were skeptical, after all she had shown them, she could demonstrate at one or two of their facilities as a trial, before they adopted the program across the board.

She smiled while she ate. How could they say no? If it wasn't going to cost more and it was better for the patients, how could they? After all, nobody really wants to punish sick, helpless people with brown slop and canned peas. Even if the administrators are secretly apathetic, they have to at least pretend they care.

She finished her salad and glanced at her watch. It was one thirty. She had to get back to the office. She walked outside into a brilliant, sunny day, then went into her own building and caught the elevator up, excited with the prospect of spilling her joy all over Shelley. Before the elevator reached her floor, it seemed to come to an abrupt stop. Her stomach lurched violently and she had the feeling that the elevator car was free-falling. She reached toward the wall to steady herself, but her fingers contacted nothing but air. She panicked, grabbing at the nothingness and feeling dizzy, but the sensation lasted only a split second before she realized she was sitting solidly in her chair at her desk.

She placed both hands flat on the desktop, wondering what had just happened. Whatever it was, it was over. She felt fine. Her computer displayed the complicated spreadsheet she'd been working on for three days. She was in the process of generating a line graph to chart arsenic levels in fruit juices. Lois, her cube mate, leaned back in her desk chair, her earbuds in, humming some sixties pop tune as usual.

Gemma tried to ignore her and concentrate on her work. The time display at the bottom of the screen taunted her. It was only one forty in the afternoon. She had nearly three and a half hours left before being released from this torment.

CHAPTER FIVE

The first thing Dani heard was a little bell ringing, a faint ding, ding, ding. She lay with her eyes closed, her head pounding, her stomach on the verge of rejecting lunch. It took her a moment to force her eyes open and take in her surroundings. She was lying on a padded table in a room with eggshell-colored walls and sterile-looking furniture—a table, counters, a couple of chairs, all of them taupe. There was light in the room, but no windows and no visible lamps or light fixtures. The light seemed to radiate from the entire ceiling.

Eventually, she turned her head and was startled to see a young woman standing a few feet away, watching her. She had a milk chocolate complexion and ebony hair, cut short and straight just below her ears. She wore a pastel blue smock and shoes that looked like dancer's slippers. She was lithe and fragile-looking with pale skin and black eyebrows that arched in the center, giving her a look of mild surprise.

Just as Dani was about to speak, the woman said, "You are awake." She was at her side instantly. "How do you feel, Daniella Barsetti?"

"Like crap." She licked her dry lips and the woman handed her a cup with a straw to take a drink. Despite the slippers, she was apparently a nurse.

"Some discomfort is to be expected," the woman said.

"Is it?" She looked down at her body to see she was wearing a loose-fitting smock that covered her arms to the elbows and her legs to the knees. She tentatively moved her legs. There was no pain. "Was I shot?"

"Shot? We injected you with an antiemetic."

"No, I mean with a gun. A bullet. Was I hit?"

"You are not wounded."

With that knowledge, Dani relaxed and lifted her head to take a sip through the straw. She looked past the woman at the seamless white wall, then searched the other walls, finding no door to the room. The walls themselves were mostly empty except for one abstract piece of art, a frameless print in midnight blue, white and yellow.

Looking back at the nurse, she asked, "Where am I?"

The woman's smile was practiced. "Dr. Swenson will answer your questions."

"Who's Dr. Swenson?"

"She is the director of this facility."

"What hospital is this?"

"Dr. Swenson will answer your questions. I am Lara. If you need anything, please ask."

Dani attempted a nod, then sucked more liquid through the straw. It tasted odd. "What is this?"

"Fortified water. Do you want something to eat?"

She shook her head. "My stomach's too upset." She peered at the colorless liquid in the cup. *Fortified with what?* she wondered.

"Your nausea will wear off in an hour or two. It is just one of the side effects." Lara took the cup from her.

"Side effects of what? What am I doing here? Am I sick?"

Lara smiled again. "Dr. Swenson…"

"…will answer my questions. Right."

She leaned her head back and stared at the luminescent ceiling, searching her memory. She'd been chasing Agent Bryan and Darius through an apartment building. Bryan had been shot. Darius escaped or was captured by someone else. She'd picked up an object, a silver tube with three blue lights. That's the last thing she remembered. Now she was lying in a hospital bed feeling like she'd been tossed into a concrete wall, her mind muddled. Maybe Darius had attacked her and knocked her out while she was preoccupied with Bryan. Maybe she had a concussion.

"How long have I been here?" she asked.

"One hour."

"Did they get Darius?"

Lara tilted her head to the side, as if perplexed. "I do not understand."

She's an odd little thing, Dani thought. "Did the police arrest Darius?"

"I do not know. Perhaps Dr. Swenson can answer that. Can I get you anything?"

"Yes. I want to see Dr. Swenson."

"I will take you to her as soon as you can walk."

Dani sat up, her head swimming. When it settled down, she swung her legs over the side of the bed and touched down on the floor. She wasn't sure she could walk and she didn't know what was wrong with her, but she was impatient for answers.

"I will tell Dr. Swenson you are awake," Lara offered. She walked toward one of the walls, which slid aside for her with a swishing sound, creating a doorway. It closed after her, blending into the wall nearly seamlessly.

Dani stood beside the bed, keeping still and willing the nausea to subside. She'd never been in a hospital room that looked like this, so stark with no machines and no sounds. And no light switches. She visually searched the walls for electrical outlets. There were none. No switches and no outlets. They must be hidden somehow. Behind a panel or inside a cupboard.

Lara returned in a few minutes with a pair of elastic-waisted pastel blue pajama pants. "Please put these on," she said.

Dani already felt stronger. She sat on the edge of the bed and pulled on the pants. They were thin, but the material felt strong, like Tyvek but much softer.

"Where's my phone?" she asked. "I want to call home."

A look of perplexity greeted her request before wan-faced Lara said, "You may ask Dr. Swenson about that?"

Dani groaned her frustration. "Fine! Take me to Dr. Swenson."

She followed Lara down a circular hallway to another door. Beyond this the hallway curved out of sight. The room they entered looked substantially the same as the first one except that it was larger and furnished more like a conference room. It contained an oval table surrounded by swivel chairs, a counter along one wall and an inset panel above it that Dani imagined might move up or down to reveal a video screen. Again, there were no light fixtures, but the room was lit. As they entered, the light level rose automatically.

"Please sit," Lara said. "The others will be here in a minute."

Dani sat in the silent, windowless room for fewer than five minutes before three people came in, an attractive woman in her thirties and two men, one young, small and dark-complexioned, the other older, about sixty, with hollow cheeks and salt-and-pepper hair. Both men were clean-shaven, and all three wore light-colored slacks and coordinating shirts of a material similar to Dani's pajama pants. The woman, whose auburn hair was thick and shoulder length, walked with self-assurance, her chin tilted up slightly, an attitude conveying the message that she was in charge. Dani rose to her feet, noting that she still felt shaky. With a welcoming smile, the woman held out her hand. "Hello, Officer Barsetti," she said, her voice composed and even-toned. "I'm Pamela Swenson."

So this was Dr. Swenson, the woman with all the answers.

"This is my associate, Dr. Gavin Hale." Swenson indicated the young man, who put on an unconvincing smile and reached in to shake Dani's hand limply. "And this is Filbert Moon."

Moon, trim and alert-looking with bushy sideburns that might legitimately be called muttonchops, gave her hand a quick shake. He did not smile and his eyes betrayed concern. Dani noticed that Swenson's introduction of Filbert Moon neglected to identify his role. She also noticed a small device attached to his left ear. Hearing aid? Glancing at Gavin Hale, she saw that he had a similar device on his ear. Because of Dr. Swenson's hairdo, her ears were out of view.

All of the newcomers sat at one end of the table near Dani, forming a close-knit foursome.

"I'm sure you have a lot of questions," guessed Swenson. "So do we. Are you feeling better?"

"Yes, thanks."

"Before we answer your questions, which is going to take some time, I'd like you to clear up a few things for us. First of all, where is Agent Bryan?" She leaned toward Dani, folding her hands together on the table.

Dani was completely thrown by the question. Up until now, she had thought she was in a hospital and would be meeting with her doctors. Now she had to start over figuring out what was going on.

"You know," she said cautiously, "maybe it's just my police training, but I'm not comfortable with the whole Q and A thing just yet. I don't know where I am or who you are. I don't know how I got here or what happened to me. All my stuff has been taken, including my badge, my weapon, my wallet and my phone. I want all of my stuff back. And I want to see some ID from you three before we go any further."

Swenson gave her an indulgent smile, then glanced at Moon, whose face remained passive.

"I understand how you must feel, Officer Barsetti. We will answer all of your questions in time, believe me. But, please, where is Frank Bryan? We are his colleagues."

"You're FBI?"

She shook her head. "No. Neither is he. He's undercover. The FBI story was designed to get the cooperation of local law enforcement. Frank was on a very important mission. He should be sitting here with us now instead of you." Her tone had become stern. "We want to know how that happened. Why are you here?"

Dani didn't know how to answer the question. From the expressions around her, the narrowed eyes of the older man and the antagonistic set of the young man's jaw, she felt that she was being accused of something.

Swenson nodded at Hale, who placed a silver, lipstick-sized tube on the table, the same device Dani had found next to Bryan's body. The blue lights were dull, no longer glowing.

"When you arrived," Swenson said, "you had this. It belongs to Frank. How did you get it?"

"Look, I don't remember *arriving*. I don't even know where I am. Where is this place? At least you could tell me where I am."

"It's San Francisco, Officer Barsetti," offered Moon matter-of-factly. "You're in San Francisco."

That was a relief if it were true, but it wasn't very specific. She began to believe that nobody here would tell her anything until they had the answers to their own questions. She had nothing to hide anyway, she thought, whoever these people were.

"I picked that thing up," she said, nodding toward the silver tube. "Maybe Bryan dropped it. He called for backup and my partner and I answered the call. Darius shot him just before I arrived. As far as I know, Bryan's dead. This thing was lying beside him. The blue lights were glowing. I picked it up to see what it was. That's all I remember."

Swenson's eyes widened in shock. "Dead?" She glanced at Hale, who also looked stricken.

Dani realized she had just dropped a bombshell on these people. She had forgotten that they knew Bryan, that he was their coworker and, probably, friend. She remembered her own similar recent loss. "Oh, geez, I'm sorry," she said. "I'm pretty sure he's dead," she reiterated more gently.

Swenson stood and walked toward a blank wall, facing away from the group. Hale lowered his head. Moon seemed unmoved. Perhaps he had not been a friend of Frank Bryan's. He simply stared at Dani with displeasure.

"What about Darius?" he asked. "You said Darius shot Bryan. What happened to him?"

"I'm not sure. The SFPD might have gotten him. We had quite a few units there. But I didn't see where he went and then…well, I woke up here."

Moon stared hard at her, his bushy eyebrows knit together. "This is a disaster!" he finally announced, then addressed Swenson impatiently. "We have to be sure he's stopped. Even if the police arrested him, how do we know they'll keep him locked up? What if they let him go? He can pay money to get out of jail, right?" His last question seemed aimed at Dani.

"You mean bail? Sure, as long as the judge…"

"That's beside the point," Hale interrupted, his voice soft and feeble. "Bryan is dead."

"I'm very sorry about that," Moon said, his eyes darting to Swenson, who still stood facing the wall. "But we still have a serious problem to deal with that is not at all 'beside the point.' Darius is still alive."

Swenson turned to face Moon, her expression cold and challenging. "What do you propose we do?"

"How do I know! This is your project. You need to fix this."

Swenson closed her eyes, clasping her hands together in front of her.

Moon stood and took a step toward her. "This is a big setback, Doctor. Not only did you lose Bryan and your chance at Darius, but now we've got *her*." He pointed at Dani, clearly unhappy about her being there.

Dani glanced from one to the other of them, wondering what kind of operation this was. She'd thought from the beginning there was something fishy going on with Agent Bryan. Who was behind him? If not the FBI, who? Some other government agency? A foreign government? Nothing about this place or these people suggested anything to her. All of the usual clues were missing. But she did gather from Moon's comment that she was a liability. This was a covert operation and she was not supposed to be here. She wondered if that put her in danger. Could they let her go without compromising their plans? She now knew Bryan had been an imposter. Her knowing that couldn't be okay with these people.

If it were true that she'd only been here an hour, it was still Monday afternoon. Gemma would be at her office, unaware that anything had happened. At least she wouldn't yet have any reason to worry. If things worked out, Dani might be walking into the apartment at the usual time and Gemma would have never had a moment of concern. Well, not the usual time. She had that appointment at the bridal shop first. She'd go pick up a carton of ice cream after that, Gem's favorite, dulce de leche.

A smile tugged at the side of her mouth as she imagined herself walking in, giving Gemma a kiss and an apology. Gemma would melt just like her bowl of ice cream. But that nice little scene depended on her getting safely out of whatever mess this was. *So, Barsetti,* she said to herself, *make yourself an asset to these folks instead of a liability.*

"If this Darius guy is really that dangerous," she said, "maybe I can help keep him behind bars. Or, if he isn't already in custody, I can put some pressure on the force to take him in. I know Bryan had information he wasn't sharing. I'm guessing you know what it was. If you give me something to work with, I can help. All I know about Darius so far is that he blew up a research lab. You obviously think he's got a bigger plan. Let me in on it. I have a few connections and I'm already on the case, right? Let me go after him."

Swenson gazed at her a moment, her expression unreadable, then glanced from Moon to Hale in turn. Neither of them reacted. When her eyes met Dani's again, she said, "We'll need to discuss your proposal, Officer Barsetti. May I call you Daniella?"

Dani shrugged. Nobody called her Daniella except her mother, but she wasn't prepared to engage in chitchat about nicknames with Dr. Swenson.

"Please give us an hour or so to talk. Meanwhile, Lara can bring you something to eat if you're hungry."

Dani glanced around the room for a clock, but the walls were empty. "How do you tell time around here?"

Swenson's eyes darted slightly to the side, then she said, "It's nearly three o'clock." Dani looked in the same direction and saw nothing but a blank wall.

"You know, I'm supposed to meet my sister this afternoon. Do you think we can hurry this whole thing up a little?"

Another indulgent smile from Swenson. "We will do our best. Lara will let you know when we're ready for you."

Dani wished she could stay around for this discussion. She had a bad feeling about all of this. She couldn't help believing there was no way in hell they were going to let her walk out of here alive, wherever *here* was. She wasn't supposed to be here, they didn't want her here and at least one of them, Muttonchop Moon, was fuming about it.

CHAPTER SIX

Young Dr. Hale brought Dani back to the room she'd awakened in, leaving her there with the request, "Please wait here."

Once he had gone, she conducted a thorough search of the room, looking for her possessions. Not only didn't she find them, but she found no drawers, no cupboards and no closets. There was nothing of interest in this room, which was probably why she was being kept in it. Deciding to go exploring, she stepped toward the door just as it whooshed open.

Lara came in with a tray, which she placed on a wheeled cart by the bed. "Dr. Swenson said you might want to eat."

Dani's stomach was still a little queasy. Besides, the contents of the plate did not look all that tempting. "Naw, I had a big lunch earlier, which I'm sort of regretting now." She peered at the food, a beige cube about two inches high and some green things that looked like baby pinecones or bumpy Brussels sprouts. "What is this stuff anyway?"

"This is a protein portion," Lara answered, pointing to the cube. "Soy-based with teriyaki flavoring. And the vegetable portion is rukor."

"Rukor?"

"You are not familiar with rukor?"

Dani shook her head.

"Most people enjoy it."

"What's in the glass?"

"That is peach-flavored tea. I will be back in a moment." Lara left the room.

Dani took a sip of the tea. It reminded her of something from a juice bar that she would never have ordered. All in all, the food was right up Gemma's alley. She stabbed the vegetable with the fork and, out of curiosity, took a small bite. It was okay. She wondered if Gemma knew about rukor. She'd be thrilled and impressed if Dani introduced her to a new vegetable. She put the fork down and pushed the cart up against the wall.

She realized she felt a lot better than she had when she first woke up in this place. The nausea and headache were nearly gone.

Lara returned with Dani's uniform and let her get dressed, for which she was grateful. She felt like herself again in her own clothes. Her utility belt, which contained her weapon and her phone, was not returned.

"I am sorry," Lara answered when Dani asked for it.

"Look, I need my phone. I just want to call my sister. She's expecting me this afternoon and I need to tell her there might be a delay."

"I am sorry," Lara repeated, her expression indicating no sorrow, just the same perverse smile and arched eyebrows.

"Then could I use your phone?"

Lara shook her head. Dani pondered twisting the woman's arm, literally, to get her phone back but decided against it. The time for violence had not yet come. When it did, she felt confident against this group. She'd seen nobody so far who could pose any physical threat to her. Two small women, a spindly nerd and an elderly man. If she had to break out, she was sure she could do it.

By three forty-five, she was led to the conference room with the same group as before. They all looked so serious, it made her nervous. She didn't know what to expect, if she was in danger or why she had the persistent feeling she wasn't in San Francisco after all. The two rooms she'd been in had no windows. For all she knew, she could be anywhere. And she didn't trust anybody here to tell her the truth.

"I see you're wearing your uniform," Swenson said with a thin smile, taking a seat. "More comfortable?"

Dani nodded and sat in the same chair she had previously occupied.

When they were all seated, Swenson placed the silver tube on the table between them again, as if it embodied the group's subject of interest. "This is going to be hard for you to understand, Daniella. But please try to keep an open mind. We've decided to trust you."

Moon snorted, causing Swenson to amend her statement. "*I've* decided to trust you."

"Even though there are no records we can check to attest to your character," Moon grumbled.

"What do you mean?" Dani asked. "You can check with the police department. You can check my academy records and my DMV record. You can even look at my Facebook page if you want to. I've got nothing to hide."

"We could have checked those things," he replied, sounding disgruntled, "if we'd known you were coming. But not anymore. You, Officer Barsetti, are now a blank page, and all we've got to go on is what you say."

"Huh?"

"As you can see," Swenson intervened, "Mr. Moon has some misgivings, but he did agree to bring you in. So he'll keep his objections to himself." She stared him down, then turned her attention back to Dani. "I believe that you being here is an accident and that you played no part in Frank Bryan's mission failure or his death."

"I was on his side!" Dani insisted. "I was trying to help him."

"Yes, I understand. But you don't really know what he was trying to do. Unfortunately, he wasn't able to be completely honest with you. But there was no way he could have foreseen this outcome. His intention, and our intention, was to create as little disruption as possible. You and your colleagues were never to have known the truth about Frank Bryan's mission." She rolled the device under her forefinger, averting her eyes, as if she were still reluctant to trust Dani. Eventually, she said, "This item is a sort of homing beacon. When it's activated, the person holding it is transported back to wherever he or she came from. Frank was trying to get home—back here, you see. He must have activated this after he was shot, but then dropped it."

Dani looked around the drab room. "And where exactly is home for Frank Bryan?"

"This is...*was* his workplace. This is a scientific research facility that houses the equipment that transported you here."

"You've got a transporter?" Dani laughed, looking from one grave face to another. Nobody else looked even a tiny bit amused.

"Yes, we do. It's what we do here. We experiment and refine this transporter technology."

Visions of Spock and Captain Kirk fading into sparkly dust played across Dani's mind. Apparently she was not understanding what Swenson meant by "transporter." And she still didn't know who these people were. "Is this a government project?" she asked.

"Not directly, but there is government funding and oversight. We're an independent collective of scientists. At least Dr. Hale and I are. Mr. Moon is a government representative."

"So he's here to make sure you're not wasting the taxpayers' money."

Moon grunted.

"Something like that," Swenson replied.

"Well, it's really cool that you've got a transporter and all that." Dani stood, anxious to get away from these people. "Considering how lousy it made me feel, I think I'll just call a taxi to take me home, if you don't mind, and skip the whole beaming back experience."

"Please sit down, Officer Barsetti," Swenson said commandingly. "There's a lot more you have to know." She held her hand out to indicate the vacated chair. "Please, Daniella," she urged more softly.

Dani reluctantly took her seat, thinking it had been a mistake to let this woman call her "Daniella." Because of it, she felt obligated to obey her.

Swenson pushed a lock of auburn hair back from her forehead, sweeping it behind her ear. Dani saw that she too was wearing an earpiece like the others. "You can't take a taxi back to where you came from."

Hale huffed, seeming amused at the taxi reference.

"I thought we were in San Francisco," said Dani.

"We are." Swenson hesitated, focusing her gaze steadily on Dani. "But you've traveled forward in time. This is the year 2221. You're over two hundred years from where you were earlier today."

Dani glanced around the room, ready to burst out laughing. Again, nobody else seemed to think this was funny. Did they really think she was going to believe this?

"Look," she finally said, "if this is some kind of con, you can't pull it over on me. I've seen them all. My grandfather Antonio Righetti was a master con artist. He taught me how to spot a con from the word go. And this is an amateur job. You lock me up in a windowless building, give me some weird food to eat and wear funny-looking clothes, and based on that lame demonstration, you expect me to believe I've traveled into the future? I suppose next you're going to show me a newspaper with the year 2221 on it."

"There are no newspapers," Hale said haughtily. "There are no printed magazines or books anymore."

Dani slapped her palm to her forehead. "Of course. What was I thinking? Two hundred years into the future, everything's digital, right?"

"I told you she was too ignorant," Moon remarked.

"Hey!" Dani objected.

"That isn't helpful," Swenson said pointedly to Moon. She turned back to Dani. "Obviously, anything digital we show you won't be convincing because we are all aware of how easy it is to manufacture digital information."

"Sure. Even in my time we've got Photoshop. So take me outside and show me the cool flying cars and robocops. I'd love to take a look at the skyline and see if I recognize anything. Is Coit Tower still there? What about the Golden Gate Bridge? Still standing? At least it was in the *Star Trek* movies set in the twenty-third century." She chuckled. "I don't know what you're after or why you've targeted me, but I do know a con when I see one, and I'm pretty sure you've given me something to dull my reasoning so I'll go along with this line of bull. Well, it's not going to work. So why don't we just cut to the chase?"

"It *is* still standing," Hale said with a hint of a smile.

"What is?"

"The Golden Gate Bridge. Beautiful old relic. It suffered some damage in the great quake of..." Moon clamped his hand down hard on Hale's arm and gave him a terse shake of his head. He smiled sheepishly, then returned his focus to Dani. "Yes, it's still there and it still gets its regular coat of paint. It's not used for transportation anymore, of course, but people do still walk on it because of its historical significance. It's a tourist attraction."

"Unfortunately," Swenson said, "we aren't authorized to show you anything. Moon hasn't yet reported your presence to his superiors because we don't know if you'll be going back. This doesn't happen every day, a visitor from the past, so we're not completely sure how to proceed."

"It's *never* happened before," Moon corrected. "We don't have a policy for this. It could get very messy."

"If I'll be going back?" Dani asked. "What does that mean?"

"That's what we're here to discuss, whether or not we will be sending you back."

"With your nifty time machine?"

"Right. We'll need some time to prepare you, equip you properly and brief you on your suspect. It shouldn't take too long, so we were thinking tomorrow. We can send you back to the same day, nearly the same time, so you won't have lost the time you've spent here. But there's a catch."

"There always is." Dani leaned back in her chair with a sigh.

"You can go back temporarily, but you can't stay in your own time for long."

"Why not?"

"You'll die," Hale offered bluntly. "When you came through the portal, you were imprinted with a temporal signature for this time. It's part of the process of reentry. We never expected anybody from the past to come through. It wasn't designed for that."

"Sorry, you're going to have to explain that so a cop can understand it."

"Yes, well, how to explain temporal mechanics to a…cop." He regarded her with disdain.

"I've seen it done in movies," she offered.

He turned beseechingly to Dr. Swenson. "Oh, Pamela, this is hopeless. How am I supposed to convey even the simplest concept of our work to this woman?"

Swenson gave him an impatient frown. "According to the scans Lara made, this woman is of above average intelligence for her time."

"For her time," he repeated. "Yes, exactly, that's my point."

"Just try…please."

Hale released an exasperated sigh and turned to Dani with a thin smile. By now, she had pegged him as a smug little prick.

"Okay," he began, talking with his hands. "About the movies, that's just going to confuse you more. Your popular culture is full of time travel fictions. In those old films, people went back in time and met themselves at a younger age, for example."

"Sure."

Hale shook his head. "That's not possible. People or animals or any life form can only exist at one point in any temporal plane. If you leave one position, you can appear in another, but you can't exist in both at the same time. There's only one of you after all, and you're traveling through time, traveling being the key. Just like if you were in a train going from Chicago to Los Angeles. Once you got to Los Angeles, you wouldn't still be in Chicago. Despite the theories of infinite dimensions and infinite universes and the Belchner hypothesis of refractory mirror planes…"

"Gavin!" Swenson gave him a stern look. "The point, please."

He nodded, looking slightly miffed. "Even if there are infinite universes and all of them contain one of you, they don't intersect. A parallel universe is not the same thing as another point in time, that's what I'm saying. We're talking about the time dimension, time along one plane in one universe. All of our experiments, theoretical and applied, have proven that there can never be more than one of you in a single timeline. If it's possible, we haven't yet imagined how. We would be the first to admit that we still have more to learn about time and time travel. But what we do know is that when you left your time, you became a reality in ours and ceased to exist back then. Right now, you are not living your life in the twenty-first century. Not only did you cease to exist there when you came here, but you *never* existed there. You exist here now and, for all practical purposes, you always have."

Did they really think she was going to believe any of this? She pondered his words while the three of them silently observed her, seeming anxious for her response. For the purpose of hearing them out, she said, "So if I go back, I'll exist there again. Right?"

Hale, who seemed to be playing the resident expert on time travel, took up the question. "No. You don't understand the part about the temporal signature. Sending you back in time doesn't alter that. The process assumes you belong here, that you originated here. If you go back, you can't stay in the past for long. Because you don't belong there, because you're out of temporal sync with your environment, you'll begin to degenerate, atom by atom, until you die from the breakdown of your organs."

Wow, they had really thought this wild story through, down to the fine details.

"What about Bryan?" she asked. "How was he able to live in the past?"

"He would have come back as soon as he completed his mission. He was there about a week altogether. The degeneration begins immediately. The shorter the time spent in the past, the better."

"The longest anyone's been gone is two weeks," Swenson added. "There was significant neurological damage and major organ failure. She was an intern who volunteered. A young woman. She was unforeseeably detained during her trip to the past. We didn't yet know about the effects of temporal asynchrony, as we had never sent anyone for more than a couple of days."

"Temporal what?"

"Temporal asynchrony," Hale said. "Being out of sync with the temporal environment you're inhabiting."

"Unfortunately," Swenson said, "the young woman died a few hours after coming back. There was nothing we could do. So, you see, we've lost two people already. This is a dangerous endeavor. It's not something we do casually. The danger to us and the danger of unraveling an important historical timeline are both critically important. As you can see for yourself, Frank is...gone and here you are, permanently ripped out of your time."

"And Darius is still a threat," Moon reminded them.

"If time traveling is so dangerous," Dani asked, "why did Bryan do it? What's the big deal about Darius? He's just a punk eco-terrorist. We can take care of him ourselves."

"A punk eco-terrorist," Moon sputtered to himself.

"If you can go back and change something," Dani asked, "why not go back and stop Hitler or Osama bin Laden or save JFK?"

Hale looked disgusted and shook his head. "You're still at the movies, Barsetti. What makes you think we didn't already go back and stop Hitler? Did he win? And what about JFK? Maybe we or somebody in our future went back to assassinate him. Maybe that was our solution to something worse. How do you know that his death didn't stop a nuclear war?"

Dani was alarmed. "Did it?"

"That was just an example. It might even have happened that way. We would never know it. If someone in our future went back and altered reality, we'd be completely ignorant of it, so there's nothing I can say about history with absolute certainty. As far as we know, it could have been changed already innumerable times by time travelers yet to come. That's the thing you're not getting. Once it's changed, there's no record of what it was before. That reality never existed. Just like you never existed back there. Your own mother has no knowledge of you now because she never had you."

Thinking about her mother not knowing her, Dani felt a painful jab at her heart. That was inconceivable. Tension gripped her body before she remembered what a load of crap all of this was. She shook off the unease.

Swenson appeared momentarily sympathetic as she gazed into Dani's eyes. "Leo Darius," she said, "concerns us because, although he may seem like a punk eco-terrorist so far, he will become something much worse in the future."

"We *must* stop him now while we can," added Moon emphatically. "Before he kills millions of innocent people."

"Millions of people?" Dani asked. "A future Hitler?"

"Worse than Hitler," replied Swenson, her expression somber. "If you judge evil by the number of lives taken. Darius is an evil genius, a maniac."

"How did he do it, kill millions of people?"

"Biological weapons targeted very specifically at humans."

Dani sat silently regarding the faces of these people, trying to figure out what their game was. So far, none of this made sense. Clearly they wanted her to believe them. But how could she? Still, she was curious to find out what they were really up to, so she decided to play along, at least for a little while.

"You said I could go back. What do I have to do?"

Swenson tapped her fingertips together. "Have you ever killed anyone, Daniella?"

"No."

"Could you?"

Dani considered the question. It wasn't the first time she'd thought about it, of course. In her job, it was a real, daily possibility. She hoped she would never have to kill anyone. That was probably the one aspect of her job she most dreaded, the need to use deadly force. But if her life, the life of her fellow officers or the lives of innocent people were in danger, she knew she was capable of it. She was trained for it. "Yes, I could do it," she answered. "If people were in danger."

"A lot of people are in danger from Darius. Could you kill him?"

Dani nodded. "Yes, if I couldn't take him into custody. If it was necessary."

Mr. Moon rolled his eyes. "What did I tell you?"

Swenson smiled gently at Dani. "You don't understand. He has to be stopped. He has to be killed. Custody is not enough. You witnessed his first murder. There will be so many more. I can't begin to describe the horrors that will result from his actions. His ultimate goal is no less than to annihilate the human race."

"Why would he do that? Bryan said he was an environmentalist, that he wanted to stop the polluters, stop the destruction of the rain forests and all that. He wanted to make sure there was clean air and water and natural, healthy crops...*for people*. It doesn't make sense that he would attack Genepac if he wants to destroy the human race."

"Did you miss the part about him being a maniac?" asked Moon sarcastically.

"Exactly," Swenson agreed. "Darius started out like any other planet-friendly protestor. But he evolved. His ideas became dangerously twisted. He began to believe that reformation wasn't possible, that any progress would be too little, too late. So he turned to destruction as the means of achieving his ends, to return the planet to its natural state. He wanted to remove what he saw as the most destructive poison threatening the Earth. Humans. He believed that the only way to save the planet was to eradicate humanity."

Dani stared.

"In a way, he's right," said Hale with a half-hearted shrug. "I mean, obviously, humans have raped and pillaged the planet for centuries. Species have gone extinct, ecosystems have been destroyed."

"We are all aware of that," Swenson said. "As a species, we've made huge mistakes and we've been selfish, but we have turned it around. We're on the right track now. We're doing much better as shepherds of this planet. And we will continue to improve. Even Darius realized that humanity will get it right eventually."

"But not quickly enough for him," Hale added. "In the twenty-first century, the planet endured devastating losses. Recovery, naturally, will take centuries. Darius thinks humans have had the reins too long."

"You all seem to know Darius very well," Dani remarked, her gaze on the smug little scientist.

He shot a glance at Swenson, who laughed bitterly.

"Of course we know him well," she said. "What would you expect? His legacy is huge and monstrous. Every kindergartener knows his name, the twenty-first century's mastermind of mass murder!" She paused, composing herself. "So you see why he has to be stopped? Completely stopped."

Dani mulled this information over for a silent moment. "So I would have to kill him."

Swenson leaned back in her chair. "Yes. You can never be sure what will happen in your so-called justice system. We can't leave any room for doubt. The stakes are too high for both your world and for ours. And we may not get another chance."

"To put this in perspective," Moon said, "we have never taken on a mission like this before. This is our first. Of all the monsters in all of human history, we've targeted this one man."

Dani looked from one to the other of them, still trying to figure out what this con was all about. "Yes, I could kill a man like that."

"Good," said Swenson. "Then that's what we're offering you. We don't have anyone else to send right now. Nobody who's right for the job anyway."

"What I want to know," Dani said, "is why you don't just hire somebody, a hit man or whatever."

Swenson licked her lips, looking like she was trying to formulate an answer. "It would be very hard to find someone here with the skill and predisposition to do this job, especially with so little time. Besides, this is a top secret installation. Very few people are aware of our ability to travel through time. It wouldn't be wise to bring in anyone else unnecessarily. You already know about us, obviously."

"Whether we like it or not," added Moon.

Swenson frowned in his direction, then turned a gentler expression toward Dani. "You said you could do it and we think you might have a chance. You're strong and know how to use a weapon. Like you said, you're already on the case. You were working with Frank. You certainly know the historic city and how to work it to your advantage. Also, there's another reason we're considering your offer to go back. You can only return for a few days, you understand. After that, you'll come back to us and live out your life here. I'm sure there are people you'll miss in the twenty-first century."

Dani thought of Gemma and Tucker, of her sister, brother, parents and friends. What if she really did have to leave them all? That was unimaginable and something she didn't want to think about. She didn't *need* to think about it. She was being manipulated, obviously lied to. She had to keep reminding herself that nothing she was being told could possibly be true.

"It would be your chance to say good-bye," Swenson explained. "We thought that was the best we could do for you. You could see the people you love again, then the next time you transport out, you'll do it with understanding, on your own terms. The way this happened, well, we're very sorry and we feel that we can at least give you a chance to adjust to the idea by giving you a short trip back."

"But, remember," added Hale, "nobody will know you. To them, you'll be a total stranger."

An involuntary shudder took hold of Dani's body. *No!* she cautioned herself. *Don't let them get under my skin.*

She leaned back in her chair, shaking her head and pushing her doubts away. "This is the biggest can of bullshit I've ever heard. But you people do it well, I've got to say."

Swenson smiled appreciatively. "Daniella, I understand your skepticism, but it doesn't matter whether you believe us or not. If you agree to go home, you'll see for yourself. And I'm certain you will want to help us stop Darius. You are, after all, a police officer. It's your duty to protect the public from this monster. The only thing is, you won't have time to mull it over, and you may find it difficult to rely on local law enforcement for help. It will be up to you to take him out, you alone. You'll have no more than two weeks, so whatever you need to do back there, you'll need to do it quickly."

Moon slapped a palm on the table. "I don't like any of this! This isn't how it's supposed to happen. You need to find somebody else. What about Dr. Hale here?" He leaned toward the delicate young scientist, who looked suddenly terrified and began to stutter.

"I'm the only one who knows how to operate the machine," he blurted.

Swenson stood, calm and self-assured, and said, "Daniella, do you mind stepping into the hallway for a moment?" She flashed Dani a smile meant to be reassuring, but it was bordered by the hard, cold edge of resolve. She could hardly hold the smile for more than a heartbeat. Swenson was nothing if not cool.

Dani left the room. The door slid shut behind her. She stood outside it for a few moments. Whatever was going on inside was inaudible. She looked down the curved, featureless hallway in both directions. *What's to stop me from walking right out of here?* she asked herself. Whatever this con was about, she didn't like it and didn't intend to fall for it. Why not just leave?

Having come from the left, she decided to head right. New territory. She jogged until she had lost sight of the conference room, passing identical doors along the way, meeting nobody. How did they not get lost in here? she wondered. She reached a Y junction and randomly chose to go left. Shortly after the junction, she came to a metal door. There was a label above it that said "Exit." *This is the one*, she thought. The door didn't open automatically like the others. She pushed on it. There was no response. A panel on the wall contained six buttons. One of them said "Open." *Simple enough*, she thought, then pressed it.

A beam of soft white light passed over her face. Then a buzzer sounded and a section of the ceiling opened above her. Before she could retreat, a greenish light enveloped her, freezing her in place. She struggled, but all of her strength was sufficient to move her body only a fraction of an inch. She tried to move her hand toward the wall, pushing as hard as she could and achieving a paltry result. She was like a mosquito caught in a drop of amber.

The buzzer still sounded, but it was muffled by the force surrounding her. She struggled a moment longer, but soon realized there was no point. As soon as she let her body go limp, she saw Hale, Moon and Swenson running toward her. They stopped six feet away, Moon panting and the other two gazing with displeasure at her.

"I told you we couldn't trust her," said Moon, his voice sounding wavy and distant.

"Unfortunately," Swenson replied, "we have no choice. She's all we've got right now. Once she realizes the truth, I believe she'll do the right thing."

CHAPTER SEVEN

The first thing Dani was aware of was a dog barking in the distance. Then the moist cool cushion under her body. She had a splitting headache and felt like she might throw up if she moved a muscle, even an eyelid muscle. Finally, the unmistakable smell of bubblegum roused her from the deep nothingness she inhabited. She managed to coax one eyelid open. Inches from her face, a pair of clear azure eyes peered down at her from a cherubic face, puckered mouth working rhythmically on a wad of gum. Dani opened the other eye. The girl was about seven, her face framed by blond curls. A tiny silver unicorn suspended from her neck swung within a micron of Dani's nose. A pea-sized pink bubble appeared between the girl's lips, then grew steadily larger until it was the size of a lime. It popped and she swept the remnants back into her mouth with her tongue.

"Are you okay?" she asked in a small, sweet voice. Then she sat back to observe.

Dani looked past the girl. A canopy of trees above formed a lacework of sunshine. Well-maintained grass stretched out in all directions. She nodded at the girl.

"I thought you were dead," she said matter-of-factly.

Dani put a hand to her forehead. "No. I just feel like it." With effort, she sat and pulled her knees up to her chin.

The girl held Dani's cap in one hand. She thrust it toward her. "Are you a policewoman?"

"A police officer, yes." She took the cap and brushed a few blades of dry grass from it. "My name's Dani. What's yours?"

"Bailey."

Dani squinted at the park-like landscape. She could hear cars honking and music playing nearby. And the dog was still barking. "Where are we?"

"Bunny Meadow."

Dani knew the place. Golden Gate Park, San Francisco. She gingerly rose to her feet, pushing through a wave of nausea. "Thank you for your concern, Bailey. Are your parents nearby?"

The girl pointed vaguely toward a group of people with lawn chairs, a well-stocked picnic table and a volleyball net.

"Why don't you go on over there? I need to get back to work." Dani ran a hand through her hair, then set her cap gently over it.

"You sure you're okay?"

"I will be." Dani flashed her a smile to reassure her.

"Bye!" Bailey ran across the lawn to her family.

Dani stood where she was, trying to remember what had happened. This reminded her of her college days, waking up with a raging hangover in some strange place with no idea how she'd gotten there. But that hadn't happened in a long time. She hardly ever drank these days and when she did, she didn't drink much. So what was she doing here, passed out flat on her back in a public park?

In a sudden panic, she reached for her holster. Her duty weapon was in place and still secured. She heaved a sigh of relief, then stepped toward the road, her legs weak and unsteady. When she reached the sidewalk, she walked toward the Panhandle, fighting the fog in her mind and trying to piece together the events of the day.

She and Perkins had been on patrol. They'd pulled over an elderly man driving erratically. Some kind of medical issue.

Mr. Cavanaugh, that was his name. An ambulance took him to the hospital. About a quarter after one, dispatch issued a call for assistance from Agent Bryan, the FBI man in charge of the Genepac Industries task force. He was in pursuit of the suspect, Leo Darius. She and Perkins had responded. She remembered racing up the stairs of a ten-story apartment building. When she got to the top, Bryan was lying on the roof, shot once in the chest, his blood pooling around him.

After that, things got fuzzy.

She took out her phone to see what time it was. Three o'clock, Monday, October 3. Had that been only an hour and a half ago? It seemed so much longer.

When she reached Stanyan Street, she automatically looked for Old Gustav and his pony Comet. Their spot was vacant. Gus's sign, offering pony cart rides in the park, wasn't there either, but there were a few pieces of shattered red and yellow wood in the gutter. The pony cart? Had something happened to Gus's cart?

She heard the strains of a bluesy saxophone nearby. She followed it to where a young man sat on a low wall blowing on the horn, his eyes nearly closed, his face adorned with a nose ring and a precisely trimmed goatee. His instrument case was open on the sidewalk. There were a few dollar bills and some coins on the blue velvet lining of the case. When he opened his eyes, he acknowledged her with a nod but continued to play. She waited for the song to end.

"How'd you like it, Officer?" he asked.

"Nice. I haven't seen you here before."

"I move around." He hopped off the wall. "Is there a problem?"

"No, no problem. I was wondering if you'd seen an old man with a pony and cart. He's usually right there on that corner giving rides. His name is Gus."

The young man's smile faded. "Gus, right. I don't think he's coming back, at least not for a while."

"What do you mean?"

"It was…yikes." He bared his teeth, then shook his head gloomily. "I saw it myself. It was right there, earlier today. I guess you didn't hear about it."

Dani tensed with dread. "What happened?"

"A car ran up on the curb and plowed right into them. Demolished the cart."

"Oh, my God!"

"Yeah, it was a mess. I ran over and tried to help. The little horse was hurt and the old man was crying, trying to comfort her. I don't know if she had a broken leg or what. He, Gus, that is, had a cut on his face, but I don't think he was hurt too badly because he kept arguing with the ambulance guys that he wanted to go with the pony instead of to the hospital."

Poor Gus, Dani thought. *Poor Comet!*

"The old dude driving the car was acting nuts. Like he didn't know what was going on. He must have passed out or something and lost control of the car. His name was Cavanaugh, I think. He wasn't hurt from the accident, but they took him to the hospital too because of how he was acting."

"Cavanaugh?" The feeling of dread turned into a profound chill running up Dani's spine. "What did the car look like?"

"It was a tan Toyota Camry. Old guy like that shouldn't be driving. He was so mixed-up, he didn't know where he was. I'm not even sure he knew he'd just run over somebody."

Dani felt pretty mixed-up herself. "This happened this morning?"

The musician nodded. "About eleven forty, forty-five. Just a little before noon. I hope the horse is okay."

Dani stared at Gus's corner, remembering how she and Perkins had pulled Mr. Cavanaugh over and sent him away in an ambulance. That was eleven thirty this morning. At eleven forty, forty-five or even noon, he wasn't in his car, wasn't driving. He was being treated at the hospital. But it couldn't have been another Mr. Cavanaugh in the same type of car with the same type of disorientation.

Am I losing my mind? Dani wondered. The sax player seated himself again. As he started to play, she walked quickly away, disturbed by what had happened to Gus, not just because it was a horrible blow to the old man, but because of how impossible it was that it had happened at all.

Anxiety crept over her skull as unsettling images played across her consciousness. She was gradually remembering the dream she'd been having while lying in Golden Gate Park. It was wild. She'd been in a strange circular building where the rooms had no windows. The people, there were four of them, wore unusual clothing and little doodads like Bluetooth earpieces. Frank Bryan, the FBI man who'd been shot, was one of their colleagues, they said. He was a man from the future. He'd been sent back in time to kill an evil genius named Leo Darius before he could commit the atrocities history attributed to him. Classic sci-fi stuff. Dani was a sucker for movies like that. She and Gemma had watched *Planet of the Apes*, the original one, just a couple of weeks ago.

She shook her head. *Funny how your subconscious weaves bits of reality into your dreams.* For sure, Agent Bryan had been in her thoughts. The disturbing image of his bloody body was vivid in her mind. But she still couldn't remember what had happened between that moment and the moment when she had awakened in the park.

Suddenly all she could think of was the comfort of hearing her wife's voice. She pulled out her phone again and speed-dialed Gemma's office. Nothing happened. She then pressed the code for home. Same thing. She opened the address book. It was empty. There were no names, no numbers. She checked her text messages. Nothing. Not only were there no new messages, but there were no messages at all. She clicked on the icon for photos. That folder was empty as well. All her nutty selfies and pictures of Gemma and Tucker were gone. Had she wiped out all her data during whatever this drunk-like blackout was? Or had somebody else wiped her phone?

She dialed Gemma's cell number manually and waited anxiously for her voice, but the phone didn't dial. Checking the display, she saw the message, "No Service." How could that be? Her service was paid automatically each month. Irritated, she tucked the phone into a compartment of her duty belt. There was something else there. She removed a silver tube from the pouch. On the side of it were three translucent blue windows. She recognized the object. She had picked it up on the roof beside Agent Bryan's body.

As she stared at the device, she remembered that this too had made its way into her dream. The nerdy young man, Dr. Gavin Hale, had told her it was a transport beacon, that it would return her to the future. "Turn the top of the device clockwise. That will turn it on. To activate it, cover the pinhole at the top with your thumb. Once you do that, you will be transported instantly back through the time portal."

She was frustrated that she was remembering more and more details of the dream, but nothing more about actual events.

She stared hard at the device. Obviously not a ticket to the future. Then what was it? Some kind of flashlight? She considered rotating the top to open it, but decided against it and put it away. She'd take a look at it later.

The silver tube made her wonder if she could still be dreaming. Listening to traffic, she realized there was nothing at all dreamlike about her surroundings. The sidewalk felt solid beneath her feet. She decided to walk to the Richmond Station and find out what had happened in the last couple of hours. It was unlikely, but maybe Agent Bryan had survived his wound. Maybe Leo Darius had been apprehended and was behind bars.

She walked past the familiar landmarks of her life. The reassuring sights and sounds around her made her feel better. Everything was fine. Everything was normal. There was a logical explanation as to how she had ended up in Golden Gate Park under the scrutiny of a seven-year-old girl.

At the door of the station, she met Bradley Nelson on his way out. "Hey, Brad, how's it going?" she called. He looked at her pointedly, wrinkling his brow, no recognition on his face. Then he gave up and said, "Hey," before walking off. She stood just outside the station door, a slow chill moving down the length of her body. *He didn't recognize me*, she realized. How was that possible? They'd known one another two years. They saw each other every day at the morning briefing and sometimes more than once a day. She turned to look at herself in the reflection of the glass and saw what she always saw, a tall, slender, fine-looking woman in a police uniform.

It was just one guy, she told herself, shaking off the uneasiness. Maybe he had something on his mind. Maybe the sun had blinded him.

She pushed through the door to the inside and walked across the lobby to a side room where she knew she could grab a cup of coffee. Two female officers sat inside talking. She didn't recognize them, so she just smiled as she filled a disposable cup. On a table by the window was the collection box for their Make-A-Wish sponsorship. They were collecting to send a ten-year-old girl, Lydia, to London. Her picture, sweet little kid with braids, was on the front of the box, superimposed over a skyline scene that included Big Ben and the London Eye. Lydia had leukemia. To send her family to London for a week would cost about ten thousand dollars. According to the hand-drawn thermometer beside the box, they were creeping up close to one thousand. It was slow going. Dani wondered if that poor kid would ever see Buckingham Palace.

After a deep swallow of coffee, she left the room, having decided to find Sergeant Hudson. He'd fill her in on Darius. At the security door, she swiped her ID badge over the reader and banged up against the door, spilling some of the coffee when the door unexpectedly resisted. The light on the reader remained red. She swiped her badge again more carefully and watched for the green light, but it remained stubbornly red.

She took a step back, noticing her anxiety returning. *There's something wrong with the reader,* she told herself. No need to panic. It happened sometimes. She wiped the coffee from the floor with her napkin, then looked around at the bustling station lobby with its cops and citizens going about their business like any other day.

As she was trying to decide what to do next, the security door opened and Sergeant Hudson himself stepped through. She felt her body nearly physically lift off the ground in relief to see him. "Sarge!"

He turned to face her, his weathered, clean-shaven face expectant. "Yes, Officer, what can I do for you?"

There was no recognition in his face. Dani balked, thrown off guard. She stuttered, having forgotten what she wanted to see him for.

"What's on your mind?" he prompted.

She recovered herself enough to ask her question. "Sarge, what's the situation with that bomber Darius? Did we catch him?"

He pursed his lips and shook his head. "Somehow he got away. But we're all over him. Don't worry, we'll get him."

"What about our guys? Is everybody accounted for?"

"Yeah. We never got near him. Agent Bryan of the FBI, though, that's another story. None of our people got there in time. Perkins found the body."

Perkins, she thought, bewildered. But *she* had found the body, not Perkins. He arrived after her.

Hudson put a hand on her shoulder paternally. "Carry on, Officer."

He strode across the tile floor, his shiny shoes clicking out a regular beat. Sweat broke out on Dani's forehead and her palms went clammy. Everything looked normal. Everybody was acting as if it was an ordinary day. But there was nothing normal or ordinary about this situation. She was becoming truly frightened now.

She walked up to the duty officer, a young man she knew only slightly, and, trying to sound casual, said, "Can you look up something for me?"

"What is it?"

"I ran into this officer of the twenty-first precinct and want to verify her ID." She made sure her badge was obscured from his view through the window.

"Name?"

"Daniella Barsetti. Badge number 65991."

After a moment of intimacy with his computer screen, he replied without looking up. "No such officer."

Dani managed to suppress her alarm, though she could feel her throat closing in.

The rookie looked at her and said, "Impersonating an officer? Do you want to file a report?"

She shook her head. "Not yet. Thanks." She forced a smile, then turned and nearly ran from the building.

Back on the street, she leaned shakily against the wall of a building and cradled the mysterious silver tube in her palm, trying to wrap her mind around what was happening. According to the police department, Officer Daniella Barsetti didn't exist. The young scientist in the future, Gavin Hale, had said even her mother wouldn't know her. She must still be dreaming. That was the only explanation. She closed her eyes and willed herself to wake up. Sometimes that worked. But it didn't work this time.

It was now nearly four o'clock. Her sister was expecting her to help pick out her wedding dress. She had only a half hour to get to the bridal shop. She checked her phone. Still no service. *Damn!* She needed to call Gemma just to hear her voice and hear her say, "I love you." If only she could hear Gemma's voice, she knew everything would be okay.

When she got to the bus stop, she waited alongside a man in a cheap business suit who was talking on his phone. The faint but unmistakable odor of urine wafted by every few seconds, bringing back the nausea. Dani glanced around to see a crumpled heap of dark clothing in a doorway. No doubt there was somebody sleeping there. Like any big city, this one had its problems. But it was also beautiful and vibrant. Dani had never lived anywhere else and had never wanted to. As a kid, she had read *The Wizard of Oz*, and when she came to the description of the Emerald City at the end of the yellow brick road, she pictured San Francisco at the end of the Golden Gate Bridge, the water at its feet sparkling like precious gemstones. This was her home and she loved it. She loved the city and she loved her life. At the moment, anxiety barely under control, she loved it more passionately than ever.

When the man in the suit had finished his call, she asked, "Sir, can I borrow your phone for a minute?"

He looked momentarily surprised, then thrust it toward her. "Sure, Officer."

She dialed Gemma's office, waiting for her assistant Shelley to answer with her customary greeting: "Mettler Consulting, this is Shelley speaking." But it wasn't Shelley who answered. It was a recording. "We're sorry. Your call cannot be completed at this time." *What?* She ended the call and dialed Gemma's cell phone number instead. It went to voice mail and Gemma's recorded message. "I'm not available right now. Leave a message." Even if Gemma hadn't answered, it was so good to hear her voice! Dani gulped back the emotion, determined not to give Gemma any reason for concern.

"Hi, honey," Dani recorded. "It's me. I just wanted to say hello and let you know something's wrong with my cell phone, so you won't be able to call me back. I'm on my way to meet Rachel at the bridal shop. Wedding dresses, yuck! See you later. I love you."

She returned the phone to its owner and asked, "How much longer until the bus gets here?"

"Fifteen minutes."

If she waited for the bus, she'd be late. It was quicker to walk anyway, she decided, and she took off on foot. Walking made her feel better. She nodded to people she passed and they nodded back. It was a beautiful day.

When she arrived at the bridal shop, Rachel was already there and already wearing a gorgeous white gown with lace everywhere, a train of satin on the floor at her feet and two middle-aged women fussing over the details. Dani stopped short in the doorway, stunned at how beautiful her kid sister looked with her hair tucked into a filmy headdress and her face flushed with excitement. Her brown eyes shone with a glossy mist. The scene took Dani's breath away.

All three women looked up as Dani entered. She hadn't had time to go home and change, so she swept off her cap to diminish the impact of her official appearance.

"Rach," she said brightly, stepping inside. "You look gorgeous!"

Rachel looked directly at her, one eye squinting in concern. She looked about to speak when another woman came out from behind a rack of dresses holding another dazzling white beauty on a padded hanger. Her long black hair dropped to her petite waist, which was encased in a tightly fitted, thigh-length purple dress. It was Patty, Rachel's best friend. *Why did I have to come if she was going to be here*, Dani wondered with annoyance. *Rach knows I don't like this kind of thing.*

"Look at this one!" Patty announced, then stopped short when she caught sight of Dani. "Oh, what's going on?"

"Can I help you, Officer?" asked one of the older women.

Rachel was still staring at her with mild curiosity and absolutely no recognition. Dani swallowed, not knowing what to say. She couldn't get over the way Rachel was looking at her. Everyone waited for her to explain her presence.

"Sorry," she finally said. "Wrong shop." She stepped backward toward the door, noticing the puzzled look on Rachel's face. She must have heard Dani say her name. Maybe she'd think she had misheard it. "You're very beautiful," Dani said. "That's a magnificent gown. Congratulations."

"Thank you," Rachel replied uncertainly.

Dani quickly exited out of sight of the shop windows and pressed herself against the stone wall, in need of support. *Oh, God*, she thought, *this can't be happening! How could my own sister not know me?* After a few moments watching and listening to the traffic, she was able to gather herself together enough to walk away from the shop.

What should I do now? she wondered. *Where should I go?*

She got out her keys. Her apartment key was there on the ring where it always was. So was the car key and all the rest. She could go home, have a shower, hug Tucker and think through what to do next. Gemma would be home in about an hour. She wanted so badly to see Gemma.

It was too far to walk, so she waited at the Muni stop with an elderly woman and a young man with an unkempt beard and a worn brown coat.

When the bus came, she let the other two board ahead of her, then passed her Clipper card in front of the reader. It didn't register, so she held it more precisely, but the card wasn't recognized. "Shit!" she muttered under her breath, then reached into her front pocket to see if she had any change. She came up with a quarter, two pennies and a lint-covered Tic-Tac. She looked apologetically at the driver, a no-nonsense woman with metallic black hair and bright blue eighties-style eye shadow over languid brown eyes. The woman jerked her head toward the back of the bus. "Go on," she said flatly.

"Thanks." Dani walked down the aisle as the bus pulled into traffic, drawing the glances of the other passengers, who must have wondered what a uniformed cop was doing riding the bus. She found a seat at a window beside a young woman in a pink sweater and white-rimmed glasses. She was engrossed in her phone and didn't look up, no doubt hoping that whoever it was would move on.

Dani stepped over the woman's knees to get to the open seat, then settled in for the ride. She was sure she'd put a twenty somewhere and began to systematically search the compartments of her duty belt. She hoped she could find it because at this point she was beginning to worry that she was about to learn the hard way that her debit and credit cards were not going to work and she'd be cut off from her bank account. A twenty wouldn't go far, but it was something.

When she got to the glove pouch, there were no gloves inside. Instead, there was a thick wad of money. She unrolled it to find that all the bills were hundreds, hundreds of hundreds, all of them worn, circulated. That's when she remembered the woman in charge of the science lab, Pamela Swenson, handing her the cash, antique paper money that they'd gotten from some archive, carefully selected to predate the current year. Money like this wasn't that rare, she'd said. It turned up all the time inside walls when old buildings were torn down and in containers buried long ago in people's yards. It was worthless as currency in the future, Swenson had told her, and not worth much more even to collectors. "You might need to buy a few things," she'd said.

Dani glanced at the woman beside her, who was staring at the money in her palm in astonishment. She quickly folded the loot and stuffed it back in the pouch, then looked out the window, pretending nonchalance. In her mind, she couldn't have been farther from it.

When the bus made it to Cow Hollow, she got off and walked another block to the apartment. All she could think of now was getting home. If she could just get home and lie down in her own bed, when she woke up this nightmare would be over.

Walking up the steps, she thought what she always thought. The house needed a little TLC. The windows, with their wavy old glass, were so hard to open and close that she and Gemma rarely tried to shift them. A fresh coat of paint would have worked wonders on the place, but the landlord, an elderly Polish man, had lost interest in the property long ago. He had his own troubles. Dani kept meaning to paint the building herself, but she hadn't gotten around to it. She was sure the old guy wouldn't care.

She put her key in the front door lock and turned it. It didn't budge. She tried again, but no luck. Her key didn't work. She examined it to make sure it was the right one, the Schlage. Then she stared at the lock. She'd replaced the deadbolt four months ago, but this lock was tarnished and scratched. In fact, it looked exactly like the lock she had replaced. She rubbed her face with her hand, feeling like her brain was going to explode.

The key wasn't the only thing bothering her. Normally, when somebody was at the front door, Tucker would run to it and bark. She listened and heard nothing. She banged on the door in case he was asleep. Still nothing. She rang the doorbell and waited. There was no noise inside. She sat on the steps, sitting in front of her own home, locked out. An unwelcome thought occurred to her. Maybe it wasn't her home. If she no longer existed in this time, maybe Gemma didn't live here anymore. Anything could have happened. Gemma might have given up the apartment when her mother moved to the nursing home. Gemma might be living with someone else, somewhere else.

That can't be true, though. It just can't!

Not knowing what else to do, she decided to wait for Gemma. Today was the day she had her interview with North Bay Healthcare Services. Dani was sure it had gone well. Gemma had a good system and she came off as sincere, passionate and capable when she talked about it. She'd be home any minute. Then they'd go out to dinner to celebrate. It would be great. It would be fine. Everything was fine.

Dani sat on the front steps and thought back over the last few days and the events leading up to today, all of which she remembered clearly. What was less clear, however, was where reality left off and dreaming had taken over. On Friday she'd met FBI Agent Bryan for the first time. He called a task force together to capture a dangerous man, Leo Darius, a man he described as "an evil genius." That was the day Darius had blown up a building. But did Leo Darius even exist? For that matter, did Agent Bryan exist? In her dream, he was a visitor from the future. Maybe he had only existed in the dream. Maybe her dream had already spanned several days.

She checked her phone for the time. That was about all it was good for. Gemma was late.

She sat with her muddled thoughts and watched ordinary life in progress, feeling numb. Cars went by. People came home from work and left for evening activities. They rode bikes and walked their dogs. They went about their non-dreamlike activities on a lovely, mild October evening in San Francisco. In the twenty-first century.

CHAPTER EIGHT

Gemma read through her email, delighted that the final hour of the workday had finally arrived. Lois typed rapidly on her keyboard while streaming tunes from her iPod. There was an expression of serene satisfaction on her shiny round face. And of course a barely audible humming issuing from her throat. Gemma tried not to listen, tried to block it out. Lois believed she was being graciously polite to her coworkers by listening to her music, all oldies, all the time, in silence. Except that she wasn't silent. There was the ever-present hum. Sometimes it became distinctive enough that Gemma could actually make out the song, invariably something by Elton John, the Bee Gees or the Eagles.

Her fifty-something neighbor had other annoying habits too, but the humming was the most irritating of all. Gemma had tried to drown it out with music and earbuds of her own, but was only minimally successful. Lois would be retiring soon, or so she promised, and Gemma would inherit a new cube mate. She both happily anticipated and dreaded that day; the new coworker invariably would have his or her own bad habits, and for some reason, the new, unknown bad habits seemed potentially scarier than the known ones. Gemma was sure she too had bad habits that annoyed people. People who lived alone were especially prone to that, she had heard. Even more so, women who lived with cats.

All in all, she liked Lois, except for the humming. She was single too, long divorced, with two grown kids. She was pillowy with the shapelessness of middle age and had wiry, bronze hair with nearly perpetual storm-gray roots. Her eyelids drooped down over her eyelashes, giving her a somewhat mournful look when her face was in repose, but she wasn't a mournful person. She was garrulous and upbeat and seemed fond of Gemma in a maternal sort of way. The workplace did this to people, threw you together day after day with someone you should never have known, someone you would never have spoken to or come across in your regular life. And over time, somehow, with your excruciatingly opposing political, religious and social views, you became two people who had a genuine emotional attachment to one another. You knew more about this person than you knew about your own parents and siblings because you spent all your days together for years and years. Gemma had been rooming with Lois for years here at the FDA's district office.

Her phone ringing broke through her irritation with Lois. "Hello?"

"Hi, Gem," said her friend Miko. "I've had a hell of a day. Can you meet me at Stormy's for a drink?"

"Sure. I've got no plans." Gemma chuckled. "Like I would have plans."

"People say miracles do happen."

If you were a student of sarcasm, Gemma thought, *you would do well to study at Miko's feet.*

"See you there."

After ending the call, she noticed she had a voice mail message. "Hi, honey," a woman's voice said. "It's me. I just wanted to say hello and let you know something's wrong with my cell phone, so you won't be able to call me back. I'm on my way to meet Rachel at the bridal shop. Wedding dresses, yuck! See you later. I love you."

"*Hi, honey,*" she thought. *Obviously a wrong number.* Also, she knew nobody named Rachel.

Lois removed her earbuds as Gemma put her phone down. "Going out tonight?" she asked hopefully.

"With Miko," Gemma replied.

"Oh." She sounded disappointed. "Well, that's nice. But, really, Gemma, you should get out more, find a woman to settle down with."

Gemma turned to catch Lois's eye. She grinned. She liked to show how open-minded she was by making remarks like that. But Gemma hadn't forgotten that five years ago when they first met, Lois had been extremely uncomfortable with the idea of sharing a cube with a lesbian. She tried not to show it, but it came through in subtle ways. She seemed to be afraid that Gemma was some kind of sex maniac who would attack her and, somehow, maybe with witchcraft, force her to do unspeakable things with women.

As if! Gemma thought, rolling her eyes. Five years later, Lois seemed to have evolved. Maybe because Gemma was single. *A lesbian who doesn't sleep with women isn't all that offensive to anybody. Maybe I don't even deserve to be called a lesbian,* she thought. Although she had not been celibate the entire five years, not completely. There was the occasional date that turned into two or three dates before everything blew up in her face. But Lois knew nothing about those dates. To her, Gemma was a safe and cuddly kind of lesbian. Didn't give offense. Easy to love.

"How's your mother?" Lois asked.

"I've got her in a new place, River Gardens. It seems okay, so far. Except, of course, for the food. I take her homemade things as often as I can. I just don't understand why institution food has to be so bad. Maybe in prisons it makes sense. After all, it's prison and things aren't supposed to be high class, but in a nursing home, why can't people get some fresh fruit or a salad now and then? Everything's preservative-laden, highly processed, monotone brown stuff. I've tasted it plenty of times, so I know how bad it is, and it would be even worse if you had to eat it every day."

"I know what you mean. My father was in one of those places for a while. That was the main thing he complained about, the tasteless food. When you have an eighty-five-year-old suffering from a dozen different ailments and the food is his main complaint, something is seriously wrong with it."

"Why can't somebody do something about that?"

Lois shook her head. "It's probably just too big a challenge. They have to feed a lot of people with a small budget and staff."

"I know, but there ought to be some improvements possible within those parameters. Somebody with some drive and a few good ideas could really make a difference."

Lois nodded thoughtfully, then put her earbuds back in and proceeded to hum.

* * *

Miko placed a glass of chardonnay in front of Gemma, then took her seat and settled her own glass beside her plate where four cherry tomatoes had been pushed to the side as she had eaten her salad. Gemma had a hard time understanding somebody not liking tomatoes, but Miko had her quirks. She crossed her legs, adjusted her blouse, then picked up her glass for a sip. Miko always looked ready for a photo shoot—her flaxen hair was shiny, clean and orderly under a royal blue tam-o'-shanter, and her makeup, expertly blended with her natural skin tone, looked freshly applied. Miko liked hats and they helped show off her mood and personality.

Miko took a lot of trouble with her looks, and maybe the end result was worth it. She was always lovely, well-groomed and well-coordinated. She was one of those women who had to have two hours to get dressed in the morning. Maybe that was the reason she still lived alone, Gemma surmised, tasting her wine. In Gemma's experience with lesbians, they didn't have much patience for Miko's style of "getting ready." A lot of them were ready five minutes after you said, "Let's go." They wriggled into a sports bra, shoved their feet into sandals, and they were out the door. Gemma was somewhere in between, and she had heard her share of exasperated sighs, jangling keys and toe tapping. Sometimes she was ecstatic that she was single. *Sometimes.*

"Thanks for having dinner with me," Miko said. "After that reaming by my boss, I needed to vent. He's just such a jerk. How was I supposed to know that girl was somebody? She looked like a hooker. So why would I give her the royal welcome? Then she turns out to be somebody's bitch of a daughter and he says, 'You should have known. It's your job to know.' Really? It's my job to know everybody's kids' names?"

Stormy came by to collect their plates and the glasses from their first round of drinks. "Anything else, girls?" she asked, her voice raspy from decades of smoking. Stormy was a tough-looking fifty-year-old with straw-like hair held back in a tight ponytail. She had dark roots and dark eyebrows, but even without the roots, the dye job wouldn't have fooled anybody. She wore a sleeveless top, exposing her tanned, hide-like arms and a classic barbed wire tattoo around her bicep. The barbs, like the arms themselves, had lost some of their definition over time.

"No, thanks," Gemma said. "This'll be it."

"I'll get your check." Stormy withdrew.

"What was her name?" Gemma asked.

"Whose name?"

"The girl you threw out this afternoon?"

"Ashley Roth Livingston." Miko pronounced the name with her nose in the air. "I'm not going to forget that name now, believe me."

Gemma fingered her napkin thoughtfully, avoiding Miko's eye.

"You know who she is!" Miko guessed.

Gemma shrugged. "She's the daughter of our state senator, possibly on her way to becoming the daughter of California's next governor."

"How do you know that?"

"I watch the news. Sorry, Miko. Maybe you shouldn't automatically assume every grungy-looking young woman is a prostitute. The shabby look is very popular these days. The kids want a hairdo that looks like they took a weed whacker to it."

Miko narrowed her eyes skeptically. "Is that the look you're going for? Shabby chic?"

Gemma looked down at her clothes, the pants worn almost through at the knees and the shapeless sweater with a small stain over the left breast. She hadn't noticed it until she was at work. Dabbing at the stain with a wet paper towel in the restroom had done no good. "So you're going to attack me now, your best friend?"

"Sorry. You look beautiful, as always." Miko fluttered her eyelashes, making Gemma smile. "But your hair..."

Gemma stroked the back of her hair self-consciously, thinking, *It isn't that bad.*

"You really should make more of an effort."

"Why?"

"Because that's how you're going to attract your dream girl, that's why. You're not some princess in a fairy tale where some gorgeous dyke is going to ride in on a white horse, take one look at you and fall madly and forever in love. You have to put in the effort."

Gemma sighed. "If I see anything remotely resembling a gorgeous dyke on a white horse, I'll put in some effort. But for the last few years, they've all been toads, so why bother?"

Miko smiled. "All the more reason to try harder. There aren't that many good ones out there."

A rush of cool outside air drew Gemma's attention to the door as it opened. A police officer stepped inside and took off her cap, revealing wavy sable-colored hair with bangs hanging down over her left eye. She swept the bangs aside and glanced around the room, her gaze lighting on Gemma. She seemed momentarily startled, but she held Gemma's gaze, looking at her as if they knew one another. The cop was nicely proportioned and attractive with well-defined cheekbones, a generous mouth and deep brown eyes with naturally thick eyelashes.

Miko leaned across the table and whispered, "Look what just walked in!"

"I saw it." Gemma turned back to her table and took a sip of wine.

"Nice, huh?"

Gemma watched out of the corner of her eye as the cop walked up to the bar and slid onto a stool, facing away from them. "If you like that kind of thing," she said indifferently.

"You mean a hot-woman-in-a-uniform kind of thing?"

Gemma shrugged.

"Look at her," urged Miko. "She looks terrific in that uniform."

Gemma looked at the straight back of the police officer. "Yeah, so what? Take off the uniform and what have you got?"

"You got lucky!" Miko laughed her shrill cackle, drawing a glance of curiosity from the cop.

"You know what I mean," said Gemma quietly. "I prefer brains to brawn."

"Girl, there is no rule that says you can't have both. If you're not interested, she's all mine, which is more than fine with me."

"Go for it," Gemma said with a wave of her hand.

* * *

God, this is painful, Dani thought, resisting the urge to turn around and look at Gemma again. She looked just as she had this morning when they had said their strained good-byes. She was beautiful, her light brown hair framing her face in soft waves. It was a face Dani knew better than her own, a face she had awakened to each morning and fallen asleep with each night for the last four years. But when their eyes had met, there was no recognition there. In fact, there was no interest either. When Gemma had turned away just now, Dani had felt like somebody had stabbed her in the heart.

Maybe coming here was a bad idea. But after an hour of waiting at the apartment, she had decided to try looking for Gemma at one of their hangouts with both hope and dread

building in her mind. By this time, Dani was forced to admit
to herself that she was either still stuck in an incredibly realistic
nightmare or the unthinkable really had happened. She had
known on her way over here that it was likely Gemma would
have no more familiarity with her than anyone else had, and
that was going to hurt like hell. Still, how could she resist?

She had at least been able to prepare this time, but preparing
intellectually did little to cushion the emotional impact.

When Stormy came over to take her order, she said, "Hey,
Storm, how are you?"

She took a long look at Dani and said, "Do I know you,
Officer?"

Geez, what a dipstick I am! For a moment, Dani had forgotten
that nobody knew her in this nightmare. She had to be more
careful.

"I've been around before," she said, "but it's been a while.
Nice to see you're still here. Officer Daniella Barsetti. You can
call me Dani." She set her cap on the bar. "I'll have a club soda
with a lime twist."

"This isn't an official call, is it?" Stormy asked.

"No, no. I'm off duty. Just need to relax."

Stormy's upper lip lifted to reveal her top row of teeth in
her characteristic grin. She popped open a can of club soda and
poured it into a glass. Then she went about her business, leaving
Dani to slowly make her way to the bottom of the pretzel bowl.
She was close enough to Gemma's table to hear Miko's piercing
voice, but not close enough to hear what she was saying, not
over the noise of the squeaky electric fan running behind the
bar. Like a lot of San Francisco buildings, this one didn't have
air-conditioning. It wasn't normally needed. It had been a warm
day, but not hot enough to need a fan running at top speed. But
Stormy always ran hot lately. Sometimes she'd put an ice cube
between her boobs and let it melt there, much to the amusement
of customers. The fan was for her, not them.

Miko laughed frequently and Dani's nightmare began to take
on new levels of horror as she considered that without herself

in the picture, Miko and Gemma might actually become…or might already be…lovers.

"Miko and I could never be more than friends," Gemma had said more than once. It was the sort of thing you said to your wife to reassure her. Not that Dani had ever worried about Miko. Those two had been friends since high school. They loved one another, but it just wasn't like that and it never had been. It never had been in *her* reality, she cautioned herself, but who knew what could happen in this one?

She took a surreptitious look in their direction. There was no ring on Gemma's left hand. Not Dani's and not anybody else's. She glanced at her own hand, at the wedding ring Gemma had placed there. They'd told her that inanimate objects could go back and forth unchanged, that she would be wearing whatever she wore when she transported, that objects in her pockets could travel with her. That was why she was able to bring the transport beacon with her, a device that had obviously not yet been invented in this time.

She shook her head. She would never understand all the bullshit Hale had given her. Probably because that's what it was, bullshit. It wasn't like she was stupid or something. She wasn't stupid enough to believe that line of time-travel bullshit, for instance.

Even if—so far—everybody was acting just like Swenson and Hale said they would.

She put her hands below the bar and slipped off the ring, tucking it into a case on her belt.

"Rough day?" Stormy asked, coming by to check on her.

"Very rough day."

"Want to talk about it?"

Dani had to laugh. "Yes," she said, "but you wouldn't believe me, so, no. Thanks."

Stormy shrugged and stepped away. As Dani turned again to glance at Gemma, they caught one another's gaze. Gemma smiled. It wasn't the comfortable smile of a good friend nor the shy smile of a self-conscious lover. It was the polite smile of a stranger. Dani tried to smile back, but was sure it fizzled. She turned back to the bar, feeling devastated. After a few seconds, she pinched her forearm. Yep, it hurt. What was that supposed to prove? she wondered.

As her drink disappeared, she began to consider the possibility that this was reality after all. What if she were awake and this had really happened to her? Was this how it would end for her and Gemma? A polite smile in a restaurant? She would never have known her, never have kissed her? In fact, nobody would ever have known her or kissed her. It would be like the first twenty-nine years of her life had been erased.

Oh, God, Gemma, this can't be happening!

"Hey, Dani, you okay?"

She realized Stormy was the only person in this world who knew her name. She didn't know her well, but she had already started to know her. *What about Gemma?* she thought. In the few days Dani had here, could they get to know one another again? Could they get close enough so that saying good-bye would actually mean something? At least she could say, "Good-bye, Gemma" and get a look from her that wasn't the polite smile of a stranger. That would be something to take away, something to treasure.

"Dani?" Stormy asked again.

Dani looked up from her puddle of grief to see Stormy looking concerned.

Seeing that look nearly made Dani cry with gratitude. She composed herself and said, "I'm fine. Just a rough day, like I said. But I'll be fine."

A moment later Miko was standing beside her. "We haven't seen you in here before, my friend and I," she said, thrusting out one hip and jerking her head toward Gemma, who was looking out the window, unconcerned with them. "This is sort of our hangout."

"It seems like a nice neighborhood place," Dani replied.

"Can I buy you another one of whatever that is you're drinking?" Miko batted her mascara-thickened lashes.

"No, thanks. I'm just having the one."

"Then how about buying me another glass of wine?"

Miko stood very close, her vampire eyes penetrating deep into Dani's. If Dani had not been so upset, she might have laughed.

"What about your friend?" she asked.

"Naw, two's her limit."

Dani shrugged. "Okay, sure. Stormy, can you set up my friend here with another?"

"I'm Miko," she said, smiling.

"Dani." She glanced back at the table where Gemma still stared out the window, as if she were determined not to show any interest.

Stormy set the wineglass in front of Miko, who climbed up on the stool next to Dani to set her seduction routine in motion.

Dani took another gulp from her glass and put a hundred-dollar bill on the bar, pushing it toward Stormy. "Sorry, it's all I've got."

"No problem, hon," Stormy replied. She took the money to the register and brought back change.

Dani stuffed a twenty into the tip jar.

"You're not leaving, are you?" Miko asked.

"Yeah, I've gotta get going."

Gemma appeared behind them with her purse hanging off her shoulder. "I'm taking off," she said to Miko.

"Stay a while longer, both of you. The night is young."

"Still," Gemma said, "I have to work tomorrow, so see you later."

Gemma gave Dani a noncommittal look, then slipped out of the restaurant. Dani stood and grabbed her cap off the bar.

"Sit down, Dani," Miko said. "Let's talk."

"Sorry, I've got to go too. Nice to meet you, Miko. See you around."

Miko shook her head, her lips set in an exaggerated pout. Dani knew she would sit there and drink and get sad. That was her MO. After four glasses of wine, Stormy would shove her out and she would stumble down the street to her apartment building.

Dani dashed outside into the cool, breezy evening air and trotted along the sidewalk to catch up with Gemma at the corner where she waited for a green light.

"Hey," she said.

Gemma looked startled. "Yes?"

"I thought you might let me walk you home."

"Really? What makes you think I'm not driving?"

That threw her. "Uh, well, you wouldn't, would you? Not after two glasses of wine. Because then I'd have to arrest you. My name's Dani, by the way."

"Gemma. And you're right. I'm walking, but I hardly need a police escort." The light turned green and Gemma turned away and crossed the street.

Dani dashed across to join her. "I'm sure you don't. But I'm feeling a little vulnerable myself and wouldn't mind some protection."

Gemma laughed spontaneously, then looked into Dani's eyes as if trying to read her. She shrugged, then headed toward home with Dani at her side.

"Wasn't that a little cold to walk out on Miko?" Gemma asked.

"It would be colder to sit there and make her think I was interested."

"You're not into women," Gemma stated flatly.

"I am, actually. She's just not my type."

"What is your type?" Gemma asked in her cynical voice.

"Somebody a little more quiet. An introspective sort not prone to road rage."

"Sounds like you summed her up pretty fast."

"Was I wrong?"

Gemma smiled in that way she did when she was trying not to. "No. She's the original Road Rage Diva."

"I also like a girl who's comfortable sticking her hands in mud and sliding into home plate. Miko doesn't look like she'd do either."

Gemma laughed. "She wouldn't."

They stopped at another light.

"But you would?" Dani asked.

"I've been known to dig up a bait worm now and then."

When the light turned green, Dani held her arm out toward Gemma, who hesitated, then smiled and took it.

Dani couldn't help thinking about the day they'd met four years ago. Their meeting was flirtatious with an undercurrent of barely contained euphoria. They both liked one another immediately and both of them hoped they were correctly sensing that it might turn into something real. But this was so different for Dani. It was hard to keep in mind that she and Gemma had no history, at least in Gemma's mind. Their four years together was completely unknown to her. Dani struggled not to allow her despair to show when she looked into Gemma's eyes and saw interest, but no love, no deep connection. It's hard to quantify the subtle ways couples evolve together over time. In many ways, Gemma felt like a stranger to Dani too. The way she looked at her, her body language, even what she said, were all lacking the intimacy that was simply a part of daily life, not something Dani noticed much normally. But she definitely did notice the lack of it.

"You seem to have a knack for sizing up a person," Gemma noted.

"It's just training. Sometimes a cop has to decide fast who she can trust and who she needs to shield herself from."

"You'll find I need a lot more time than five minutes to know if I can trust someone."

Dani smiled to herself. That was true! Gemma was cautious and did not trust easily. Dani found it hard to ask her questions because she already knew all the answers. Like what do you do for a living? But she asked anyway.

"I'm a nutritionist," Gemma replied.

"Really?" Dani said. "What do you do exactly?"

"I work for the FDA. Mainly studies on food safety. It's okay. Secure. Pays well."

Dani stopped abruptly and stared. "The FDA?" she asked, incredulous.

Gemma stopped too and observed her with puzzlement. "Yes."

Dani was stunned. That was the job Gemma had had when they met. That was the job she'd left to start her own business, to rehabilitate institution food in the health care industry. Apparently, in this reality, that had not happened. Dani didn't know what to say. She finally realized her reaction must look truly strange to Gemma, who laughed nervously and asked, "Is something weird about that?"

Dani shook her head, coming to grips with this bombshell. "No, no, not at all. Sorry. I was actually thinking about something else. It was a very strange day and I'm still trying to leave all that behind."

Gemma nodded understandingly. "I'm sure you have a lot of strange days."

"Maybe none so strange as this one," Dani stated. "How long have you worked for the FDA?"

"Eight, almost nine years."

Dani adapted quickly and they continued their walk. "So… you're a nutritionist, huh? I guess you could tell me how to eat better."

Gemma looked Dani up and down quickly. "You seem to be doing okay."

She had always wondered if you met someone you loved at a different time in your life, would you still fall in love? Maybe four years wasn't that much of a difference, especially if Gemma was still single. She lived in the same neighborhood, had the same best friend. She might not have changed much from the day Dani had met her four years ago. She still had the same job, after all. Her face seemed a little fuller than it had this morning. During the last four years, Gemma had gotten fitter, lost a few pounds and muscled up. The two of them kept up a rigorous fitness routine together. Apparently this Gemma, the one who'd never met Dani, wasn't as keen on exercise. Still, she looked fabulous and beautiful, and Dani wanted nothing more than to take her in her arms and kiss her.

"I've got a weakness for hamburgers," she admitted. "But my job is pretty active."

"And dangerous." The left side of Gemma's mouth creased slightly, a subtle indicator of her misgivings.

The danger of Dani's job was always a concern and often a source of tension between them. Gemma was already putting a check mark on the "Con" side of her list, Dani just knew it.

"I should tell you," Gemma said, stopping at a corner, "I don't really go for cops."

She had said something similar four years ago when Dani was a spanking new rookie. At that point, Dani was ready to change professions for her. She would have delivered newspapers to get this woman into bed. She was crazy about Gemma. But she'd won her over then without making that sacrifice. She could win her again, she knew it.

"I'm not just any cop," Dani said in her sexiest come-on voice.

Gemma was friendly and clearly attracted to her, but she was her public self in all respects. The private woman that was cleaved to Dani's heart was nowhere to be seen. Gemma asked about her interests and hobbies, and if she was into any sports.

"I love to kayak," she said. "I don't get to do it often. But I do run at least once a week, along the Embarcadero most Sundays." *With you*, she longed to say. Then, with a painful realization that she knew nothing about Gemma's life in this reality, she asked, "Do you run?"

Gemma nodded. "Now and then. My friend Miko, the one you just met, you couldn't get her to run across a room unless she was trying to get away from a spider. It's actually pretty hard to find a running buddy. To be honest, I don't run much. In college, I was very consistent with it, but not so much anymore."

"I love it," Dani said, thinking about their Sunday runs with Tucker. "I've been training for a half marathon later this month."

Gemma looked impressed. "Wow. I could never do that."

Dani smiled to herself, deciding there was no point contesting that opinion.

"Do you have family in the city?" Gemma asked as they walked side by side toward their building.

"Yes. My parents have lived here all their lives. And there are quite a few of the extended family. My family actually goes back to the eighteen hundreds in San Francisco. My brother

Nick goes to Cal Poly, but my sister still lives here. She's getting married in less than two weeks."

"That's exciting. Younger or older?"

"Younger."

She thought about her parents. They wouldn't know her either. She would never have been born to that family. Was there some other family in the future that she had been born to? This was all too complicated for her. She knew nothing about physics or temporal mechanics or whatever science was screwing her over.

"You ever been married?" Gemma asked.

Dani shook her head. "But I've got nothing against it. If I met the right woman, I'd do it in a heartbeat." She winked.

Gemma rolled her eyes.

She had to remember to ask Gemma questions too, she reminded herself. "What about your family?"

She listened distractedly to the answers, thinking about how absurd it was to be on a first date with her wife of four years.

"I was an only child. My parents were in their early fifties when I was born. My father died a few years back and now my mother is in a nursing home. She has Alzheimer's."

"Oh, I'm sorry. That's gotta be rough. Is she nearby?"

"Yes. She's at River Gardens, here in the city. It's not far. I see her often."

River Gardens? Dani pictured the place in her mind. This morning Harriet had been at Palm Terrace. River Gardens was the place she had lived six months ago. Dani realized nothing could be assumed in this timeline.

As they approached the apartment, she braced herself for what she would see—none of her stuff, nothing of herself. The experience of being obliterated from one's life was devastating. The people she had known, the city she had occupied, were all here as familiar as ever, but she…she had never disturbed a molecule of this timeframe. She realized she was finally starting to believe it. It was the look in Gemma's eye that convinced her, the lack of tenderness, the lack of love, the lack of knowledge. It was a look she knew she couldn't dream because it had been so long since she'd seen it, she had forgotten it completely.

At the steps to their front door, Gemma stopped and faced her. "Do you need to be somewhere? Or…" She smiled nervously. "Do you want to come in?"

Do I need to be somewhere? Wow, Dani thought. *What a question!*

"There's nowhere I need to be. I can come in. I'd like to."

Gemma smiled and stepped up to unlock the door. Dani followed her inside, steeling herself for what she would see. The apartment looked almost identical to how it had the first time she'd been inside, sparsely furnished, neat, clean, somewhat subdued on the personality side. Dani was the messy one, the big, loud personality. Gemma was quieter and took up less space in the world.

Out of habit, she glanced around the floor, expecting Tucker to appear at her feet, tail wagging, looking up at her with his loving soft brown eyes. He didn't appear.

"What are you looking for?" Gemma asked.

"Oh…I…I thought you might have a dog." She laughed uneasily. "I sort of figured you as the Boston terrier type."

Gemma looked at her quizzically. "I'm actually more of a cat person. I have two cats, Smokey and Bear."

"Smokey and Bear," Dani repeated. "That's cute."

"Do you like cats?" Gemma tossed her keys in the yellow glazed bowl on the kitchen counter.

"Sure."

"Funny you should mention Boston terriers, though. Miko has one. A rescue that we came across two years ago. She really loves that dog. He's a sweetheart too."

Dani swallowed hard, trying to push back her disappointment. So Miko had Tucker. *What did it matter?* she asked herself. Miko was a good dog parent. Even if Gemma had taken Tucker in this timeline, what would it have to do with Dani? They'd taken Tucker at her insistence, so it should be no surprise that Gemma had passed on him. Too bad for her. She adored that dog.

"What did she name him?" Dani asked.

"Oreo."

Dani shook her head, managing to suppress a disapproving grunt. "Does she walk him?"

Gemma looked puzzled. "Yes, she walks him. She takes very good care of him. Would you like to see the apartment?"

"Sure."

The master bedroom, their bedroom, was first on the tour. Dani entered it tentatively, noting with dismay how much it had changed since morning. It looked remarkably like it had the first time she'd seen it. The same country quilt covered the bed, and the same pictures were on the walls, landscapes chosen by Gemma's mother. Harriet's rocker, still white like before she had painted it, sat in the corner with a shawl neatly folded over the arm and a gray cat curled up on the cushion. The room was much neater than the last time she'd seen it. The whole apartment was neater. *I'm a slob*, she realized. She ran her hand over the soft fur of the cat's head and he stretched one foreleg out in front of him, then pulled it back and settled back into his resting posture.

At the back of the apartment was the kitchen with its cheerful yellow wallpaper and red accents. She'd never made much of an impact on the kitchen, considering it Gemma's domain, so it looked much the same as it always had.

"It's a nice place," Dani said.

"Thanks. Do you live in the City?"

"Yes." She stopped, not knowing what else to say. *I live here.*

"Whereabouts?"

"Potrero Hill." It was where her parents lived, so as close as she could come to another home in the City. "I grew up there."

"Oh. With a name like Barsetti, I thought maybe North Beach." She smiled flirtatiously. "I grew up in the Central Valley."

Dani nodded, feeling uncomfortable. *This is bizarre.*

She stepped toward the kitchen window just as Gemma turned around, putting them face to face and close together in the narrow room.

"Sorry," Dani said. "I just wanted to get a look at your view."

"Not much of a view. Just the fence and the house behind."

They stood silently gazing at one another. Dani looked deep into Gemma's eyes, trying to persuade her to remember. She had that look on her face, the soft hazy look that meant she felt vulnerable. Dani reached out and caressed her cheek. Gemma put her hand up, clasping Dani's fingers, as if afraid to let them roam freely. Overwhelmed with her closeness, Dani slipped her other arm around her waist and drew her body tenderly nearer. She kissed her, tasting her familiar lips, imbuing the kiss with as much love as she could, hoping that the perfection of their mouths together would stir something in her. Dani had the idea it would be like magic, like the prince kissing Sleeping Beauty, that with this kiss of true love, Gemma's memory would awaken and she would remember everything.

When Dani released her mouth and looked into her eyes, she saw that she had stirred something in her—desire, but there was still no recognition.

"Wow," breathed Gemma. "You're an excellent kisser."

I should be, Dani thought. *I've kissed you a million times. I know your mouth like my own name.* But she said nothing. Instead, she put both arms around Gemma and held her tightly against her chest, then kissed her again, deeply and sensuously, the kind of kiss she knew would light a fire in her. She could tell by the way her mouth and body came alive that Gemma wanted her. She pressed into the small of her back, closing the gap between their hips, eliciting a sigh from Gemma, who tilted her head back, exposing her neck. Dani knew how sensitive Gemma's neck was, how quickly she responded to being kissed there. But as soon as her lips touched the magic spot, Gemma pulled abruptly away.

She caught her breath and looked startled, backed up against the counter, unable to move more than a couple inches from Dani. She seemed to shake herself, then put her hand to her forehead, as if she felt dizzy. "I'm sorry," she stuttered. "This is too fast. We met less than an hour ago."

"I know," Dani said gently. "But I feel very connected to you already. I think there's something powerful between us. Do you believe in love at first sight?"

Gemma laughed. "No."

"Are you sure? Because that would explain how I'm feeling."

She wished she could tell her the truth, but she couldn't think of any way to prove it, and she knew Gemma well enough to know that if she made the attempt, she'd be immediately thrown out as a lunatic. The first time around, it had taken three weeks to win her over. She might not have time...

"Besides," Gemma said, turning away, "I have a thing about cops. I told you. I don't date..."

"I know," Dani said.

"What do you mean, you know?"

Dani knew about Gemma's Uncle Pete. He used to be a cop. Now he was a paraplegic, taken down by a convenience store robber with a handgun. Gemma had every right to want to avoid the life dealt to her Aunt Trudy.

"I mean, I know how some people feel about cops. It's tough for the spouses and kids."

"Spouses and kids?" Gemma frowned. "Whoa. Hold up, there, Fatal Attraction." She moved to the other side of the room, putting the dining table between them.

"No, I didn't mean...I'm just saying, I understand there are drawbacks to getting involved with a cop. But there are advantages too." *Didn't I say these same words four years ago?* she said to herself. "I'm going to make it my personal quest to prove to you that a cop could be the love of your life."

"You're not only fast, but you're cocky too."

Dani chuckled. "Okay, okay. But I really like you, Gemma, and I know there's something special happening between us already. I deserve a chance."

Gemma smiled. "I let you walk me home, didn't I?" She turned her head sideways in that adorable way she had. So sweet and so Gemma. It made Dani's heart ache. "But I think you should go now, Officer Barsetti."

Dani sighed. She knew Gemma was serious. She didn't play games, and trying to take this seduction farther tonight might alienate her altogether.

"Can I see you again?" she asked.

"I'll think about it. Give me your number."

She was about to rattle off her cell number when she remembered she had no service. "I know this is going to sound strange, but I don't have any mobile service right now. Maybe I can call you. Or maybe we can get together tomorrow if you're free. Dinner?" She gave Gemma her most adorable smile, hoping to coax her into falling in love again.

"Okay," Gemma relented, trying to suppress her smile.

She likes me in spite of herself. Of course!

Gemma gave Dani her phone numbers on a piece of note paper. They were the same numbers they had always been.

"I'll see you tomorrow night," Dani said, putting on her cap. "Six o'clock."

Gemma held the door open. Dani kissed her cheek on the way out, then skipped down the steps, hearing the click of the dead bolt behind her. She was encouraged that she could woo Gemma all over again. It wasn't a fluke that they had fallen in love the first time. They really were soul mates.

But where am I going with this? she asked herself. If she had to leave soon, never to see Gemma again, what was the point of winning her heart just to break it? Maybe she shouldn't have come here. Maybe she should never have spoken to Gemma. But there were things she had been told by the curious crew in the future that she wasn't ready to believe. Like she couldn't stay here. Maybe they just said that. Maybe it was their way of insuring that she'd do the job. Maybe she really could stay here where she belonged and start all over. Maybe nothing would happen to her at all if she stayed. Then she and Gemma could be together just like before. The only difference would be that they had lost four years, that Gemma had lost four years. Dani would remember it all. How could she keep such a thing from Gemma? That would be hard. But if it was the only way they could be together, she had to do it.

And what would those people care, really, if she stayed, as long as Darius was stopped? That's all they cared about. Dani was just a problem for them, a person out of time. If she stopped Darius and saved the world from a mega-terrorist, she should be free to return to her life.

She'd forgotten all about Darius, about the reason she'd been sent back. She still needed to figure out how to find him. But before she could do that, she'd need a place to stay, somewhere they took cash and didn't ask any questions. As a cop, she was familiar with places like that. She'd also need a change of clothes and a phone. Fortunately, money was not an issue. Her hand went instinctively to the pouch containing the roll of hundreds. Worthless in the twenty-third century, but invaluable to somebody traveling into the past.

Like me, she said to herself, tentatively acknowledging her identity as a time traveler. Unless she woke up soon, she would have no choice but to believe it.

CHAPTER NINE

Whatever Dani had hoped she would see when she opened her eyes in the morning became rapidly irrelevant as she took in the dim, dingy details of a third-floor room of a long-neglected hotel in the Mission District. The first thing she saw on the opposite wall was a painting in muted browns and reds of a crowd in a street, fleeing for their lives. A huge bull, nostrils blazing, chased after them. The bull seemed larger than life. The people were screaming, mouths agape, and at least one man was on the ground, trampled, not by the bull, but by the heedless mob. Others were scaling walls on either side of the narrow lane, and one of them had clearly been gored through the torso, dying while clinging with both arms to the top of the wall. It was a terrifying and horrific scene. If the artist had been trying to capture the spirit of Pamplona, he or she had fallen well short and had delivered Armageddon instead. Who would hang up a painting like that?

She sat on the edge of the bed and took in the rest of her new home. The wallpaper, something from the forties, she guessed, was stained and peeling. The bathroom was a tiny box crowded with a pedestal sink and a toilet you had to practically step over to get to the shower. The floor was covered in warped linoleum, and the room smelled of mold. The pipes rattled so hard when she turned on the faucet, it seemed they would shake themselves apart.

She brushed her teeth, then ripped open a new package of underwear and changed out of her new royal purple pajamas and into her uniform. The uniform was conspicuous, but it would allow her some freedom of movement.

Swenson's group had given her two pieces of equipment, the transporter beacon and a DNA detector. The latter was to be worn like a wristwatch and had a small screen displaying a faint grid. She didn't understand what they had told her about how it worked. She did understand that it could detect an individual in range by his unique DNA signature. It was programmed to detect Leo Darius. She had seen one of these before, on Frank Bryan's wrist. It made sense. He'd been going after Darius just like she was. That solved the mystery of how Bryan had located the suspect all by himself.

Dani put it on her wrist and turned it on. It flashed to life and displayed a blue dot in the center of a grid. That blue dot represented her. If Darius were near, they had explained, he would show up as a green dot, but he had to be within five hundred feet. No sign of him yet. No surprise. He could be anywhere in the city. He could be anywhere in the world, actually, and she had no idea where to start looking.

She grabbed a bagel with a cream cheese smear at the corner coffee shop and ate it on the walk to the BART station. A long-faced man sat on a stool and played a guitar near the ticket machines, appropriately "Ticket to Ride" by the Beatles. Dani wondered if Swenson and her colleagues knew the Beatles. Did they even have pop music, and if so, what was it like? Leaping two hundred years into the future might be really interesting, though she wasn't crazy about the food, not what she'd seen of it so far anyway. She had a sneaking suspicion they'd all gone vegetarian in the future. That alone was enough to make her want to stay here.

She got on the Daly City train and ignored the stares. What was a city cop doing riding BART, the commuters had to be thinking. *Maybe I need to get a car,* she thought. Problem was, she wouldn't be able to rent or lease one. When they ran a DMV or credit check on her, everything would come up blank. She'd have to pay cash. Not that big of a problem, as it happened. She had counted the money last night. She had fifteen thousand. She couldn't buy a new car, but a decent used car should be no problem.

She got off at the end of the line, Millbrae station, then went out to the street and hired a taxi to take her to Genepac.

"You lose your cruiser?" asked the driver, grinning like he'd made a smart joke. He was a wiry older man with a few tufts of white hair on the sides of his blotchy bald head.

"It's a long story," she said.

It wasn't far to the site. She had the driver let her out a block away, then she walked over to the burned-out building. It was surrounded by crime scene tape and investigators. She glanced at her DNA detector watch. No green dot. Too bad. A lot of these terrorists liked to watch the aftermath of their attacks. It made them feel like a big man. She looked around the buildings surrounding the site. He could be watching from one of them, just too distantly for the device to register, watching them while he chowed down on a chicken shawarma wrap. *Man, that sounded good!* she thought, thinking about her favorite menu item at the Mediterranean deli in the Financial District. *You practically had to eat the thing over a bowl; it was that juicy.*

Surveying the activity around the building, Dani saw Sergeant Tyler heading across the street and away from the team. *Smoke break,* she guessed. She was glad to see Tyler. *She won't know me from Lady Gaga,* Dani realized, *but I know her, and maybe that's enough to get her to talk.* Tyler cupped her hand to shelter her cigarette as she lit it. Dani walked over to her position, a good vantage point from which to survey the team at work on the ruins of Genepac.

"Hey, Sarge," she said, "could I bum a smoke?"

Tyler regarded Dani briefly, glanced at her name tag, then put her cigarette pack in her hand. "Sure," she said. After she'd taken one, Tyler lit it for her and she took a long drag to get it started. She sucked the smoke into her lungs, savoring the sensation, the smell and the taste.

Wow, this brings back memories! she thought. She used to smoke. She gave it up for Gemma. She was almost positive that two hundred years from now, nobody would smoke cigarettes, so there wasn't much danger of starting up again based on this one butt. Even today, smokers were becoming an endangered tribe, at least in California. Smoking used to be cool. Now it was the opposite, and Dani knew the kind of loyalty that sprung up between individuals in an outcast minority. So this cigarette was her way of softening Tyler up and getting the job done.

"Thanks," she said. "Left mine back at the station. It was a hectic morning."

"I don't know you, do I, Barsetti?"

"No. I'm on loan from the twenty-third. Unfortunately, I also missed the morning briefing."

Tyler took a drag from her cigarette. When she exhaled, this time she didn't make any attempt to blow her smoke in the other direction. Now they were smoke sisters.

"What's the D stand for?" Tyler asked, vaguely pointing toward Dani's name tag.

"Dani."

"What's Dani stand for?"

"Can't it just be Dani?"

Tyler gave her one of those sideways glances she did so well.

"Daniella," Dani replied, trying not to sound resentful about it.

Tyler took another puff, then said, "What do you know about this case?"

"I know about the bombing and that the main suspect is Leo Darius. I know FBI Agent Bryan was killed going after him yesterday."

"Agent Bryan, yes." She sounded doubtful.

"Something strange about Bryan?"

"The FBI says they never heard of him. And we haven't been able to ID him. He's in the deep freeze waiting for something to turn up. Nothing on his prints. I'm not sure I believe the feds on this one. But if they sent in a ghost agent to catch Darius, why? Why's it such a big deal? An eco-terrorist blows up a research lab. Nobody was even killed."

"Bryan knew when it would happen."

"Right. He knew a lot more than we did. The FBI's got a finger on the guy. They know what he's going to do and when. But now they're saying nothing. Not only have they never heard of Bryan, but they're telling the same story about Darius. Never heard of him." She took a leisurely drag on her cigarette.

That made sense, Dani reflected, if she'd been told the truth. This was not an FBI case. She smoked, observing Tyler's freckled face. You could almost see the gears turning. She wanted to figure this out. *There's no way, Sarge*, Dani thought sympathetically. *Whatever you can think up, it's wrong.*

"Do we have anything new on Darius?" she asked.

Tyler shook her head. "No. Nothing new and not much to begin with. Don't know what he looks like beyond the vague description Bryan gave us. He's the only one who actually put eyes on him. By the time Perkins got there, Bryan wasn't talking and Darius was gone. We had people all over that building, but there was a catwalk kind of a thing between that one and the one behind. We think he might have gone that way, got into the next building and got clear of it before we sent people in to search it. Anyway, I might have passed him on the street this morning and I would never know it."

I know what he looks like, Dani thought. She'd been shown a dozen images by Swenson. Leo Darius was forty-two, medium height, slightly built with a bit of a stoop to his shoulders. He had a full head of chestnut brown hair and, at least in the photos, a mustache. He looked non-threatening, more like a college professor than a terrorist. There was no way Dani could explain her knowledge to Tyler, so she kept it to herself.

"Leo Darius doesn't exist," Tyler said. "Obviously an alias. We've got nothing but spooks in this case."

"Nobody claimed responsibility?"

She shook her head again. "Nothing."

"That's strange."

"Right. What kind of terrorist doesn't want credit?" She stamped her butt out under her boot. "Why don't you help Stanecek inside? He's with Dr. Ruben, one of the scientists. They're trying to get a catalog of what was destroyed. Second floor, west side."

Dani nodded and put out her cigarette underfoot, observing the damage to the location Tyler mentioned. Blackened walls and blown-out windows.

"Hey, Barsetti," Tyler said, "don't take the elevator." She laughed at her joke.

Inside the main entrance of the building, the smell of smoke and dampness hit her. But the lobby looked otherwise undamaged. She found a staircase and went up to the second floor. The damage was much worse there. Walls were charred, and glass and other debris littered the floors. Dani found Dr. Ruben in a large open room with minimal damage, seated at a table with a clipboard and a scattering of papers. There was no electricity in the building, so the table was pushed close to a bank of windows for light. The rest of the room was choked with boxes and plastic containers on tables and on the floor, stacked atop one another. Dr. Ruben, a bald, clean-shaven, middle-aged man, wore a white coat and glasses and looked undeniably glum. His expression did not change at the sight of Dani.

"Officer Barsetti," she announced, approaching his table. "How's it going?"

"Tragically, Officer Barsetti, tragically. The losses are insurmountable. Our freezers were destroyed, for one thing. Thousands of DNA samples were lost. Seventy percent of our seeds were lost. Some of these can never be replaced. Others... it would take decades to reassemble this collection of plant biodiversity, if it's even possible."

"At least nobody was hurt. Thanks to Agent Bryan, we got the building evacuated in time."

Ruben sighed melodramatically. "I'm glad nobody was hurt, but in my opinion, the loss was much greater than the value of any member of the staff. I include myself in that assessment. We can be replaced."

"But your data…you've got to have backups. Why can't you just re-create the experiments? Splice some genes together and make whatever GMO thingy you made before?"

He stared, looking perplexed. "Do you have any idea what we do here?"

"Yeah, sure. You genetically engineer crops to make them disease resistant, hardier, better, bigger." She laughed. "Monster tomatoes, that sort of thing."

Ruben remained somber. "That may be what this Darius fellow thought. Otherwise, why would he have done this? I can't see what quibble anybody would have with us, especially not an environmental activist."

Dani thought back to what Bryan had told her about Genepac. Maybe she had misunderstood him. "What are you saying? You don't do genetic engineering?"

He shook his head. "No. We do genetic sequencing. We're here to preserve genetic biodiversity. A very important part of our work is sequencing the genome of extinct or nearly extinct plants. If we can't preserve the plant itself, at least we can save its genetic code and maybe, some day, find a way to resurrect it. If it turns out to be worth the effort."

"What do you mean, worth the effort?"

He stood and stretched, looking pained and clearly tired. "Officer, plants are essential to life on this planet. They provide food and shelter and clothing to all the animals, directly or indirectly. We don't know the half of it yet. Do you know there's a tree in the Amazon basin that may hold the cure for COPD? That tree is going the way of so much of the flora of the Amazon. It's disappearing at an alarming rate, disappearing before we even know what's there. So many of our most effective medicines come from nature, from plants, animals, bacterium. Penicillin, for instance. Bread mold. You've heard of it, I assume."

He walked away, his hands clasped behind his back. Dani felt like she was at a lecture.

"You collect those plants here?" she asked.

"Yes. We save their seeds and their DNA. Not *monster* tomatoes, but heirloom tomatoes. One of the most popular tomatoes today was nearly obliterated from the planet until we found it growing in a few family gardens in Kansas. We collected the seeds and grew the tomatoes on our farms, then collected those seeds, and so on. With the resurgence of heirloom varieties, these tomatoes are growing all over the country now."

"Your farms?" Dani asked.

"That's right. We partner with farmers, sometimes even restaurants with a kitchen garden. They grow the endangered crops and give us the seeds. That way, we keep our supply viable. So, you see, we aren't engineering new crop plants. We're resurrecting our ancestral crops, the primitive cultivars that are on the verge of disappearing." He shook his head. "This Darius is an idiot. He's certainly not very concerned about being precise, if his message is to protest genetically modified food."

"Maybe he's just nuts," she suggested.

Ruben shrugged.

A man in a hazmat suit wheeled a cart through the clear plastic sheets covering the doorway, then pulled off his respirator. It was Stanecek, his earnest face and deep-set eyes well known to Dani. "You here to help?" he asked her.

"Yes, sir," she said. "Barsetti."

"Okay, Barsetti, suit up. The bomb ripped up a bunch of old flooring and kicked up some asbestos, so we're stuck with this gear. Besides, the critters in all the doc's test tubes were set free in the explosion. Who knows what kind of mutants are in there waiting to squirm their way into your body and lay eggs in your brain."

Dr. Ruben rolled his eyes, clearly exasperated. "They're plants!" he protested.

"Hey," Stanecek replied, "I've seen *Little Shop of Horrors*." He picked up a box from the cart and found a spot for it among the others.

Dani helped him unload the cart, then put on a suit and went into what used to be a laboratory and storage rooms. Pieces of wood, glass, metal, plastic, ceiling tiles and broken ceramic floor tiles covered the space. Their job was to sift through it, looking for evidence, any remnants of the bomb or anything that might link the location to the suspect. In the process, they turned over any intact containers to Ruben, trying to placate him, as he wasn't allowed into this section of the building and was frantic to know what could be salvaged.

The work proceeded slowly and methodically over the next two hours. The freezer, acting like a vault, had protected its contents well. Most of the samples inside were undamaged. At least the containers were undamaged, but the freezer had been powered off since the explosion, so everything had thawed and, according to Ruben, been destroyed. He was overjoyed whenever they turned over a box containing seeds, as these were salvageable, but there weren't many still intact. The entire lab had been destroyed, all of the equipment melted. The rest of the building, including another lab downstairs, had suffered only minimal damage. Obviously, Darius had targeted this suite of rooms specifically.

Dani was no expert on bombs or terrorists, but she knew this case didn't fit the usual profile. It seemed less about a political statement and more about taking out this one lab, or maybe the storerooms, the mutant critters, as Stanecek called them. If they were just heirloom tomato seeds, why would anybody care? Maybe Dr. Ruben wasn't being straight with her. Maybe there were secret experiments going on here, and why would Ruben tell her, just another cop, about it? Maybe Darius knew the score and he'd hit exactly what he had intended to hit.

There were a lot more questions than answers in this case. A lot of mysteries. All of that was something for the police to puzzle through, she reminded herself. Things were different for her. What had happened to Genepac didn't concern her. She was here only to get a lead on Darius. His reasons for blowing up this particular place didn't matter. What mattered was that he would do it again and develop a real taste for it. He wanted to punish people for polluting the planet. He would become a fanatical maniac who would cause the deaths of millions and somehow elude law enforcement for decades. Unless she could find and stop him in the short time she had here. "*Stop him,*" she thought, acknowledging the euphemism. *Kill him.*

CHAPTER TEN

Dani was more than happy to get out of the hazmat suit when lunchtime came around. *If you want to sweat off a few pounds*, she thought, *wrap yourself in plastic for a couple of hours.* Stanecek asked if she wanted to join his crew for lunch, but she begged off. She wasn't planning on spending the rest of the day here working. She wasn't getting paid, after all, and she was getting no closer to Darius by sorting through this debris.

As she pulled her arm out of the Tyvek sleeve, a flash of green caught her eye. She stared at the device on her wrist. There were two dots, a blue one and a green one. Though this was what she had been waiting for, actually seeing it momentarily stunned her. Darius was here! She grabbed her jacket, belt and cap, then ran downstairs where a couple of detectives were working. She looked at her Darius detector again. No change. If he's closer than fifty feet, she'd been told, the green dot would be blinking. It wasn't.

Outside, she scanned the grounds, seeing a group of officers piling into a black-and-white. What if Darius were posing as a cop? That would make it easy for him to move around the target zone. Just like it did for her. Dr. Ruben stood beside a BMW at the curb across the street. He'd taken off his white coat and replaced it with a brown sports jacket. He was talking to somebody who was mostly blocked from view by the car. Dani walked out to the street to get a better look. Standing beside Ruben was a trimly built man in brown pants and a pale green, short-sleeved shirt. His brown hair was unruly, blown by the wind, and his shoulders were slightly stooped. As Dani reached the curb, he glanced her way, revealing a mustache and close-set eyes. He looked unconcerned, then turned back toward Ruben. In that brief glance, Dani recognized him from the many images she'd been shown. And if she had any doubt about his identity, the green dot on her device was now blinking.

Darius reached out to shake Dr. Ruben's hand, then broke off the handshake and seemed preoccupied with his wristwatch, staring at it as if he had just realized he was late for an important appointment. He looked up and swung his head toward Dani, who was already walking rapidly in his direction. He took off in the other direction, running toward the numerous commercial buildings. She pulled her weapon and broke into a run after him.

"It's him!" she called to a bewildered-looking Dr. Ruben as she passed him. The other cops were gone already, and the detectives inside the building couldn't hear her from this distance. Her instinct was to radio for backup, but then she remembered that she was alone on this assignment. She wasn't a cop today. She was a hired killer. It was better that there were no other cops around.

Darius ran as if he wasn't used to it, awkwardly and inefficiently. Dani knew she could catch him. He dashed toward a side street, clearly intending to round the corner and disappear from view. "Shoot and ask questions later," she'd been told. She had to ignore her training. She would kill him, then activate her beacon and disappear before she could be apprehended. In the future, she would be a celebrated hero. That's what they had told her. She would have taken out one of the worst monsters of all time. She regretted that she would have no chance to see Gemma again and say a proper good-bye. That was probably best for Gemma though.

She sprinted toward the corner, arriving a split second after Darius had rounded it. She spotted him just ahead. He turned to catch her eye, looking alarmed, then broke for a passage between two buildings. She planted her feet and fired just as he ducked out of sight. Then she resumed pursuit, following his trail around the building into a small side street. He'd disappeared. He must have gone inside one of the buildings. She stood still and listened, her heart thumping insistently in her chest. She knew the gunshot would alert the officers still in the Genepac building. She had to get Darius before they arrived.

She flattened herself against the wall of a building, realizing she was an easy target from any of a dozen windows on the opposite side of the street. She eyed one window after another, watching for movement and primed to shoot.

She moved with caution past doorways, hoping to catch him hiding in one. Just one bullet, she thought, and the world would be rid of this menace for all time.

"Darius!" she called as loudly as she could. "Make this easy on yourself and give yourself up!" No response.

Just then two detectives rounded the corner, guns drawn. They saw Dani and joined her in a doorway alcove.

"He came into this street, then disappeared," she said.

"It's Darius?" one of them asked. "Are you sure?"

She nodded.

"How'd you ID him?" asked the other.

Uh, yeah, that was a tough one, she thought, thinking of the device on her wrist. "He matched the description and ran when he saw me. Let's search these buildings. He's got to be here somewhere. Brown pants, green shirt, brown mustache. Medium height, thin build."

"I'll take this building," she said, jerking her head toward the door behind them.

When they had moved on, each of them disappearing into apartment houses, Dani consulted her watch. The green dot had gone out. Darius was no longer here. He wasn't hiding in one of these buildings after all. He must have kept running. He had escaped again.

She holstered her weapon and walked back to where Dr. Ruben still stood beside his Beemer.

"What happened?" he asked.

"He got away."

"Who is he? Why did he run?"

"He's Darius, the guy who blew up your lab."

Dr. Ruben's mouth fell open. "But I...he said..."

"What did he say?"

"He said he was a scientist. He wanted to know how bad... how much we lost." Ruben was obviously disconcerted. He rubbed the top of his bald head.

"He wanted to know how successful his bomb was," Dani surmised.

"He didn't seem like...that wasn't how it sounded. I thought he was genuinely sympathetic, actually, to hear how much irreplaceable..."

"Have you ever seen this man before?"

"No. I think I would remember him." Ruben took off his glasses and pinched the bridge of his nose. "He asked particularly about the black beetle beans, if they had survived."

"Black beetle beans?"

"It's a kind of bean that's native to China. They're shiny black and resemble beetles. The species is believed to be extinct now, and it's possible we have the only existing seeds in the world. I mean, we *did* have. I'm almost positive they were destroyed in the blast. That's what I told him."

"Why did he want to know about a bean?"

"He said he had hoped to get a sample from us. He wanted to propagate and study them."

Dani shook her head. "Probably just a story he invented to go along with his cover. So you wouldn't suspect him."

"I didn't! I didn't suspect him at all!" Ruben's eyes widened as he realized he'd been completely taken in and had been talking to a dangerous criminal.

"No. So why did he run? One minute he's perfectly comfortable talking to you, then suddenly he takes off like he's been found out. Why?"

"He saw you."

She shrugged. "So what? A few minutes ago a half a dozen cops were out here on the street and it didn't bother him."

"I don't know." Ruben shook his head as if he were extremely weary.

The only difference between Dani and those other cops was that she had a device that could ID Darius. But he couldn't know that. He couldn't know about this device from the future. So it had to be something else. He'd never seen her before. Yesterday on the roof, when she arrived, he was moving away from her and never turned around. She only saw the back of his head. She couldn't make any sense of it, why he had run, especially when running would have given him away automatically.

"Are you on your way to lunch?" she asked Ruben.

"No, I'm going home for the day. This has been very trying."

"Where's home?"

"Mountain View."

"I'm going the other way. Could you give me a lift to BART?"

He nodded. Dani was anxious to get away before news of the Darius sighting hit the airwaves. She needed to keep a low profile.

Once they were in the car and moving, Ruben said, "It's kind of odd about the beetle beans. That it was that particular thing he mentioned. If it was a random thing, I mean."

"Why odd?"

"On Friday I mailed a package of those same seeds to a Berkeley professor who wanted them for an experiment."

"You give them out like that, something that rare?"

"We'll give them out up to a certain percentage, always with the condition that in return, we get some back, new ones. That way, we keep the supply robust and viable. After all, seeds don't last forever."

"Yeah, that makes sense. Did you tell Darius about those seeds?"

"No. I only just now remembered."

"Do you know what kind of experiment this professor wanted to do?"

"Not exactly, but she's worked with us before. She's a cancer researcher, so I assume she's looking for a new cancer treatment."

"Is that likely?"

He shrugged. "From this bean? Who knows. But any plant can yield medicinal properties. Look at taxol, for instance. It comes from the Pacific yew tree. Very interesting things are being discovered on a daily basis by researchers looking at common plants."

"But this isn't a common plant."

"Not anymore. Nevertheless, she must have some reason for thinking it could be useful."

He turned off the road toward the parking lot at the train station. "Pharmaceuticals are not our business at Genepac, but obviously that's one of the primary reasons for preserving plant biodiversity, so we work closely with people doing this sort of research."

Dani asked for the name of the Berkeley professor. "I'd like to speak to her."

"Gail Littleton. It's ironic, but I put the seeds in the mail not an hour before we heard there was a bomb. She'll probably get them today. If I hadn't done that, we'd have lost them all. Considering what's happened, I'm going to want them back. Professor Littleton will soon be in possession of the only ten black beetle beans in existence." His eyes widened as he realized the significance of the package leisurely making its way through the Bay Area postal channels.

"I'll let her know you want them back," Dani said. "Thanks for the lift."

She didn't know what, if anything, bean seeds had to do with Darius and his plans, but at the moment, it was the only lead she had. As she settled into a seat on the train, listening unwillingly to an obnoxious woman on her cell phone talking about what she should make for dinner, she decided she really did need a car. Traveling this way was too slow. She needed to keep a step ahead of Darius, for one thing. That would be a lot easier if she knew where he was and what he was planning next. Just sitting around waiting for his next attack didn't seem like much of a plan. It might be months. But at least now she knew he was still in the area and that the fancy doodad on her wrist actually worked.

CHAPTER ELEVEN

After buying a burner phone and a new ride, a rough-running 2006 Volkswagen Jetta with a dent in the rear fender, Dani headed toward Highway 101 to catch the Bay Bridge over to the East Bay. Gail Littleton was expecting her at her office. As soon as she'd bought her phone, Dani had called the university, gotten Littleton's number and made an appointment for three thirty. The route brought her right through Potrero Hill where her parents lived. She found herself turning toward their street, almost subconsciously. She had a few extra minutes and couldn't resist at least taking a look at the house, the place she'd grown up, her home.

The last time she'd been here was almost two weeks ago. She and Gemma had come by for Sunday dinner as they frequently did when Dani had Sundays off. The topic of conversation had been all about her sister Rachel's wedding. Rachel was marrying a great guy, Luke. Not Italian as their parents would have liked, but they'd gotten over that mild disappointment. After all, if they were cool with their firstborn daughter marrying a lesbian, how could they object to Luke? Since Rachel was pregnant, what choice did they have anyway? If he wasn't marrying her willingly, they would have leaned on him hard to do it.

She drove uphill, noting the view in her side mirror of downtown San Francisco in the distance below. The skyscrapers of the Financial District dominated the picture, with the Transamerica Pyramid easily distinguishable. The bay itself beyond that was just a blue-gray haze.

The Jetta, black and ordinary, was at least inconspicuous. The young woman who had taken her money had seemed relieved to get the sale. She got a nice deal for a car with so many miles on it. It didn't matter to Dani if she paid a little more than it was worth. She couldn't see how she'd be able to use up that wad of cash in two weeks anyway.

She parked across the street and a few houses down from her parents' townhouse, a pale yellow tri-level with bay windows facing the street on the first and second floors. On the third floor was a balcony hemmed in by a wrought iron railing. From that balcony, she had often leaned over the railing to look down the street toward downtown. It was a terrific, though indirect view that had left her precariously teetering on the top bar of the railing, her feet off the ground. Rachel had done the same often enough, not so much for the view as the sensation of balancing on that narrow support digging into her stomach. Sometimes Dani had held her by the feet so she could point her head down even farther, arms out at the sides, looking like she was about to take flight. Incredible that Rachel had trusted Dani so completely. She smiled to herself, thinking they'd been lucky neither of them had ever fallen over.

She stood on the sidewalk looking at the house with its familiar white front door, her mother's Lincoln in the driveway. Her father would be at work. The drapes were open in all the windows. Her mother always wanted to bring as much light in as possible. As Dani stood watching, her mother came into view on the second floor. Dani bit her bottom lip as her heart leapt to her throat. Her mother wore one of her favorite outfits, a black and red print blouse and black pants. If she went out, she'd put on the white jacket that completed the outfit. She walked past the window and out of view. Dani bolted to the front door, craving her mother's guaranteed love.

What now? she thought, holding her finger poised over the doorbell. *What if she doesn't know me? How devastating would that be?* She couldn't decide whether to ring the bell or turn and run. She didn't know how long she stood there before she heard the dead bolt pulled back and her mother opened the door, her expression one of concern. She looked exactly as Dani had last seen her, her frothy black hair parted on the right and held in place on the left with a tiger's eye barrette. Dani gazed into her brown eyes, searching for her mother. It's so strange how much recognition is conveyed in the eyes and face and even the body posture of a person who knows you well. You can't know that fully until it's absent. Her heart sank, seeing her mother looking at her with the eyes of a stranger.

"Can I help you, Officer?" she asked.

"Mrs. Barsetti," Dani said with difficulty.

She saw Dani's name tag and her face brightened. "You're a Barsetti too!"

Dani nodded, swallowing the emotion like a golf ball in her throat.

"Are you one of Marcello's kids? My husband and I have all but lost track of Marcello. Oh, we still see your grandfather Tony all the time and his daughter Lucy. She would be your aunt, wouldn't she? I haven't seen Marcello for years now. My husband Teddy would probably know which one you were. But he's at work." She put her hand to her chest. "To think Marcello's got a daughter your age…well, that's something! And a police officer." She smiled approvingly. "I'd be so proud if one of my children was a police officer." She laughed. "But that wouldn't happen, let me tell you. My daughter Rachel, she's not interested in anything but her fiancé and future career as a mother. Which is fine with me, of course. I'll be thrilled to be a grandmother, though how I suddenly got old enough to be a grandmother is beyond me! And my son Nick…" She stopped, her face clouding over, as if she had just remembered something sad.

"What about Nick?" Dani asked. "I heard he's very smart. Always did well in school."

She nodded, her fingers clutching helplessly at her throat. "Well, your parents must be very proud." She so clearly did not want to talk about Nick, Dani wanted to know why, but she was a stranger to this woman and didn't see how she could press for more information.

"Is Rachel your oldest?" Dani asked.

"Yes. She's twenty-four. She's getting married in less than two weeks and we've been pulling our hair out getting ready. She's supposed to be here, actually. When I saw you out here, I thought it was her. Not that you look like her in that uniform." She stood back and squinted her eyes at Dani. "Actually, you do look sort of like her. Same mouth." She clapped her hands together. "Well, no surprise there, is it? You're cousins. Do you have any idea what's involved in planning a wedding?"

"I have some idea," she said. "I helped out a little with my sister."

"Oh, you have a sister too. I'm sorry, I forgot to ask your name."

"Daniella," Dani answered, disturbed to be telling her name to her own mother.

"I love that name! If I had another daughter, I might have named her that. But we always thought the perfect family was one girl and one boy, so we stopped after Nick. I'm sorry, Daniella, where are my manners? Come in and visit. Tell me all about Marcello and the rest of your family. I'm sorry, but I can't remember your mother's name."

"Kathy," Dani said, remembering Marcello's wife. She knew these people only by name, by the annual Christmas cards, though she knew she had met them as a young child. At this point, she didn't know how to tell her mother she wasn't Marcello's daughter. She was having trouble speaking at all and it was actually a convenient assumption. She hadn't had the presence of mind to rehearse how she would explain her identity when her mother opened the door and didn't recognize her. She just hadn't been able to believe that was a possibility.

"I can't stay, Mrs. Barsetti. I'm on duty. I just thought I'd stop by and introduce myself."

"Call me Aunt Nora, please." She looked past Dani. "Oh, look, there's Rachel!" She waved.

Dani turned around to see her sister taking a long box out of her car. She waved up to the porch and shut the trunk.

"She's got the wedding dress!" said their mother excitedly. "Oh, you have to stay to see this."

Dani didn't think she could bear it. "I really have to go."

"Well, come back for dinner any time. And you should tell your father that we can't wait for weddings and funerals to see one another."

"I'll do that."

Dani turned to leave and her mother rushed her. "Let me hug you, Daniella." She wrapped her arms around her, and Dani stooped over her and did the same, hugging her closely, closing her eyes and enjoying the familiar smell of her perfume, the same scent she had always worn. When Dani pulled away, Rachel was standing beside her on the porch.

"What's this?" she asked.

"This is your cousin Daniella," their mother said. "Marcello's daughter."

"Really? Daniella? Sorry, I can't…" Her arms were full of the box, so shaking hands was not an option. "Oh! You're the police officer from yesterday in the shop. That's how you knew my name."

Dani nodded politely, anxious to get away.

"Why didn't you introduce yourself yesterday?" Rachel asked, her forehead wrinkled up in puzzlement.

"You were busy and I…bridal shops sort of creep me out. But I'm happy to meet you at last."

Rachel laughed. "I hope weddings don't creep you out. Mom, did you send all my cousins an invitation?"

"Of course! I sent Marcello an invitation for his entire family."

"Will you come?" Rachel asked, her eyes bright and hopeful.

"Yes," Dani said. "If I can." She moved awkwardly down the steps. "Congratulations. Nice meeting you both finally."

"Thank you for stopping by," called her mother after her. "I hope we'll see you and your sister at the wedding."

Dani skipped down the steps, waiting until she heard the door shut before turning back around to look at the house again. Was this the last time she'd ever see it? she wondered.

Feeling beat up, she returned to the Jetta. Once seated behind the wheel, she lost control of her emotions completely and began to sob. She couldn't believe this was happening. But it was true. It was really true. She had no life here. She didn't exist here. Nobody knew her. Nobody cared about her. She had been erased!

She wrapped her arms around the steering wheel and buried her face in them, letting herself cry for several minutes.

Eventually, she lifted her head, wiped her eyes and nose and composed herself. A few minutes later, she dialed Gemma's cell phone, prepared to sound cheerful. Her voice mail answered, so she left a brief message. "Hi, pretty lady, it's Dani. Looking forward to seeing you tonight." She gave her the new phone number in case Gemma needed to call.

She then took off for Berkeley.

Traffic on the Bay Bridge was just heating up this time of day, but there were no serious delays. Around the campus, Berkeley looked a little sleepy, as classes were probably mostly over for the day. Without an official police vehicle, Dani was in the streets like everybody else, trolling for a coveted parking spot. That took so much time and she had to park so far away that she was practically sprinting to reach the appointment on time. After asking a couple of students for help locating Stanley Hall, a multistory blue and gray building, she made it to Dr. Littleton's office four minutes late.

The professor rose from a swivel chair to greet her with a cordial smile. She was a tall, slender and elegant woman in her thirties with carefully styled black hair and a flowing, long-sleeved orange blouse that perfectly complemented her bronze skin. Taupe-colored pants and espresso-colored T-straps completed the outfit. She wore makeup, including lipstick, but none of it was overstated. With large, almond-shaped eyes, she was a striking-looking woman. Tall women unnerved Dani, as it was unusual to run into one taller than herself. Professor Littleton met her eye to eye, but she was wearing two-inch heels. Barefoot, Dani would have edged her out by about an inch, and that knowledge sat well with her.

"Officer Barsetti," she said in a pleasant low voice, "nice to meet you. Please sit down." She motioned to the only other chair in the room, molded plastic, no doubt the chair where ardent students sat to do their begging, complaining and worshipping. Littleton then shut the door and sat gracefully in her desk chair.

Dani sat, noting how the chair put her several inches shorter than the professor. The office contained unruly piles of books and folders on shelves, but the long desk was neat with organized stacks of paper, a desktop computer and a healthy-looking jade plant. A two-drawer filing cabinet was beside that. On top of it sat a printer. On the wall above the desk were three framed certificates, Littleton's degrees. Dani noted that one of them, issued from the University of Southern California, contained the phrase "Doctor of Medicine" in bolded type. The other two were PhDs, but the lettering was too small for her to make out the subjects. On this side of the closed door was a yellowed poster with tattered edges and mod style lettering that said, "Make Love, Not War." The o's had peace signs in them. Dani found herself staring at the poster until Littleton said, "That belonged to my predecessor and I decided to keep it, a memento of the campus legacy. Besides, when it comes right down to it, I would much rather make love than war myself."

Dani faced her to find a smirk on her lips and a faintly suggestive look in her eye.

"What's this about, Officer?" Littleton asked, becoming serious. "You said something about black beetle beans over the phone."

"Yes. Dr. Ruben said he mailed you some."

"I haven't gotten them yet."

"Probably tomorrow then. You've heard about the bombing?"

"Oh, yes." She shook her head. "Absolutely horrible. I couldn't believe it."

"The rest of the beetle beans were lost in the explosion, so the ones in the mail may be the only ones in existence. Dr. Ruben naturally wants them back."

This news clearly disappointed the professor. "I see. Why didn't he tell me that himself?"

"He'll probably be calling you. Right now, he's overwhelmed with all of the destruction. The only reason he remembered sending you the beans is that the suspect wanted to know if any of them had survived the explosion."

"The suspect?" Littleton's eyebrows shot up. "Really? Why?"

"I wish I knew."

"So the man who did it has been arrested?"

"No, actually, he's still on the loose. That's why I'm here asking about the beans. It could be a lead. The bomber, Leo Darius, spoke to Dr. Ruben earlier today about the beans. Ruben didn't tell him that some of them had been saved. It slipped his mind until he was speaking to me. Maybe you can tell me what's special about these beans."

Littleton crossed her legs casually. "As far as I know, and I'd go so far as to say as far as modern science knows, there's nothing special about them. They're an ancient legume that was once used as a food source in Asia, particularly in the Guangdong province of China where they were briefly cultivated in the sixteenth century. But their natural habitat has since disappeared due to encroachment by agriculture. They aren't considered a viable food crop in the modern world, being difficult to mass produce, so nobody's really noticed their disappearance. I was thrilled to find out Genepac had some in their archives."

"But why are *you* interested in them?"

"That can't be of importance, can it? I like to keep my work close to the chest, if you know what I mean. There's a lot of competition in the academic world and I don't want anything leaking out, at least not before I publish."

"It may help us understand what he's up to," Dani explained.

"I don't see how anyone else could have any interest in the beans. That's truly puzzling." She picked up a pencil and tapped the desk with the eraser. She seemed to have forgotten Dani was there. But after a moment, she looked up and said, "My interest stems from an obscure reference in an ancient text from the Han Dynasty." She gave Dani a look that said, "Of course you don't know what I'm talking about," then added, "Around the time of Christ, give or take a couple hundred years."

Dani let her know by her expression that she did indeed know what she meant by that. *Why does everybody think cops are stupid?*

"It was a tiny story," Littleton continued, "about a man who was dying from an incurable disease that might be deduced to be cancer, but it's impossible to know for sure. His doctor cooked up some beetle beans, mashed them and fed them to the man for three days. On the third day he got up from his sick bed and was completely cured." She smiled, clearly pleased with the story.

"That's it?" Dani asked. "That's why you want the beans?"

She nodded. "That's it. Of course, it's a legend. Curing cancer in three days would be impossible. You can't take a legend literally. Still, there could be something to it. I've found that a lot of ancient stories are rooted in fact. At any rate, it's worth taking a look. But I can't imagine how your bomber would be aware of this text that has never been translated into English. I only know about it myself through extensive research. I look for old references like that, for forgotten natural cures. Or even those that still linger in our folklore, like chicken soup."

"Chicken soup? But it's just an old wives' tale. It doesn't work."

Littleton shook her head. "It actually does work. At least it helps. Science ignored that bit of folklore forever, but recently, we've taken a second look. That's what I'm doing, taking a second look at the old remedies. Once upon a time, humans used only natural substances to cure diseases, and then we got modern medicine and forgot about a lot of the old, quite effective cures. But they're coming back. In fact, modern medicine is turning more and more to answers found in nature. The problem is, we've only surveyed about one percent of the plants on earth for pharmaceutical uses. With a daunting backlog like that, where do you start? That's why I look for things like the story I just told you. Humans have had tens of thousands of years before us to figure out what worked and what didn't. They knew about aloe for burns and cardamom for indigestion. We quite arrogantly shoved aside all of that accumulated wisdom. Maybe they didn't know exactly why cardamom worked, but they knew it worked."

"You think the beetle beans, based on that one legend, can cure cancer?"

"I don't know. But it's a place to start. It's more information than I'd have going into the rain forest and randomly picking a flower to study. I believe the cures are out there. We just have to find them...before we destroy their habitat. That's where Genepac has been so valuable, but they've got only a small sampling covered."

"Even smaller now."

"Yes, sadly. Why would the bomber ask about these beans when he's just blown up the world's reserve of them."

"Another question I can't answer," said Dani. "Maybe he was trying to destroy them and wanted to know if he had succeeded."

"There again, it makes no sense. Like I said, these beans are nothing to anyone. They haven't been studied. Nobody knows about them and nobody cares. Except me and some long dead Chinese poet."

"And Leo Darius," Dani pointed out. "He at least knew they existed."

Littleton shook her head, perplexed. "That's so unlikely. Who is this man?"

"Nobody really knows. The name appears to be an alias."

"You've got me really curious now, Officer Barsetti. I'd love to ask him why he's interested in black beetle beans."

Dani laughed. "He's a very dangerous man. In addition to blowing up Genepac, he shot and killed a man."

"Yes, I remember hearing about that, an FBI agent."

Dani nodded. "You'll be lucky if you never meet Leo Darius."

"I expect I never will. Since he doesn't know about the beans Dr. Ruben sent me..."

Dani stood. "Right. He knows nothing about that or about you. Whatever his interest is in black beetle beans, he believes they've all been destroyed. As soon as the beans arrive, put them somewhere safe, call me and I'll be over to get them. I'll return them to Ruben myself."

Littleton sighed and pursed her lips. "This is very disappointing."

"By the way," Dani said, opening the office door, "what do you teach?"

"Biochemistry, microbiology, that sort of thing. And gender studies now and then."

"Gender studies?"

The professor gave her a knowing smile. "Hope to see you soon, Officer Barsetti."

Dani left the campus and returned to her car, checking her DNA detector on the way. No green dot. She realized her pursuit of the beans was probably not going to lead her anywhere near Darius. But she didn't know where else to go. Maybe tomorrow she'd go back to Genepac and hope to pick him up again on this ingenious scanner. But for now, she was off the clock. She had a date with her wife. For Gemma, she reminded herself, it was their first date, so she needed to make it special.

CHAPTER TWELVE

"I love African violets!" exclaimed Gemma, taking the pot from Dani. "How did you know?"

She shrugged. "Just thought you might like it."

It seemed a little like cheating to use insider knowledge with her, but the first time around, Dani hadn't, and she'd fallen for her then, so speeding up the process wasn't the same as pulling a con on her. Which is why Dani wore an outfit she knew Gemma would like—black jeans, a white blouse with ruffles around the neck and down the front placket. Over the blouse she wore a black and white print vest. Gemma always liked Dani best in black and white. So striking, she said. Dani wasn't surprised to see Gemma wearing the same outfit she'd worn on their original first date, an emerald green blouse and taupe pants over black, heeled boots. She'd had her hair done too and wore her favorite cloisonné earrings. She was making an effort and she looked fantastic.

It had bothered Dani again when she walked up the steps to the door that Tucker hadn't barked eagerly on the other side. His absence in this apartment was huge. The cats were so subdued in comparison.

Gemma put the violet plant on the kitchen counter, then turned back to Dani. She regarded her with a satisfied smile. "You look great tonight," she said.

"You too."

They took the Jetta to their favorite Italian restaurant, a place in North Beach they'd discovered together over three years ago. It was new to Gemma in this timeline.

"The carbonara here is terrific," Dani told her as they read the menus. "They really do it right."

Gemma gazed at Dani with curiosity. "It's one of my favorite dishes."

"It's the best vegetarian option, though the pesto primavera isn't bad."

"How do you know I'm a vegetarian?" Gemma asked, putting the menu on the table.

Dani smiled self-consciously, wondering how she was going to make it through this evening without some serious missteps. "I just guessed. You're a nutritionist and a lesbian. You're either a vegetarian or a vegan, and I saw a yogurt container in your trash yesterday, so not vegan."

"You're very observant." The answer seemed to satisfy her.

They ordered their meals and a bottle of wine and settled down to conversation. Gemma told stories Dani had heard before, and she retold her own that were now new to Gemma. *How long will it be*, Dani wondered, *before I see a look in her eyes that belongs just to me?* It was hard to be a stranger with her, and Dani slipped up a couple of times, like when she said, "You know how my mom and dad argue." Then she had to backpedal and explain. But overall the meal went well. Gemma was clearly having fun. She was talkative and engaged. And Dani got better at the flirty posturing of a first date as the meal wore on.

"You said your sister's getting married soon," Gemma said over dessert. "Are you in the wedding?"

"Yes. Maid of honor."

"Why are you rolling your eyes?"

Dani chuckled. "It's just my mother. We had a very big fight the day Rachel and I decided on my outfit for the wedding. Actually, it's not unlike what I'm wearing tonight, except that the blouse is blue, a bit more frilly, and there's an embroidered jacket. My mother said I looked like a bullfighter in it and she threatened to call the entire wedding off if I didn't wear an appropriate dress."

Gemma giggled.

"I know, right? Can you imagine?"

Still grinning, Gemma shrugged. "You could probably pull it off."

"No, I couldn't! Believe me. We had this same fight over my high school graduation. That was the last time I wore a dress, and I only finally agreed because I had a graduation gown over it during the public event and nobody could see it."

Gemma put her fork down, finished with her tiramisu. "You won the argument this time, then?"

"After a few sofa pillows flew around the room, Rachel intervened and put her foot down. She said it was her wedding and she would decide. So I'm wearing pants." Dani felt her smile fade as she recalled that she was no longer a part of that wedding. She wasn't even a part of the family. "Rachel's always been terrific, a lot of support. She was there for me when I first came out to my parents. It wasn't easy. Nobody could have a better kid sister." The serious, compassionate look on Gemma's face told Dani she was heading down the wrong path. She wanted to keep it lighthearted, so she changed the subject back to Gemma's job.

"At work, do you have an office or do you work in a cubicle?"

"Cubicle." Now it was Gemma's turn to roll her eyes. "With a cube mate named Lois. Older woman. She drives me nuts every day. I don't want to talk about her."

Fine with me, Dani thought. *I had my fill of hearing about Lois back at the beginning of our relationship.* "Do you ever think about a different kind of career, about working more independently?"

"It's funny you should ask that. Yes, I've thought about it a lot. My mother has been in nearly every memory care facility in the city, and almost all of them serve practically inedible food. Nothing fresh anyway. There are a lot of bad things about institutionalized living—lack of privacy, no quiet, living among strangers, many of them sick and nuts. No closet space. I don't see how to fix most of that. But it seems like something could be done about the food, to bring a little zing into the mostly dismal lives of the patients."

"So why don't you go for it? Why shouldn't it be you who transforms institution food? After all, you'd be starting a revolution just by sticking an orange or a bunch of fresh grapes on their plates, right?"

Gemma's mouth fell open. "Right! That's exactly it. That's what I always say to myself. Just a piece of fresh fruit. How hard could that be? And then an actual salad, a fresh salad. They're already prepackaged in all the stores. Why not in the nursing homes?"

Dani smiled to herself, seeing Gemma's enthusiasm. They'd been through all of this before, a long time ago. Back then, Dani had persuaded Gemma to follow this dream, to take a risk and believe in herself. She'd needed the push. Maybe nobody else had given her one in this reality.

"I'm sure it could be done," said Dani. "I'm sure you could do it."

Gemma smiled self-consciously. Dani knew it would take more than one conversation along these lines to persuade Gemma to take the leap of faith. It would take several. Dani didn't have time for that, but she hoped the short time she had here would at least get Gemma to think more seriously about starting her own business. Her life was so much better because of it. Her work was important to her and it gave her a powerful sense of self-worth.

When it was time to go, Dani reached into her pocket for one of the hundred-dollar bills she'd brought with her. Her fingers contacted the smooth metal casing of the transporter beacon as she did so. Always carry it, she'd been told. It could save your life if you get into a tight spot.

After leaving the restaurant, they went to a club where they used to go dancing. They didn't go out dancing anymore, she realized. They both liked it, so why had they stopped?

"It's so strange," Gemma said when they walked onto the dance floor. "It's like you know all about me, the way you get everything right."

"We're destined to be together," Dani said with a smile.

They danced close and slow, and she could tell Gemma was projecting herself ahead to the moment when they got back to the apartment. She would ask Dani to stay, she could tell. Dani pressed her close and nuzzled her neck, wanting her more and more. The heat between them rose to a palpable level as they moved their feet in perfect synchronicity. That's how it would be with their bodies too, Dani knew, later when she would make love to Gemma in a way that would blow her mind. It would be perfect, as if they had been lovers for years.

After they'd danced through three songs, Gemma looked into her eyes and said, in her bedroom voice, "Take me home."

Dani was happy to do so. Gemma talked about her dream career on the way, but Dani barely listened. She didn't have to. She had heard it all before. Her mind was busy on what was to come, and her body was humming in anticipation.

As soon as they were inside the apartment with the door closed, Gemma approached Dani, offering her lips, and Dani took her in her arms and kissed her passionately. Gemma wasted no time taking Dani's clothes off, and they left a trail of clothing from the entryway to the bedroom where Gemma fell onto the bed laughing. Dani knelt beside her and took her legs in her hands, one at a time, and slid off her boots. She caressed Gemma's silky smooth calves as she finished undressing her, admiring her body in the dim light from the hallway. Gemma lay with her hands over her head, grinning, her gorgeous body quivering with anticipation and desire. Tonight Gemma was smooth, sculpted, buffed and polished. She'd served herself up like dessert, and Dani tingled with excitement at the thought of taking her for the first time all over again.

With Gemma's foot still in her hand, she kissed her ankle softly, then got into bed, covering Gemma's body and mouth with her own. They kissed, both of them needy and urgent. Gemma's body rose up to meet her, and they were soon overcome with desire. Dani touched Gemma the way she knew she liked to be touched. She kissed her where she liked to be kissed.

Be very careful, Dani reminded herself, *not to say, "I love you."*

* * *

Dani woke to the sound of an unfamiliar phone ringing. She opened her eyes, seeing that it was daylight. She was in her bedroom, the bedroom she and Gemma shared. Gemma wasn't in bed, but she could hear her in the kitchen and smelled coffee. Was everything back to normal then? Had it all been a horrible nightmare after all? For a split second, she was euphoric. Until, with dismay, she saw the burner phone she had just bought on the nightstand beside her. She glanced around the room, seeing the old quilt folded on a chair, the quilt they had gotten rid of a couple of years ago. The chair was white, not yellow as it should have been. And the dresser was neat and well organized. None of her stuff was there. Her heart sank. She answered the phone just as Gemma appeared in the doorway in a pink nylon bathrobe.

"Hello," she said into the phone, smiling purposefully at Gemma, who placed a mug of coffee on the nightstand next to her elbow.

"Is this Officer Barsetti?" asked the woman on the phone.

"Yes."

"This is Gail Littleton. I'm calling to let you know that the package arrived. It must have come yesterday afternoon, but it didn't make it to my campus mailbox until late. I found it there this morning."

Gemma crawled into bed and snuggled up close to Dani's side.

"Great. I'll be over to get it. What time will you be available?"

"I have class until ten thirty. Then I have an hour free. I'll be in my office."

Gemma kissed the back of Dani's neck softly.

"See you then," Dani said, then clicked off the call.

"Good morning," Gemma said. "Do you take milk or sugar?"

"Nothing, thanks."

The bathrobe fell open above the belt to reveal Gemma's naked body underneath. The full roundness of her breasts presented themselves to Dani, the nipples barely out of view behind the cloth.

"Was that business?" Gemma asked.

"Yes. I have an appointment about eleven in Berkeley."

"That gives us just under an hour. Unless you have to go home to get your uniform."

Dani tasted the coffee. It was the same brew Gemma had been drinking when they met. "Actually, my uniform is in the car."

"Oooh!" Gemma frowned. "You were very sure of yourself, weren't you?"

"I just like to be prepared." Dani chuckled.

The look Gemma gave then, full of tender affection, warmed Dani through. That expression was the one she'd been waiting for. Gemma was falling in love all over again. Dani took her hand, pressed it to her lips, then clutched it between them.

"Good coffee," Dani said. "You're good at so many things."

"You too." She laughed lightly.

Dani put down the mug and kissed her, then slipped her hand inside the robe to caress her cool skin. Gemma pressed herself closer, kissing her mouth hungrily. Coming up for air, Dani said, "Don't you have to be to work too?"

She nodded, a soft smile on her lips. "I called in to say I'd be late. I wish I could stay here all day with you."

"Maybe we can meet up tonight?"

"I'd like that." She kissed Dani once more before rolling out of bed.

Dani showered quickly and got dressed, and the two of them left the apartment at the same time. Gemma left in her car and Dani in the Jetta after one more lingering, reluctant good-bye kiss. Gemma was clearly in the magic haze of new love and Dani felt some of the same. It *was* a new love for one of them, and that made it thrilling for both.

CHAPTER THIRTEEN

When Dani arrived, Professor Littleton's office door stood open wide enough for Dani to see a young woman sitting in what Dani thought of as the underling's chair. She sat straight-backed and attentive, her eyes large and focused on the woman speaking to her. A student, no doubt. Dani waited in the hallway, looking out the second-story window at the sprawling UC campus teeming with young people and at the Berkeley hills beyond. Her thoughts were all on Gemma and how anxious she was to be back in her arms. Last night had been magical. It couldn't have gone any better.

When the student left, Dani peeked through the doorway to see Littleton seated before her computer monitor, typing on the keyboard. She looked as elegant today as she had yesterday, similarly attired in a pantsuit with a long silky blouse. It was apparently her standard costume.

"Hello," she said, noticing Dani. She swiveled to face her.

"How are you today, Dr. Littleton?"

"I'm fine." She stood and opened a filing cabinet. "I have your package." She took a large padded envelope from the drawer. "I spoke to Dr. Ruben before I called you this morning and tried to talk him into splitting this treasure with me, but he refused. There are only ten seeds here. And some of them may not germinate, so he's feeling nearly desperate about them. I can't blame him, especially after everything he's lost." She smiled ruefully and handed over the envelope. "Oh, well, perhaps one day he'll be able to spare them again for science. For now, I assume these, and anything else that escaped destruction in the explosion, will be secreted away in a vault somewhere until they can rebuild. That could be a while."

"So what will you do instead?" Dani asked, peeking into the envelope at a clear plastic box inside.

"I'll go on to the next thing. I'm sorry to lose this opportunity, but the truth is that there's no shortage of interesting plants in the world to study. There's a yam from western Africa, for example, that I've had my eye on. Fortunately, I don't have to rely on Genepac or any other seed bank for that one. The yam is not extinct or even all that rare."

Dani pulled the plastic box out of the envelope to see a zippered bag inside containing ten shiny black beans. "Ever since I heard about these, I can't stop thinking about Jack and the Beanstalk."

Littleton smiled. "You never know. The magic bullet against cancer? Or just another legume for your sixteen-bean soup?"

Dani tucked the box back into the envelope. "Thanks. I'll get these back to Ruben. If anything else comes up, call me."

"I will, but is the number you gave me still good? I called you back earlier to let you know you could come this afternoon if it was more convenient, but you didn't answer and it didn't go to voice mail. Just kept ringing."

Dani fished her phone out of her pocket and saw that it was dead. She tried to turn it on, but it didn't respond. "Damn cheap burner," she muttered. "But even if the battery's dead, it should have given you voice mail. I don't know. Something might be wrong with this. I'll give you another number. I'll be at the alternate number tonight for sure." Dani wrote down Gemma's home number. "I'm staying with a friend. This is the land line. Her name's Gemma, so if she answers, you can give her a message for me or leave it on voice mail."

"A friend?" Littleton smiled slyly as she took the paper. "Are you taken then? I didn't see a ring."

Caught off guard, Dani felt her face flush. "Oh, uh, yes, I'm taken. Gemma and I…" She stopped, trying to decide how to end her sentence.

Littleton nodded knowingly. "Take good care of those seeds, Barsetti."

After hiking back to her car, Dani drove across the Bay Bridge and headed south to the Peninsula with the seeds. She couldn't call Ruben because of her dead phone, but she figured he'd be on site at Genepac. When she got there, she saw a scene much like the one she'd seen yesterday—cops going about their investigation. She checked her DNA watch. No green dot.

She walked up to the building and found Sergeant Tyler standing by the door, taking a cigarette out of her pack.

"Hey," she said.

She recognized Dani and returned her greeting.

"Is Dr. Ruben upstairs?" Dani asked.

"He's not here. He's meeting with some eggheads in the East Bay today."

"Damn!" She wanted to unload the magic beans as fast as she could. It made her nervous being responsible for them, the only ten of their kind in existence.

"What'd you need to see him for?" Tyler asked.

She didn't want to get into the long explanation of the beans, so she said, "Nothing important. I just thought I'd give him a hand again."

"They're pretty much done with the salvage operation. In fact, we're wrapping things up here. We've spent enough time on this guy."

"Nothing new about Darius?"

She shook her head. "Not a peep. He's laying low. But at least we have a description of him now, thanks to Dr. Ruben. He spent some time last night with our artist. We've got the sketch out there. Now we just wait for his next move."

"I hope he doesn't get a chance to make a next move."

Tyler nodded. "I heard you were the one who went after him yesterday." She looked at Dani as if she were trying to see into her head. Tyler was perpetually suspicious. "What tipped you off?"

"He ran. I ran after him."

"I'd like to get you to sit down with the sketch artist too. Where did you run off to yesterday anyway? Also, where's your report?"

"Sorry. I had something personal. My CO approved it. I'll get right on that report, Sarge. As soon as I get back to the station."

She nodded, looking halfway satisfied. "I was just going to have a smoke. Want to join me?"

"No thanks." The last thing Dani needed was more questioning from Tyler. "Another time. I've gotta get going. I've got a report to write."

On the way back to the City, she noticed she had a headache. She never got headaches, normally, but nothing was normal these days.

When she got back to her room at the hotel, she plugged in her phone to charge the battery, then changed into civvies and went out to find something to eat and buy a few more changes of clothing. Even if Gemma was going to immediately rip them off, she had to show up tonight wearing something different.

On the walk to the Westfield Mall on Market, she tried to imagine what her next move would be with Darius. When Tyler saw there was no report from her, she'd check her out. She'd discover that Dani was an imposter, and her naturally suspicious nature would come up with two possible conclusions. Either Dani was in cahoots with Darius, disguised as a cop to keep an eye on them, or Dani *was* Darius. Nobody but Bryan had known what Darius looked like before yesterday and Tyler already had doubts about Bryan. Dani had been the one who fingered Darius. Tyler might conclude that was a smokescreen. Since they hadn't caught the guy, they couldn't find out one way or another if he really was Darius or, as he had said, just some science geek commiserating with Dr. Ruben. It wouldn't be long, Dani concluded, before her description was out on the streets. Maybe even as soon as tomorrow. She had to be careful, lie low and go it alone from here on out.

She hit the food court at the mall before clothes shopping, sitting among the throng of shoppers with her shish kebab plate—grilled chicken, peppers, onions, tomatoes and saffron rice. The place was noisy and crowded, but it was handy and the food was great. She glanced at her wrist gadget every few minutes. She was getting obsessive about it now, hoping against reason that Darius would walk into Bristol Farms to buy himself a bouquet of tiger lilies and a Black Forest ham and brie sandwich.

She knew that wasn't going to happen. He wasn't going to come to her. She had to figure out how to find him. In the meantime, maybe she'd just move in with Gemma and resume their life together. She could live with that. She sucked up the last of her soda, dumped off her trash and headed for Victoria's Secret. That huge wad of bills was burning a hole in her pocket. She may as well pick up something nice for Gemma while she was shopping. Something red and lacy. She smiled to herself.

CHAPTER FOURTEEN

Every time Gemma called Dani's cell, it rang like an old-fashioned land line. No answer, no voice mail. She needed to get hold of her because she was going to be late coming home. She hadn't finished the report she was working on, and it had to be to the director when he arrived in the morning.

Damn! Why today? She'd been so looking forward to seeing Dani again. She was so cute and so fun. And she was so incredible in bed! Gemma's body ached to be touched by her again. *Oh, well,* she thought, *it's only a couple hours later. I can survive that, even if I haven't been laid in a couple of years, as Miko continually reminds me.* But she didn't want Dani sitting on her doorstep wondering where she was.

Dani was incredible. Gemma was surprised at how much she liked her already, at how quickly she had taken root in her mind and heart. One date and she was soaring, daring even to let her thoughts roam into the scary realm of marriage. Of course, it had to be too good to be true. Dani had to be too good to be true. There was some deep, dark secret she was hiding, surely.

Gemma cautioned herself to expect that, but her hopes still flew to the heavens.

Again Dani's number just rang and rang. "What the…"

"What's the matter?"

Gemma jerked her head around to see Lois enter the cubicle. "I thought you were gone."

"I forgot my sunglasses." Lois snatched them from the top of her disorderly desk. "Why are you cursing at your phone?"

"I'm trying to get hold of somebody. I have a…an appointment with this police officer. I wanted to tell her I'd be late. She's not answering her cell phone and there's no voice mail. It's the only number I have for her."

"Did you get burgled or something?"

"No, it's…it's nothing. Just a car accident I witnessed." Gemma had no intention of telling Lois anything about Dani. At least not until they were married, and then she'd tell everybody. But until then, she'd keep it to herself. She didn't want people asking questions or offering sympathy if it didn't work out.

"Just call the police department," suggested Lois. "They can always relay a message to one of the officers."

"Thanks. That's a good idea."

Lois smiled and settled the sunglasses over her nose. "See you tomorrow."

Gemma looked up the non-emergency number for the San Francisco Police Department. After being transferred twice, she finally got someone who said he could help her.

"I need to get a message to one of your officers," she explained. "It's important and I have to be sure she gets it before she leaves for the day."

"Yes, ma'am," the officer said. "Do you have a badge number?"

"No, but I have her name. It's Daniella Barsetti."

"Hold on one moment," he said.

She waited impatiently, tapping her toe on the floor.

"How do you spell that last name, ma'am?"

She spelled it for him, just as she'd seen it on Dani's name tag. Another minute passed before he said, "I'm sorry, ma'am, there's no officer with that name."

"That's not possible. Can you check again?"

"Ma'am, I'm looking right here at the database. There's no Daniella Barsetti. There's no Barsetti at all. Could it be another department, like Daly City or South San Francisco?"

Gemma was stunned and unable to speak.

"Ma'am?" asked the officer.

She roused herself enough to say, "Sorry. I must have made a mistake. Thank you." She hung up and slumped in her desk chair, dumbfounded.

What did this mean? she asked herself. She had a uniform, a badge. Gemma was certain that the patch on her arm said "San Francisco Police." Dani's smile, her laugh, the way she tilted her head when she asked a question replayed in swift images in her mind. Was it all a lie?

Gemma finally realized she'd been sitting motionless for several minutes watching the cursor blink on the computer screen. She had to get this report done. After that, she could figure out how to deal with Dani. With every minute that went by, however, she got more and more angry, thinking about that smug, self-satisfied woman who had lied to her. She also remembered what Miko had said about how lesbians love a woman in a uniform. No doubt Dani had counted on that when she'd decided to impersonate a police officer. What made Gemma most angry was that she had fallen for it. Normally, she was the queen of suspicion. Nothing got by her. But she'd been duped by a pretty face. She was angry at herself for letting her defenses crumble so easily.

The woman was smooth, attractive and intelligent. She didn't even need the uniform. She could walk into any lesbian bar and walk out with the best-looking woman in the place. Why had she put on that masquerade?

When Gemma finally finished her report and emailed it to her boss, she shut down her computer and tried Dani's cell phone one more time. This time, surprisingly, it went to voice mail.

* * *

Dani wrapped a towel around herself and stepped out of the shower, then went to the bed where she had dropped several store bags. She had to figure out what to wear for tonight's date. One of the items was colorfully gift-wrapped. That was her gift for Gemma, a brilliant red teddy that she knew would encourage Gemma to turn into a seductive vixen. Clothes could transform her mood and character so completely she seemed to have multiple personalities. She would have been fabulous onstage if she had been drawn to the theater.

Dani decided on black jeans and a gray long-sleeved blouse. She did not expect to be going out tonight. She was certain Gemma would plan to stay in, would greet her in bedroom clothes with a glass of wine. Good thing she'd had a big lunch, she decided, as there would be no dinner tonight.

Before dressing, she checked her phone on the nightstand where she'd plugged it in to recharge. It appeared to be working again. She had a voice mail message from Gemma. Thinking it would be a sweet precursor to their evening, she listened immediately. The message was the opposite of what she expected.

"You lied to me!" Gemma accused, her voice quavering with that particular type of anger that included a deep hurt. "The SFPD has never heard of you. You're not a police officer. You think every girl falls for a woman in uniform? Is that your game? You can fuck the hell off, *Officer* Barsetti!"

Oh, shit! This was not good. Gemma hated liars. She hated falling for a con even worse.

Anxious to start damage control, Dani immediately called her. There was no answer, so she left a message.

"Gemma, it's Dani. I didn't lie to you. I *am* a police officer. It's just that the truth…it's so complicated. Please…please call me back. Let me see you." Dani wanted so badly to say "I love you," but she knew exactly how Gemma would take that. It would sound like a ploy so soon after they'd met, so she said, "I really like you, Gemma. Don't throw this away over a misunderstanding."

She sat on the edge of the bed, dejected. This was a major setback. Gemma would need time. She was hurt. She felt betrayed, and she didn't get over things easily. Dani glanced around her miserable apartment, gauging the prospect of spending the evening here alone. But no matter where she went, even among family and friends, she would be alone. She was so sorry she'd ever picked up that stupid transporter beacon.

CHAPTER FIFTEEN

The landscaping around River Gardens, a thin strip of vegetation between the building and the sidewalk, was awash with color from blooming flowers and illuminated with borders of solar lights. Dani walked up the steps and waited for the leisurely automatic doors to open wide enough for her to pass through. She knew her way around the place, so she didn't stop at the front desk or linger in the lobby with its oh-so-unconvincing eight-foot waterfall tumbling over polyurethane boulders. Besides, the woman on night shift rarely paid any attention to people coming and going. When you buzzed at the front gate, she automatically pressed the button to open it, not stopping to ask your business. The security here was nonexistent, despite the gates, the perimeter fencing and the cameras. But, then, Dani always figured the security, what there was of it, was designed to keep people in rather than out.

Instead of seeing Gemma again, as planned, she'd decided to visit her mother instead. Gemma had not returned her call, and Dani had decided to give her a little time to cool off. She just hoped Gemma wouldn't take too much time, as Dani had no time to waste.

It was strange to be coming here again. In Dani's reality, Harriet had moved from this place six months ago. She couldn't be sure she'd be in the same room or have the same roommate, she realized, thinking of the treat she had brought for roommate Grace.

After scoping out the parking lot, she was reasonably sure Gemma was not here visiting Harriet, but she peered cautiously around the doorframe of her mother's room first just to be sure. It was the right room after all. It was all just as it had been six months ago.

Harriet was sitting up in bed watching television. Her roommate, Grace, sat in her one chair reading a *Sunset* magazine through thick glasses. The two halves of the room were mirror images of one another, furnished with twin, adjustable hospital beds, side tables, one easy chair each and a wheelchair at the ready. The difference between them: Grace got the window and Harriet got proximity to the bathroom. At a certain age, Dani had been told, proximity to the bathroom was preferable to a view. Harriet's pale, lined face was upturned to the TV mounted on the opposite wall where *The Andy Griffith Show* played. There was a faint, distracted smile on her lips. She wore a white gown with diminutive pastel flowers and a lace collar. Her hair, snowy and fine, had not been brushed today, which meant that Gemma had not been to visit.

"Hello!" Dani called boisterously, getting the attention of both women.

Harriet's mouth fell open in delighted surprise. It was her characteristic greeting to one and all, an adaptation she had devised during her institutionalization, designed to persuade all comers that she recognized them even when she didn't. Of course she couldn't recognize Dani, not this time, but Dani was heartened by the response anyway. Even if Harriet didn't know her, she would act like she did, and that was the closest thing Dani had seen to friendship in a while.

She slung one arm around Harriet's shoulders and gave her a squeeze. Then she waved across the room. "How are you tonight, Grace?"

"Not bad, not bad."

"What did you bring me?" asked Harriet, eyeing the paper bag Dani carried.

"You'll see." Dani put aside the bag and took a package of licorice twists to Grace.

"Ooh!" said Grace, taking the package. "Thank you, Poopsie! How did you know?"

Dani chuckled and returned to the chair beside Harriet's bed. "For you," she said, "I've got..." She pulled a six-pack of Sprite out of her bag, popped open a can and handed it to her mother-in-law. "And your favorite." She held up a bag of Cheetos.

Harriet clapped her hands together and said, "Cheetos!" The joy on her face was like that of a child.

Who knew how long it had been in this reality since Harriet had cheesed up her fingers with her favorite salty snack? Gemma did not approve of soft drinks and Cheetos and had probably never brought them. Dani smiled to herself to think that if anybody could miss her since she'd been zapped out of this timeline, it would be Harriet.

She opened the Cheetos bag, then scooted the chair close to the bed so they were sitting side by side.

After she had sampled both the Sprite and the Cheetos, Harriet said, rather formally, "It's so nice to see you again."

Dani laughed. Harriet had learned a few things about appeasing people. One thing for sure, people hated it when you didn't remember them. It was easier to pretend you did and not disappoint them. Dani settled back to watch TV. Opie and his "Pa" were having a serious chat in the sheriff's office about responsibility.

"Do you like this show?" Harriet asked.

"Yes."

"Me too." After another swig of soda, Harriet let loose with a rip-roaring belch.

Both of them laughed, but Grace shook her head disapprovingly from the other side of the room, a piece of licorice dangling from her mouth.

Harriet couldn't always remember words, so she had become less and less talkative as her disease progressed. Asking her questions usually led to frustration and sometimes anger, so Dani sat quietly by her side, eating Cheetos and licorice whips, watching the show and sharing smiles. It almost felt like she was back in her own life again. It felt great.

"Harriet," she said when the show was over, "can I tell you about my week?"

"Yes, yes," she nodded, looking hopeful. Another thing that was true when you were losing your faculties was that people didn't care to have real conversations with you. So of course Harriet was starved for ordinary adult conversation.

Dani crossed her legs and got comfortable. "It started with a pursuit. I'm a cop, you see, and I was with an FBI agent named Bryan. Well, I thought he was an FBI agent. More on that later."

Harriet's eyes widened, anticipating the reveal.

"We were chasing this suspect named Leo Darius up to the roof of a tall building."

Dani continued her story, telling Harriet about her trip to the future and how nobody here knew who she was, not even her mother. Harriet shook her head sadly at that. Mostly she listened wordlessly, enjoying having someone talk to her, and nodded now and then, showing no more surprise than if Dani had been talking about a trip to the dentist. She left Gemma out of the story, worried that she would disturb Harriet, and focused on the hunt for Darius. It felt good to talk about it, to get it off her chest.

"I don't know how to find him," Dani said in the end. "This thing is practically useless." She held up her wrist to show Harriet the device.

Harriet patted her arm. "I'm sure you'll find him, dear."

Dani smiled to herself, seeing that Harriet's attention was on the TV again. This time it was *The Donna Reed Show*. Dani sat back to watch. Periodically she and Harriet shared a look or laugh. The show was slow-paced, charming and innocent. Dani wished she could walk into Donna Reed's living room and escape her present disaster.

After the show was over, she cleaned the orange stains from Harriet's fingers with a washcloth, then she got the hairbrush out of the top drawer of the side table and brushed her wispy hair. It seemed to remind her of her daughter.

"Is Gemma coming today?" she asked.

"Not today."

"Do you know Gemma?"

"Yes," Dani answered. "She's a wonderful woman."

Harriet nodded in agreement. "She's the lady who brushes my hair."

Dani closed her eyes briefly, feeling sympathy for Gemma, then patted Harriet's shoulder and put the brush away. *Maybe it feels the same to Gemma*, she thought, *having her mother not knowing she's her mother, as it feels to me now, having Gemma not knowing she's my wife.* The thought made Dani's eyes sting. She blinked back her tears.

After a little over an hour and two TV shows, during which Grace had fallen asleep in her chair with black stains on her lips, Dani got up to go. She hugged Harriet closely, thinking this might be the last time she'd ever see her.

"Will you come again?" Harriet asked.

Dani smiled down at her. "Sure. I stashed the rest of the Cheetos there in your top drawer."

Harriet's eyes twinkled mischievously, as if they had pulled off the great Cheetos caper.

"Sleep well." Dani kissed Harriet's cheek and left.

CHAPTER SIXTEEN

Dani sat on a bench in Dolores Park, eating a roast beef sandwich and reminiscing about the times in her life she had been here before. This was where they staged the Dyke March every June, where all the women gathered for speeches and general partying before taking to the street. Dani could see it in her mind. The place was wall-to-wall women every Pride weekend, full of loud music, loud women and raging female power. Today, however, it was nearly empty and quiet, except for the ever-present hum of city traffic in the atmosphere. The sun had just disappeared behind one of the towers of the basilica and the temperature had immediately dropped.

It was Thursday afternoon and Dani had still heard nothing from Gemma nor had she gotten a whiff of Darius. How was she supposed to find him? Nothing was going well.

She picked up the second half of her sandwich, absentmindedly watching a woman walking her dog, a tan Pekinese. It reminded her of Tucker. She sure missed him. When her phone rang, she put the sandwich down and answered immediately, hoping it was Gemma.

"Officer Barsetti?" a woman's voice asked. "This is Gail Littleton."

"Oh, hi. What's up?"

"I think I may have been the victim of a con."

"What kind of con?"

"Are you busy? Could you come over and talk? It's possible I had a visit from your suspect today."

"Darius?" Dani bolted to her feet.

"Yes."

"Are you okay? Are you safe?"

"Yes, I'm fine. Nothing threatening happened at all. I'm home now."

Dani relaxed. "I'm not busy, no. I can come over. Give me your address."

Littleton lived not far from the campus in Berkeley's Elmwood District. When Dani reached her address, she found a two-story Arts and Crafts bungalow with dormer windows in the attic and two brick chimneys. It was painted brown with dark green trim and rested peacefully in the shade of three totem-like redwoods. The lawn was well kept and landscaped with hydrangeas and azaleas, the former of which were blooming abundantly. It was a peaceful, comfortable-looking house and there was no sign of trouble anywhere around it. Dani checked her DNA detector. No green dot.

She walked up to the porch and was about to ring the bell when Littleton pulled open the door. She wore a loose-legged pair of capris and a sleeveless knit top and looked much more casual than the other times Dani had seen her. She had a glass of red wine in her hand and appeared calm, greeting Dani with a warm smile.

"Come in." She stood aside to let Dani enter. "I almost didn't recognize you! You look so different out of uniform. You're not on duty, then?"

"No, not today."

"I hope I didn't interrupt something fun."

"No, I was just hanging out. I'm glad you called. I've been hoping for a break in this case."

Littleton led her into the living room, a tastefully furnished space that obviously received little wear and tear.

"Sit down. Would you like a glass of wine?"

"Sure."

"Pinot noir okay?"

Dani nodded and took a seat on the couch while Professor Littleton poured her a glass.

"I think this is a good one. I usually drink zinfandel, old vine in particular. Do you know much about wine?"

Dani took the glass from her. "No."

Littleton sat in the chair at the end of the coffee table and crossed her long legs. Dani tasted the wine.

"I like it," she said.

The professor smiled with satisfaction. She didn't seem inclined to talk business, but Dani was impatient to hear the story.

"Tell me what happened? You said Darius came to see you."

"I'm not sure it was him." She put her glass on the table and pushed a coaster toward Dani. "After my last class, I went back to my office. He must have been waiting nearby because he showed up seconds after I arrived."

"What did he look like?"

"Medium height, slim, brown hair, mustache, unshaven. In his forties. At first I thought he was another teacher. I mean, he wouldn't have looked out of place in the Geology Department, for instance. Scruffy, ill-fitting clothes. You know how they are."

Dani did not, but she did know that the description fit Darius perfectly. "Professor Littleton, what did he say?"

"Please call me Gail." She smiled in a girlish way. "And what do you go by?"

"Dani."

"Dani," Gail repeated. "I like that."

"What did he say?" Dani urged gently.

Seeing that Dani was not in a flirty mood, Gail became more serious. "He wanted the seeds. He said Dr. Ruben had sent him to bring them back to the lab."

"Did he identify himself in any way?"

"He said he was Dr. Dressell, a colleague of Dr. Ruben, and they wanted the seeds back. I told him I didn't have them anymore, that I'd given them to you to return as we had all agreed. If he wanted to get them right away, I told him, he could call you."

"And you didn't suspect he might be Darius?"

"Well, no. You told me Darius had no idea there were any more black beetle beans. He didn't know anything about my beans. Maybe I should have questioned it, but…"

"No, you're right. Darius had no way to know about that. Maybe this visitor of yours really was a courier for Dr. Ruben."

Gail shook her head. "He wasn't. On the way home, I started feeling that there was something not right about this guy. I called Dr. Ruben when I got home and he said he hadn't sent anybody and he'd never heard of a Dr. Dressell. He was expecting to get the seeds back from you, but you hadn't had a chance to connect yet. That's when I knew I'd been played the fool. That burns me, let me tell you." She took a healthy gulp of wine.

"So it *was* Darius. What was his demeanor?"

"He was soft-spoken and cordial. Nothing threatening about him at all. But I think he was ill."

"Ill? How?"

"Dark circles under his eyes and the way he moved, tentatively."

"You told him you gave the beans to me. Did he recognize my name?"

"I don't think so. He didn't react to it."

No, he wouldn't, Dani thought. He'd have no reason to connect her name with the cop who had chased and shot at him. "Then he just went away?"

"Yes. He was disappointed that I didn't have the seeds, but he didn't seem angry. Actually, he didn't seem threatening in any way. Maybe that's why I didn't catch on at the time." She shook her head, then met Dani's gaze. "But if this man really was Darius, I'm afraid I've put you in danger."

"Don't worry. It's better that he's after me now." *Much better*, Dani thought. *He'll think I'm just another city cop. He won't know I'm here to take him out.*

"He won't know how to find me, so that gives me the advantage." Dani smiled to herself. "The police won't even be able to put him in contact with me, if he has the nerve to go that route."

"Why not?"

Dani looked up to meet her eyes. *It's so hard to remember.* "Oh, I just mean they wouldn't give him my address or anything. They don't give out that kind of information."

Gail looked contrite. "I gave him your phone number."

"Good. I hope he calls. Don't worry, Gail. Earlier today, I had no idea how to find this guy. Now he's going to come to me. Perfect." Dani lifted her glass in salute and took a drink. "This really is good wine. What did you say it was?"

"Pinot noir. It's from the Santa Barbara area." Gail relaxed into her chair, smiling with her eyes. "You know, you really are a fine-looking woman. I've thought so since we met, but I think I like you even better in civilian clothes." Her lips twitched in a playful way.

Dani held up a cautionary finger. "We're not going there, Gail. I told you, I'm taken."

"Yes, all right. Sorry." She dropped the come-on look. "Gotta respect that. But you *are* good looking."

"Thanks."

"Another glass of wine?"

"No, thanks. I've got to drive back." She took her phone out of her bag. "I'd better check to see if Darius called, right?" There were no messages…not from Darius and not from Gemma.

"Maybe he called the other number," Gail suggested.

"Other number?"

"Yes, the other number you gave me when your cell didn't work, your girlfriend's number."

"What?" Dani bolted to attention. "You gave Gemma's number to Darius?"

"Yes. I gave him both numbers. I didn't know he was Darius at the time." Gail stood, looking worried. "He'll be able to do one of those reverse phone number lookups, won't he? To find the address. How hard is that?"

"All you need is a computer. Or a smart phone." Suddenly Dani was alarmed.

"I'm sorry." Gail looked at Dani for reassurance, but she had none to give.

By now, Darius could be at the apartment! While I've been sitting here chatting, Dani realized, *Darius was planning, perhaps executing his next move.* She glanced at the time on her phone. It was ten after five. Gemma normally got off work at five. In less than half an hour, she would arrive home, and there was no way Dani could beat her there. All she could hope now was that Gemma was running after-work errands.

Gail put her hand gently on Dani's arm, drawing her attention back. "Do you think she's in danger?"

"I don't know. But I've got to get back. I've got to get there before he does."

CHAPTER SEVENTEEN

"Come on, baby," Dani pleaded, listening to the ringing of Gemma's phone. "Answer!"

She wove through lanes of traffic on the Bay Bridge, hightailing it back to the City and risking a speeding ticket, not to mention breaking the cell phone law. If she got pulled over, she thought, how the hell could she explain herself when they ran her ID? She'd be taken in for sure.

For the third time, Gemma did not answer. "Stubborn…" She clenched her teeth on the curse and swallowed it. "Gemma," she said after the beep, "please listen carefully. This is Dani. Do not go to your apartment. There's a dangerous criminal on the loose and he may be on his way there. I'm on my way too, but you have to stay away from the apartment. Stay away from home. Call me as soon as you get this message. Please do as I say. This is very serious."

She put the phone on the seat beside her and focused on her driving, keeping an eye out for black-and-whites and thinking about how much she could use the boys in blue right now. The headache that had come on yesterday was worse, pounding in her forehead and making her wince.

She glanced again at the phone, willing it to ring. She hit the steering wheel in frustration. She knew Gemma. She was angry and hurt. She wouldn't answer and she wouldn't listen to Dani's message, at least not for a while. She'd assume it was another plea to see her, a lame apology. Gemma wasn't quick to forgive. She'd make Dani wait. Maybe she'd listen to her messages tomorrow. But that wouldn't do any good today.

As her wheels bounced over the last span of the bridge and hit San Francisco pavement, she realized she did have the means to enlist the force. She grabbed her phone and dialed 911 and listened to the smooth, modulated voice of the dispatcher. "Nine-one-one, what is your emergency?"

"This is Gemma Mettler," she said, trying to sound frightened. "There's a strange man outside my apartment trying to break in!" The operator began her program of questions. Dani ignored them and continued, giving the address, then a brief description of Darius. "He's trying all the windows," she went on, talking over the patient "ma'ams" of the dispatcher. "Maybe he thinks nobody's home. Please hurry. Oh, God, I hear glass breaking! Please send somebody! I've got to go. I've got to get out of here."

She ended the call, reassured that the police would arrive at the apartment within minutes, hopefully before Gemma did. Driving through San Francisco was never easy, but some streets were better than others, and Dani took a roundabout route to avoid going through the tourist areas of Pier 39 and the Wharf. Once she got on Columbus, she knew she was home free. When she arrived on her block, she found a parking space a few houses down. She jumped out of the car and sprinted to the apartment where two patrol cars were parked with their lights on, one of them blocking the empty driveway. Maybe Gemma wasn't home after all. One officer stood at the curb. Another emerged from the far side of the building as she reached the front of the house. Before approaching them, she buttoned her jacket to make sure her weapon was well concealed. She recognized the cop on the sidewalk as Gray Palmer. She took a deep breath to calm herself and stepped up to him. "What's going on, Officer?"

He looked her over coolly, then asked, "You live around here?"

"Yes, a couple houses down. I'm Gemma's neighbor."

"Woman called about an intruder at this address. No sign of forced entry. No broken windows and the doors are all locked. Do you know where she is?"

"No, I'm sorry, I haven't seen her." Out of the corner of her eye, Dani saw Gemma's car round the corner. "There she is!"

Relieved, Dani rushed toward Gemma's car as it slowed to a stop in the street. She then pulled over and parked in front of the neighbor's driveway. Dani ran over to the driver's side window.

"Gem," she called, noting the puzzled look on Gemma's face.

"What's happened?" Gemma pushed open the door and got out. "What are the police doing here?"

"There's a dangerous man on the loose. He's on his way here, to our apartment. I'm so relieved you're okay."

"*Our* apartment?" Gemma narrowed her eyes.

"Uh, your apartment. Sorry."

Dani walked with her to the sidewalk in front of the house as another officer appeared. It was Tony Sanchez. He joined them in the driveway.

"This is Gemma Mettler," Dani offered. "This is her house."

"We were unable to locate the intruder," said Palmer. "If you can give us your key, we'll check out the inside and make sure it's safe."

Gemma looked from Palmer to Dani, confused and clearly suspicious. "Intruder?"

"None of the windows have been tampered with. This man you saw…"

"Man I saw?" She turned to Dani. "I don't understand."

"Probably just a vagrant looking for a handout," Dani offered. "I'm sure he's long gone by now." She looked into Gemma's eyes, using her best pleading look.

"It's better to be safe than sorry," Palmer said. "You were right to call us, ma'am. We'll just check inside before you go in, just to be sure."

Gemma's eyes pierced through Dani angrily, but she did not speak. She handed Palmer her keys. "The lock's a little bit tricky."

After the two officers had gone to the front door, Dani whispered, "Thank you!"

"I did not call the police," Gemma said through clenched teeth.

"I know. I called them."

"You!"

"I can explain everything. After I tell you who I am…"

"I don't need an explanation. I know exactly who you are."

Dani's heart skipped a beat. Did Gemma somehow recognize her at last? "You do?"

Gemma nodded. "You're a delusional psychotic who poses as a police officer. You go around creating disturbances and phony crimes so you can show up and pretend to be a big shot. I really should be in the *Guinness Book of World Records* for having slept with the most lunatics."

Really? Dani thought, momentarily distracted by the thought of Gemma bed-hopping from one lunatic to the next. She recovered her focus and said, "Gemma, I'm not a lunatic. The danger here is real. There's a man named Leo Darius. Now, *he's* a lunatic. He's going to kill millions of people unless I can stop him."

Gemma looked at Dani with confusion and pity. "You really need help."

"I'm telling you the truth."

"Then why doesn't the police department know who you are?"

"It's simple. My data has been erased from their computers. Whoever you called, they just looked in the computer database and I wasn't there. It doesn't mean I lied."

Sanchez and Palmer emerged from the apartment, Sanchez slapping Palmer's shoulder playfully. Clearly they had found nothing amiss.

"What about these two?" Gemma asked. "Are they your buddies? Can they vouch for you?"

Dani reluctantly shook her head.

"Is there any reason I shouldn't report you to them right now?"

"I deserve a chance to explain," Dani said. "Please, Gem, I *can* explain. I'll tell you everything. I'll tell you the truth."

Gemma glowered at her as the cops approached.

Palmer handed over her keys. "You can go in now, ma'am. No sign of any trouble. Like your neighbor said, it was probably just a vagrant. Long gone by now."

Dani glanced up and down the street, planning her escape should Gemma rat her out.

"Thank you, Officer," Gemma said with a grateful smile. "I feel a lot better now."

Dani heaved a sigh of relief.

When the cops had returned to their cars, she said, "Thanks, Gem. I really appreciate that. Can we go inside and talk? I know I owe you an explanation."

* * *

A few moments later they walked through the front door and Gemma threw her keys in the ceramic dish on the hallway table. Both of the patrol cars had left, which meant that Gemma was alone inside her house with Dani. *Why did I put myself in this situation?* she wondered. But she'd only agreed to listen. She wouldn't let her emotions be manipulated. Dani had seemed so sincere a few moments ago outside. It did seem only fair to give her a chance to explain her deceptions. After all, maybe she had a good reason. Maybe she was on an undercover mission, something to do with this Darius guy she mentioned. Maybe her data had been purposely removed from the police database. But if she were undercover, why had she been wearing a uniform? Gemma would listen, but she was determined not to be deceived again.

"Can we sit down somewhere?" Dani asked, placing her hand on Gemma's elbow.

"Please don't touch me," Gemma said, moving away. She hadn't meant to sound harsh, but she saw the sadness her comment brought to Dani's eyes. She didn't want Dani to touch her because she was afraid she wasn't strong enough to resist the physical attraction between them. The truth was that Dani looked gorgeous tonight in tight black jeans and a blazer type jacket, and it would be far too easy to forget her lies and fall into her arms.

They sat across from one another at the kitchen table.

"Go ahead," Gemma said, then glanced at the kitchen clock, seeing that it was mere minutes before six o'clock. "I've got a TV show at six and I want you out of here before then."

"*You Are What You Eat*, that's your show, right?"

Gemma flinched, hoping Dani hadn't noticed. *How did she know that?* "Tell your story."

"This is going to sound crazy."

"Not a good start," she said flatly.

Dani chuckled uncomfortably and swept her bangs back from her forehead. "No, I guess not." She seemed reluctant to begin, but after a couple of unconvincing smiles and embarrassed grimaces, she finally spoke. "Two years ago you and Miko found a stray dog, a Boston terrier mix, hiding under the stairs of this apartment. He was wet and shivering. You took him to a vet but he had no chip and there were no lost and found notices about him, so you talked about one of you adopting him. Miko ended up taking him."

She shrugged. "Did she tell you that story?"

Dani shook her head. "I haven't seen Miko since Monday night at Stormy's. Actually, I was there when you found the dog. But I remember the story differently. You don't have any memory of me being there, but bear with me."

Gemma felt bewildered. She really did want to believe Dani, but so far her explanation was a disaster.

"After the two of you found the dog, I begged you to let me keep him. Miko wanted him too. You weren't so sure. You didn't do dogs, you said. Sort of like you don't do cops, now that I think about it." Dani smiled, but Gemma set her teeth firmly, determined not to fall victim to Dani's charm. "Because I fell in love with the little guy immediately, you said okay to make me happy. We named him Tucker and he lived here in this apartment with us. *Our* apartment."

Gemma shook her head in a helpless, disparaging way, wondering what kind of trick Dani was trying to pull.

"The way I remember it," Dani went on, "you and I are married. We live here with Tucker and we're very happy. We've been together four years and everything was terrific until four days ago."

Gemma rolled her eyes. "So you're trying to tell me I've got amnesia, is that it?"

"No, no, that's not it. Just hear me out…please."

Gemma glanced at the wall clock, then back at Dani, who seemed to understand that her time was short.

She then told a story about a man named Frank Bryan posing as an FBI agent, about how they'd been pursuing Leo Darius, the man who'd planted the bomb at Genepac Industries, on Monday afternoon and how Darius had killed Bryan. She said Bryan had come from the future. Dani had picked up his homing beacon and was accidentally transported to the twenty-third century where she learned that Bryan had been sent into our time to stop Darius before he committed genocide. Because Bryan had failed, Dani had been sent back for the same purpose. Gemma listened wordlessly, trying to decide if Dani was trying to scam her or if she really was crazy.

"I know how you like science fiction," Dani said. "In general, I think you get the time travel stories better than I do."

"I like my science fiction as fiction."

Dani pressed her lips together with a look of disappointment, but she continued. "They told me I couldn't come back here permanently. I don't understand the science of it, but when I went into the future, I was erased from this time. That's why nobody knows me here. I was a police officer. I was your wife. But, now, it's like I was never born. My mother…" Dani stopped, choking on her words, then put her hand over her eyes and sniffed before looking back at Gemma with actual tears in her eyes. "She didn't recognize me either." She swallowed hard. "My life here is over. If I stay, I'll disintegrate atom by atom until I die. They said I have only two weeks total. So I have to return to the future after I kill Darius."

"Kill him?" Gemma blurted, alarmed. "You mean you're really planning on killing a man?"

Dani nodded. "If I don't kill him, he'll go on to become one of the worst monster maniacs in history. That's the reason they sent me back. But I also wanted to see you, to have a chance to say good-bye." Dani looked down at her hands. "I thought I could make you fall in love with me all over again, so when I leave, you wouldn't be saying good-bye to a stranger. So you'd remember me." She looked up, her expression open, honest and full of raw emotion. "So that's it. That's my reality, and it's killing me that it's not yours."

Everything in Dani's voice and face told Gemma she was telling the truth. But there was no way she could be telling the truth. "That's quite a story," she finally said.

"Do you believe me?"

Gemma shook her head sadly. "How can I possibly believe you?"

"Gem, if I'm lying, how do I know so much about you? Your favorite flower." She pointed to the African violets in the windowsill. "Your favorite pasta. I could name all your favorite books and movies."

"I don't know how you found out about those things. Crazy people are very good at that sort of thing."

"You can ask me anything. I know everything there is to know about you, your childhood, your family. Your mother is in Room 47 at River Gardens. Her roommate is a woman named Grace who calls everybody Poopsie."

Gemma felt a chill run up her spine. "Clearly you've gone to a lot of effort to learn about me, and apparently you've been stalking me for quite a while. That's bad enough, but you'd better never go near my mother or I'll have you arrested."

Dani stood and faced her. "Please, Gem, just for a minute, can't you try to believe me? Tuesday night, when we were together, didn't it seem really right to you?"

Gemma felt like crying. "It was very special, Dani, which is why I was so disappointed to find out the truth about you."

"Okay, look," Dani said. "I can show you the thing…the transporter thing." She reached into her front pocket, then looked startled. "I was sure I put it there."

Gemma sat with her arms crossed over her chest while Dani searched all of her pockets and came up empty.

"Why don't you try saying abracadabra?" suggested Gemma.

"Not funny. I can't lose that. It's my ticket back. Like I said, if I don't go back, I'll die."

Gemma sighed. "Look, Dani, I heard you out, so please go now. It's after six."

"You don't believe any of it, do you?"

"This always happens. Women seem perfectly normal for about thirty-six hours before their sanity dam breaks."

"Gem, you have to believe me! I know it's hard, but, darling, I love you so much. We're so good together. I wish you could remember."

"I'm sorry, Dani," she said. "I wish you the best, I really do. But I want to leave and I don't want to see you again."

"Wait, wait. I have this." Dani held up her wrist. "This is the thing I told you about, the thing that's coded for Darius's DNA, to let me know when he's nearby."

Gemma peered at a plastic watch-like device, the kind they put in the claw machine at the arcade. She felt a great pall of sadness descend over her like a heavy gray blanket.

"What do you think of this?" Dani asked optimistically.

"It looks like a miniature radar screen," Gemma replied. "A cheap, plastic gadget for kids. A couple of LEDs under a plastic lens, one blue, one green. It proves nothing…except that you're out of touch with reality."

"One green?" Dani repeated. She pulled her wrist back to look at the watch. "Oh, God! He's here! He's somewhere in the neighborhood!" She grabbed Gemma by both shoulders, startling her. "You stay inside and lock the door after I leave."

I'll do that, believe me, Gemma thought, wriggling free of Dani's grasp.

"This is serious, Gem," Dani said, her eyes flashing. "This guy is dangerous. But it's me he wants. He's not interested in you. You'll be okay as long as you stay put."

She dashed through the length of the apartment to the front door, looked out the window, and pulled a gun from a holster under her jacket. *She had a gun on her the whole time?* Gemma shrank against the kitchen counter, realizing that Dani's delusions might lead to violence. If it wasn't all a hoax, if she truly believed her story, that she was on a mission to kill somebody, she might actually do it. Like so many other murderous loons with voices in their heads. Only in her case, she would not say God told her to do it. She'd say somebody from the future told her to do it. What was the difference, really? Not every lunatic is a religious nut.

Dani gave her a reassuring nod before exiting the apartment. Gemma froze, terrified, then she ran to the door and bolted it shut. Pressing her face against the windowpane, she saw Dani cautiously creeping past the garage, leading the way with her gun.

CHAPTER EIGHTEEN

Dani searched the neighborhood for several minutes without finding any sign of Darius. She began to think the device on her wrist might be faulty. Or maybe he was simply well hidden, watching her. At some point, he would have to contact her if he wanted the seeds. She decided to return to her car and stake out the street until he either showed himself or the green dot disappeared. One thing she was sure of was that she couldn't leave Gemma unprotected with Darius nearby.

On the short walk to her car, she kept picturing Gemma's cynical expression. She hadn't believed a word of it. Maybe even worse, she seemed to think Dani was a genuine nutjob, and Dani couldn't think of a way to persuade her that the story was true. Gemma did not take anything on faith. It had been a mistake to tell her. It had only made things worse. And now she had another problem to worry about. What had she done with that transporter thingy? She just couldn't remember when she'd had it last. She decided it was probably back at her room in her utility belt.

Standing beside the car, she took one more look up and down the street. Nothing. She holstered her weapon and got into the driver's seat. She'd stake out the street all night if she had to. Sooner or later, Darius would make a move.

She put the key in the ignition and turned it to the accessory position. Then she reached for the radio tuner, but her hand froze as the blinking green light on her wrist caught her attention. If it's blinking, he's within fifty feet, they had told her. Adrenaline shot through her body and she bolted to attention. He's here! she realized, peering out the windshield, then both side windows. He could be watching her, hiding behind a fence, a tree, another car.

As she reached for the door handle, she felt the cold, hard prod of metal at the base of her skull.

"No sudden moves," said a soft male voice close behind her. "Do not reach for your weapon. Put both hands on the steering wheel."

Oh, God, how did I let this happen? What a rookie mistake!

He must have been in the neighborhood all along. He must have seen her arrive. She hadn't locked the car. With all the distractions, he could have easily slipped into the backseat to wait.

She put her hands on the steering wheel and looked in the rearview mirror at the pale face and dark-circled blue eyes that met hers. His face was unshaven, his beard at least a week old. As Gail Littleton had said, he looked sick. He also looked scared, wary, maybe unhinged. He's a maniac, she reminded herself. He will become a maniac, at least. She'd been hoping he wasn't one yet.

In his right hand was a semiautomatic pistol held close to the back of her head.

"Keep your hands where they are," he instructed, then reached between the seats and under her jacket to lift the gun from its holster. When he had moved back again, he asked, "What's your name?"

"Officer Daniella Barsetti."

"Your real name!"

"That is my real name."

"I know you're lying. You're not a real police officer. You recognized me the other day at Genepac. That's why you came after me. And you're wearing a time phase detector." He held his wrist up for her to see in the mirror, an identical device. Totally identical in every way, including one steady blue and one blinking green dot. "You show up on mine," he said, "so obviously you're from the future."

"I don't understand. Time phase detector? That's not what they called it."

"Your employers, you mean? It doesn't matter what they called it. It's a time phase detector. It detects anyone who's out of phase with present time. You, in other words, and me."

"They said it was programmed to detect your unique DNA, a genome signature detector or something like that. So I would know when you were nearby."

He shook his head. "Ridiculous! I ought to know this is a time phase detector because I invented it."

Dani's mind spun, making the headache worse. "You? No, that's impossible. You must have gotten that from Agent Bryan. He was wearing it when you killed him. *He* was from the future. You, you're from this time. That's why they sent me back, to find you here in our time before you…" She wasn't sure how much to say. She didn't want to give him any valuable information. "Obviously you got that thing off Bryan after you shot him, and now you've made up some story about how it works."

"It doesn't matter," he said, sounding weary. "Give me the beetle beans and you will be free to go. That's all I want."

"I don't have them with me."

"Where are they?"

"At my hotel."

"Which is where?"

"Mission District."

"Can you drive this vehicle?"

Puzzled, Dani said, "Of course."

"Then drive us to your hotel. If you try anything, I will kill you." He pushed the barrel of his pistol deeper into her neck to convince her.

She started the car and eased away from the curb, driving carefully so as not to alarm him.

"Don't break any laws," he said, withdrawing the weapon and leaning back in the seat. "Don't do anything to attract attention. Do you understand?"

She nodded. Like him, she didn't want to attract the attention of the police. If they arrested him, he'd be out of her reach, and there was no guarantee he'd be convicted of any crime. She was the closest thing there was to a witness that he'd killed Bryan, but there was no way she could testify in court. There was no evidence linking him to the bombing either. They had nothing but Bryan's word for that, and he wasn't talking. No, she couldn't count on the law this time. She had to deal with Darius herself.

She chose Divisidero Street to take them through town. Less conspicuous and less busy than Van Ness. She wasn't overly worried about him pulling the trigger. He didn't know where her hotel was. Without her, he'd never find the beans. She didn't know why he wanted them, but it was clear he wanted them badly. She drove at a moderate pace, making the trip last longer than necessary as she tried to think of a way to disarm him. Periodically, he succumbed to a coughing fit, and it sounded serious, deep-in-the-lungs serious.

At Castro and Market, the rainbow flags were flying. Dani turned left onto Market, then jogged off onto 16th to head into the Mission District.

"How do you know the streets so well?" Darius asked. "You're driving like everything's familiar."

"It *is* familiar. I live here. I've lived here all my life. I could drive a cab if I wanted to." She glanced in the mirror to see the bewildered look on his face.

"How is that possible? You're from the future. The city's changed so much."

"I don't think I'm supposed to talk about that."

He stared at her in the mirror, holding his gun loosely beside him. "You do sound like someone from the twenty-first century. Is that training? So you'll fit in? But why would they bother for a couple of weeks? Why waste the time? The police uniform is enough to get past most people. Swenson would know that."

"Swenson? You know about Dr. Swenson?"

"Of course. She's the one who hired you, I assume. Hired you to kill me, right? You're to finish what Frank Bryan started. I've got to admit I didn't see this coming, that they'd travel into the past to murder me. That's actually very clever."

Dani had to keep reminding herself that Darius would become a ruthless mass murderer someday because right now he seemed extremely mild mannered. Those soft-spoken intellectuals are the worst, she reminded herself. Nobody could go more nuts than they could. He coughed again, rough wracking coughs. She wouldn't have been surprised to see blood.

"What's wrong with you?" she asked, hoping it wasn't a contagious disease.

"I've had some interference, delays I hadn't planned on. I've been here a week and a half."

That was a weird non sequitur. Maybe he was hard of hearing. She spoke more loudly. "I said, are you sick? What's wrong with you?"

He narrowed his eyes at her. "What year were you born?" he asked.

"Nineteen eighty-eight."

He scrutinized her from the backseat. Every few seconds she caught his gaze in the mirror. He seemed to be trying to figure her out.

"What is that?" he asked, pointing to a plastic bag on the dash.

"Beef jerky."

"Is that something you eat?"

"Sure. Hey, I know it's full of chemicals and salt, but I like it. Threaten to kill me if you want, but lay off the snacks. You're not my wife."

After a moment of silence, he said, "You really are from here, aren't you? You're an actual twenty-first century police officer."

"I said I was."

"But then why are you showing up on my detector?" She stopped at a light and caught his gaze in the rearview mirror. His eyes penetrated deeply into hers and he seemed to come to an understanding, nodding. "You're the same police officer from the other day. The officer with Bryan on the roof." He scratched his head. "You used his transporter beacon. That's how this happened, isn't it? It was an accident. Then they sent you back, telling you to finish the job."

This guy was a good guesser. How did he know all this stuff about the future and Swenson? Maybe he had gotten something out of Bryan somehow. There had obviously been more to the Darius story than Bryan had told her. These two might have had some history. Bryan might not have been on his first trip back to take out Darius. He might have already tried numerous times. Happens all the time in time travel movies. They keep coming back to the same place until they get it right. Darius might have gotten to know Bryan pretty well by the time he shot him on that roof. Whatever the explanation, Darius knew a lot more about Swenson's plan than Dani had imagined.

"Yeah, that's basically what happened," she confirmed. "I accidentally activated his beacon. They said it had never happened before. Nobody from the past had ever traveled forward in time."

"No, it never has." He looked thoughtful, calmly speculative. "You would have gotten a temporal signature when you went through, a twenty-third century time stamp. That's why you show up on my detector. So they sent you back…back home. You can't stay here, you know? You can't survive here. You'll die." For a split second, he actually seemed concerned about her.

"That's what they said. Two weeks max." Suddenly she remembered his statement that he'd been here a week and a half. She looked at his sunken eyes, his sickly skin, and the truth suddenly dawned on her. *Darius is from the future!* That's how he knows all this stuff. That's why he's got a time phase detector or whatever that thing is. *Wow*, she thought. *That puts a new spin on things.*

Swenson and company had kept this interesting news to themselves. Maybe they didn't want her to know that the guy who tried to destroy humanity was from the future. Maybe they felt guilty. Dani didn't like it that she'd been lied to, whatever the reason. She was putting her life on the line for those geeks. They had an obligation to be straight with her.

"That's the way it's supposed to work," Darius said, seemingly to himself. "When you leave your timeline, you sync up with the timeline in the future. We brought back a cat from ancient Egypt and the same thing happened to it. So we couldn't send it back to die. It's living very contentedly now in Gavin's quarters, and I suspect the British Museum may be missing a cat mummy." He smiled, distracted by his thoughts. "For all anyone knows, we can go back as far as the earth was inhabitable, but the Egypt of the pharaohs is as far as we've gone. We could go back to the Jurassic if we wanted to and bring a dinosaur into the future. That's what Gavin wanted to do. He's sort of obsessed with dinosaurs. A hadrosaur, that's what he wants to get. Now how would we carry that, I asked him. You start thinking about what's possible with time travel…it gets intoxicating." Their eyes met in the mirror and he seemed to remember what was happening in the here and now. He abruptly quit talking.

There was no more mystery about why Swenson and her cronies knew Darius so well. It was obvious from the way he was talking that they were all colleagues.

They reached her block and Dani trolled slowly along it, searching for a place to park.

If Darius stayed a few more days, she realized, he'd be dead. She wouldn't even have to kill him. But what if he transported back, recovered, then came back later to blow up something else? He could do that forever, coming back to roughly the same time frame every time, so it would seem like he had been here all along, even if he stayed away for twenty years. And he'd never be caught because he wouldn't be here between crimes. That would explain how a man could elude the authorities for so long. Wow! That blew Dani's mind. He must have a way to escape punishment in his own time because Swenson was going after him in the past. He had said that was a clever plan, so maybe it was. For some reason, he was vulnerable here in a way he wasn't in the future.

"What did they tell you?" he asked. "Why are you supposed to kill me?"

"To stop your future crimes against humanity."

He nodded half-heartedly. "Of course. They were smart to play on that cliché."

If he was from the future and he committed his atrocities in the past, did he already know what he had done? Dani closed her eyes briefly, unable to comprehend the convoluted nature of time travel.

There was no available street parking in her block, so she pulled into a handicapped spot. Yeah, she'd get a ticket, but who cared? This car belonged to a ghost, and this was an emergency.

"My room's on the third floor," she said.

"Okay. We'll go up together. My weapon will be in my jacket pocket. My finger will be on the trigger."

He put her gun in his waistband, hidden by his jacket. After they got out of the car, he took her arm and leaned into her, the top of his head reaching her chin. She could feel the gun in her side through the clothing. She hoped he didn't accidentally pull the trigger during a coughing fit. They walked into the lobby and waited for the elevator, which they shared with one of Dani's neighbors, a middle-aged man with a badly scarred face and a marked limp. He'd clearly been through some kind of hell. His last name was Molson, which Dani only knew because of the mailboxes in the lobby. They had never spoken, but he gave her a polite nod of recognition. He glanced at Darius, then stared at the closed elevator doors for the rest of the ride up.

On the third floor, Dani unlocked her apartment door and led Darius inside. He removed his hand from his pocket, revealing the pistol.

"Get the beans," he ordered.

She opened the bottom dresser drawer and took out the envelope. He snatched it from her hand, then opened it and looked inside. He sighed in triumph, then extracted the plastic bag and dropped the envelope on the floor.

"Can I ask you why you want those so badly?" Dani asked.

He gripped the baggie in his fist. "These beans can be used to make a medicine that can cure a horrible viral disease. The virus, known as MRV, is barely known in your time and causes nothing more than a few days of cold-like symptoms. In time, it will mutate to become more and more virulent. In my time, it's usually fatal. It has killed millions. It's our plague."

"Plague. And these beans will cure it?"

He nodded. "We wouldn't even know about these beans without Dr. Littleton's research. She published an article about them in…well, next year for you." He reached inside his jacket and pulled out an envelope, which he handed to her. "That's the article. As she discovered, the beetle beans killed the virus quite effectively, but none of her contemporaries cared because the virus is nearly benign in your time. Even Littleton didn't care much because she was looking for cancer treatments. This was just a footnote in her research." He held up the bag to scrutinize the beans.

"Can I ask you," Dani said, "how you knew Dr. Ruben had sent some of those beans to Professor Littleton? He told me he hadn't mentioned it to you."

"No, he didn't tell me. I've been through the Littleton archives with a fine-toothed comb. On October 5 of this year, she made an entry in her journal saying that she had received ten black beetle beans from Genepac Industries. She was excited about it because she'd been waiting for them. I realized that Dr. Ruben may have sent them before his own supply was destroyed. It was a possibility, anyway, because of your primitive system of package delivery. I was about to ask him about it when you showed up on my time phase detector and interrupted our conversation."

Dani quickly processed all of the new information, trying to make everything fit together. Suddenly she understood why Darius wanted the beans. His plan was to destroy them. These ten beans might be the only ones left in the world. If he destroyed these, along with the ones he had blown up at Genepac, the plague could never be stopped. Littleton would never be able to conduct her experiments, would never write the article and the cure would never be found. Maybe Darius had even brought the virus back with him, the killer version of it from the future. He could infect someone and they would infect others, and eventually…

He coughed again. *Oh, my God!* she thought. *He's the one. He's Patient Zero. He's infected himself and come back like a time bomb. Now he's going to destroy the cure. That's why he's got to be stopped. Why the hell couldn't Swenson have told me the truth?*

Dani began to tremble, realizing she might have already been exposed, and who knew how many others? Maybe it was already too late. But even if he had already released the plague, she could save the beans and tell the world about the cure. She had to try.

The only weapon at her disposal was her Taser. She glanced toward the peg by the door that held her duty belt. It was only six feet away. If she lunged for it, he could easily shoot her before she could get it in hand, let alone get close enough to use it.

Darius put his hand inside his jacket and pulled out a silver tube. It was identical to the one she'd taken from Bryan and the one Hale had given her to transport back. It was his ticket home. Now that he had the beans, he was ready to leave. *No!* Dani thought, desperate to stop him.

Before he could use the beacon, his body succumbed to another round of coughing. It was the best chance she was going to get. She sprang at him and tore the gun from his hand. He reeled back, then reached his right hand behind his back to get to her gun. She shot before he could complete the move. He dropped to the floor, screaming in pain and gripping his left shoulder. His transporter beacon rolled across the floor, stopping at the wall. She fell on him, pushing him facedown into the floor and planting her knee in his back. She took her own weapon from his waistband, then released him and stepped back out of his reach.

Blood oozed through the sleeve of his upper arm. He rolled onto his back, whimpering in pain. She trained her gun on his chest. If somebody had heard the gunshot, they might call the police. Once the police got hold of Darius, she'd lose control. She had to finish him now. It was the only way. She aimed for his heart.

CHAPTER NINETEEN

"Wow!" Miko said, shaking her head. "That's the craziest thing I ever heard!" She took a long sip through the straw in her piña colada. "At least that explains why she wasn't interested in me. Already married to you." Miko laughed sharply. She was clearly amused, but Gemma could find no humor in this situation.

The bar was dimly lit and underpopulated. It was a neighborhood place with sporadic clientele. At seven thirty on a Thursday, there was only one other couple on the dance floor and one old guy at the bar watching a football game with the bartender.

"Why'd you want to meet here instead of Stormy's?" Miko asked.

"Because she knows about Stormy's and I was afraid she might show up there."

"Okay, Gem, but I'm not going to quit going to Stormy's for the rest of my life. That's our place."

"I know. Just for a little while. Right now I just really don't want to see her."

"I guess she's got you pretty rattled." Miko stirred her drink with her straw.

"I'm beginning to think all women are psycho bitches." Gemma ignored her own drink, a blue Hawaiian.

"I hope you don't think that about me." Miko crossed her slender legs, sleek in sheer black leggings.

"I've always thought that about you."

Miko shrugged. "Yeah, I see that. So I guess you're not seeing her again."

"Of course I'm not seeing her again! She can kiss my ass. Everything she said was a lie. It started out so well, that's what really upsets me. She was so sweet and romantic and…" Gemma thought back to the night in Dani's arms, at how wonderful it was and how excited she had been about the idea of Dani.

Miko narrowed her eyes, then nearly spat the straw out to blurt, "You slept with her!"

Gemma glanced at the other couple to see if they were staring, which they were. Frowning at Miko, she said, "Why don't you take out an ad on TV?"

Miko spoke more quietly. "Very unlike you, girlfriend. What's her secret?"

"I liked her. A lot. She seemed to understand me so well. There was chemistry. It felt right. Now I think it was all just an act on her part. She's been stalking me, researching me, learning everything she could so she could trick me into sleeping with her."

"Trick you?" Miko widened her eyes sarcastically.

"She knew exactly how to play me. She probably does it all the time. The whole persona, like the uniform, all phony."

"If she's just a player and she got what she wanted from you, why did she want to see you again?"

"It probably threw her when I didn't want to see *her* again. She likes a challenge." Gemma shook her head disparagingly. "Time travel. Geez!"

Miko sat back in her chair, looking thoughtful. "Is it really impossible? Do we really know that?"

"Seriously?"

"Yes, seriously. Can you honestly say that time travel is impossible?"

Gemma shook her head. "How do I know? I don't know anything about time travel."

Miko waved at the bartender. When he looked her way, she pointed at her nearly empty glass. Having gotten her message across, she turned her attention back to Gemma. "Have you heard of the grandmother paradox?" She didn't wait for the answer. "It's a classic example given to show that time travel is impossible. A woman travels into the past and kills her grandmother before she's married and has kids, thus preventing the birth of her mother and of herself. But if she was never born, how could she have traveled back in time?"

"So time travel *is* impossible."

"Not necessarily. That paradox has several theoretical solutions. There's the Novikov self-consistency principle, for instance, that says that any change to the past that would create a paradox would be impossible to make. But that doesn't mean a person couldn't go back in time at all, just that she couldn't kill her grandmother."

"Okay," Gemma said uncertainly, then tasted her drink for the first time.

"There's also the solution of multiple universes," Miko continued. The idea is that if you travel back in time, you're actually making a copy of yourself that appears in one of an infinite number of parallel universes. In the other universe, you can kill your grandmother, but in your own universe, nothing has changed. So in the alternate universe, you were never born, but that doesn't affect the real you, and there is no paradox."

"Multiple universes," Gemma deadpanned. She wasn't surprised that Miko could converse on the subject of time travel on a technical level. Gemma had known Miko for a long time, and she had seen her brilliant mind in action. In college, Miko took theoretical physics. Gemma took biology. Miko took differential geometry. Gemma took algebra. She didn't just take those courses. She understood and excelled in them. A lot of people who met Miko assumed she was vacuous because of her behavior, but that was a defense mechanism she had developed long ago to avoid scaring people off.

"Another solution to the grandmother paradox," Miko said, leaning forward on her elbows, "comes from quantum mechanics where all kinds of freaky things can happen. It's hard to imagine this one on a human scale, but it appears to be possible at the quantum level. According to the laws of physics as we know them, the quantum superposition theory may solve the grandmother paradox."

"The quantum what?"

"Quantum superposition. In this solution, both conditions can exist at the same time. You can both kill your grandmother and not kill your grandmother. Both are true and exist in parallel with one another. They form a kind of time loop."

"This is fascinating, Miko, but what are you saying? Is time travel possible or not?"

Miko leaned back in her chair. "Nobody knows."

Gemma rolled her eyes. "Okay, that's enough of that. None of this is helpful. And, seriously, all this talk of killing your grandmother is depressing me."

The bartender delivered Miko's fresh drink. When he had gone, she said, "I guess the conclusion is that we don't know if it's possible, but we also don't know that it's impossible."

"Naw, it's crazy."

"I see where you're coming from." Miko held up her index finger. "But just suppose, for the heck of it, just for a minute, that it's true. She's your wife. You're happily married. You have a dog. *My* dog, improbably named Tucker. One morning she goes off to work, serving the public, staring danger in the face, but content in knowing that her loving family will be there for her whatever happens."

"Is that some kind of criticism?" Gemma asked defensively.

"No! It's just a story, right? I'm not saying it's true. I'm just saying, let's suppose. You and that scrumptious cop on a regular basis." Her eyebrows went up suggestively. "Hot, right? I could see it. Yeah, I could really see it."

"Okay, okay. Supposing it's true, what should I do? Pretend like I've known her for four years? Intimately?"

"It wouldn't be the worst thing. Hey, if you don't want her, I'll take her. I hear she likes my dog."

Gemma couldn't help but smile a little at that. Miko was good for her. Her offhanded attitude toward life helped put things in perspective. "But none of it is true. Unfortunately, she's just a nut. She's obviously been watching me for a long time. It gives me the creeps."

"It's too bad. I know you liked her, but she does sound like a total whack job. You're right to stay away from her."

"I don't think she would hurt me. I think she really loves me."

"Oh, sure, like Annie Wilkes in *Misery*, she's your number one fan." Miko lifted her glass and slurped up a mouthful of tropical slush.

"She knew exactly how to touch me," Gemma said, mostly to herself. "Like a well-seasoned partner."

"Did she use handcuffs?" Miko smiled wickedly.

"Dammit, Miko, why do I confide in you?"

"Because I'm your best friend, that's why. So, tell me, did she cuff you?"

"I'm not going to tell you anything about it."

Miko grinned and batted her eyelashes.

"No," Gemma whispered. "She didn't cuff me. There were no toys. Just…" Gemma stopped herself, on the brink of reliving the details of Dani's skilled lovemaking.

Miko examined her face intently. "She really got you good. She could teach a class. Lesbian Seduction Scam 101."

"I know what I said about her tricking me, because I was angry. But, actually, I'm leaning more toward believing it wasn't a scam after all."

"Seriously? Now you think she's your wife in an alternate reality?"

"No, no. I think maybe it wasn't an intentional scam. I think she might believe everything she told me. She seems delusional. She seems to believe she's a cop on a manhunt for this guy named Darius. I wonder if he even exists. I hope he doesn't. I'm really worried that she's going to hurt somebody. She wants to kill this guy."

"That's scary."

"I know. What do you think I should do?"

"What do you mean? You said you weren't going to see her again."

"Yes, but I should probably report her, don't you think? Before she hurts someone." She thought of Dani's beautiful face next to hers on the pillow, how serene and hopeful that moment had been, how Gemma had thought she had finally found someone.

"Absolutely." Miko nodded encouragingly. "For her own good. Not to mention this guy she wants to kill. You know, that's how all these crazies are able to go on murderous rampages. The signs are always there, but nobody wants to interfere and report them. Then after they go berserk, everybody says, 'There was something really wrong with him, I just knew it. He had a houseful of guns and went on whacked-out rants on Facebook.' Hey, did you check her Facebook page?"

"I tried. There isn't one."

"Seriously, Gem, this woman should be turned in. If she really is delusional like you think and she's got a gun and wants to kill somebody, you can't let your tender feelings stop you from reporting her. They'll arrest her for impersonating a cop, then she'll give them the story about being from the future and they'll send her to therapy to get some help. It's the right thing to do."

Gemma nodded uncertainly. She knew Miko was right. Even before talking to Miko, she'd known, but it helped to get advice from someone without "tender feelings" toward Dani.

CHAPTER TWENTY

"Stop!" Darius screamed, desperately searching her eyes. "Please, don't."

She held the gun a foot from his chest, trying to pull the trigger. Killing a helpless, unarmed man went against everything she had been trained to do and everything her own conscience told her was right. But she had to stop him to protect countless other lives.

"What kind of monster are you?" Darius breathed heavily, his eyes full of fear and pain.

"You're the monster! You were going to destroy those beans, and now you've infected me with the plague. Who knows who else you've infected during the last week and a half. I've got to get these beans back to Professor Littleton and tell her to make that medicine."

"You fool!" He lapsed into another coughing fit, his body curling into a ball. When he recovered, he spoke with difficulty. "You don't seem to have any idea what's going on here. Everything you're saying, it's nonsense. You've been lied to, don't you see that?"

"I may not understand everything," she admitted, "but I do know you blew up a building and thousands of samples like those beans, thousands of valuable plants, and at least one that could cure a plague."

Darius tried to sit up but sucked in his breath and fell back, winded by pain. "I didn't blow up that building," he gasped.

"Right," Dani said sarcastically. "Who else?"

He groaned through his teeth. "Bryan. He's the one who planted that bomb."

She laughed shortly. "Bryan? He was trying to stop it. He's the one who saved all the Genepac employees. He's the one who told us about you."

"Exactly." Darius sucked in his breath. "He told you about the bomb just in time for you to see it blow, but not in time to stop it. It was all staged so he could get you people on his side. And it worked. Please, I know you don't want to kill an innocent man." He winced and gritted his teeth. "My God, how can you people endure this kind of pain?"

Dani lowered her weapon, thinking through everything that had happened over the last few days. It was so hard to figure it all out. Darius looked pathetic on the floor, bleeding, coughing and writhing in pain. He wasn't going anywhere. Before she killed him, she had to ask herself, was there any chance he was telling the truth? Obviously, she didn't want to kill an innocent man. There was still the chance that one of her neighbors had heard the gunshot and called the police, but it wasn't much of a chance. The people living in this building weren't really the cop-calling type.

If he was wounded as badly as he appeared to be, she needed to make sure he didn't bleed out while she worked out her next move.

She knelt beside him and unbuttoned his shirt, then pushed it over his left shoulder to inspect the wound. The process of moving his arm caused a fresh release of blood. It also caused him to cry out like somebody had held his hand on a hot burner.

"Look," she said firmly, "you need to be quiet or I'm going to have to gag you."

He looked at her helplessly with tears in his eyes. She checked the wound more carefully. The bullet had nicked the deltoid muscle, cutting the shoulder open and going right on past. It was only a flesh wound. She could see the bullet hole in the wall by the bathroom doorway. She used the collar of his shirt to dab away some of the blood to see how deep it was. Darius groaned and his head slumped forward. He'd passed out. She'd never seen a man react this way to a flesh wound. She took advantage of his unconscious state to wrap one of her new shirts tightly around the wound to stop the bleeding. Then she put towels on the bed and managed to wrestle Darius onto it, laying him on his back. He moaned, but remained unconscious. Dani cuffed his right wrist to the bedframe just in case. Exhausted by the effort, she sat in a chair and watched him for several minutes, trying to figure out what to do next. Her headache had worsened, pounding through her thoughts and making it hard to focus.

After a few minutes, Darius woke up, yanking on his right arm until he saw that he was handcuffed. He met Dani's gaze and watched her steadily, clearly relieved that she was no longer pointing a gun at him.

"How bad is my injury?" he asked.

"It's not serious."

"It hurts a lot."

"So I figured, based on your hollering and screaming. I've got nothing here for it."

"Are you going to kill me?"

Dani sat back and crossed her legs at the ankles. "I haven't decided." She leaned her head against the back of the chair and closed her eyes.

"Are you feeling okay?"

She thought it was a strange question, considering his condition. "I've got a rotten headache."

"That's the first symptom."

"Of the plague?"

He shook his head. "No. I don't have the plague. It's the first symptom of temporal asynchrony. By tomorrow, you'll be nauseated and dizzy. Then you'll get steadily weaker and you won't be able to eat without vomiting."

She regarded him momentarily before stating, "So it's true. I can't live here."

"Neither of us can live here. That much of what they told you is true."

She glanced over to where his transporter beacon lay against the far wall.

"You're sick because you have temporal asynchrony," she stated, testing the idea in her mind.

"Yes. I haven't got much time left. But I don't care about that. All I care about is that those beans get back so they can be cultivated and a cure for the plague can be produced."

"This doesn't make sense. Why would Swenson want to stop you from doing that? Why would anybody want to prevent a cure for a deadly disease?"

"I myself wouldn't have believed it of her, but she's willing to see this mission fail just to get rid of me. She doesn't care about the beans. That's not her interest. Bryan went after them to prevent me from getting to them, that's all. He was trying to delay me here so he'd have time to find and kill me. And he very nearly succeeded."

"Why does Swenson want you dead?"

"I've been asking myself that. We've had our differences. She disagrees with me about how to use time travel to the best advantage of humanity. I think she may be more interested in how to use it to *her* best advantage. Obviously, I can't condone that. She may be in charge of the lab, but I'm the one who controls the machine." His voice wavered weakly and he spoke with labored breaths. "I didn't think she would kill me for it, but I was obviously wrong. With me out of the way, she'll have no opposition. Controlling a time machine gives a person a lot of power."

"Did you invent the time machine?"

He nodded. "I did, along with a team of talented scientists. Gavin Hale for one. His betrayal is hard to take, I have to say. I thought of him almost like a son. Pamela must have promised him something impossible to turn down. Maybe a dinosaur."

He chuckled involuntarily, then began to cough. When he recovered, he said, "It was my lifelong dream to conquer time travel. I've studied temporal mechanics all my life, and I've been lucky to get the resources and people to actually make it happen. After all the experiments, all of the failed prototypes, we finally had a machine that seemed to work. We sent inanimate objects back at first. Then a couple of mice." His eyes lit up, and for the moment he seemed to have forgotten his physical distress. "They survived. Then at last we sent a human. There were a few bumps along the road, but eventually we worked them out and we were ready for an actual mission. This is what we came up with, a cure for a deadly virus. I knew it would be difficult. There are so many hazards involved in time travel. Look what's happened to you, for example, and Frank Bryan."

"But *you* killed Bryan."

"I know. What was I supposed to do? It was self-defense. He shot at me. He would have killed me. You don't know how surprised I was at that. And how heartbroken. He and I were colleagues, friends. I've been sick about it ever since. I never thought I would take another man's life. It was like a nightmare. It happened so fast and seemed so unreal." He lowered his head sadly.

He seemed sincere. It was easy to believe him. Dani had been told repeatedly that Darius was very shrewd, that he could spin a tale that would keep her guessing, that she couldn't believe anything he said, that she mustn't listen to his lies. "Shoot first and ask questions later." Had she received those instructions so he couldn't manipulate her or because Swenson had not wanted her to hear what he had to say?

"When I started on this mission," Darius said, his voice soft, "I certainly didn't expect to be running for my life away from my own people. And I never imagined anyone would die. We've made many advancements in the field, but it's still very risky, and I'm not sure it ever will be any easier. I'm beginning to think it's *too* risky. This seemed like such a simple mission. Just go back, grab some beans and return. Save the world." He shook his head wearily. "I was naïve."

"Why would Swenson go to such elaborate means if all she wanted was to kill you? Since you both live in the future, why not just poison your coffee or something?"

He looked momentarily puzzled, then seemed to understand. "Things are different in the future. You can't just go around poisoning people and get away with it. Murder is virtually unknown."

"Really? Human nature has evolved that far in only two hundred years?"

He looked like he might have laughed if he wasn't in such distress. "It's not evolution. It's technology. There are many types of deterrents. Various kinds of monitoring. And there's the brain implant."

"Brain implant?" Dani leaned forward.

"It serves a number of useful purposes. It's like the chips you have in your pets except that it's always active. For example, nobody can ever get lost because it transmits your GPS location. It also monitors your vital signs and sends an alert if something's not right. It allows you to communicate with certain types of machines. Well, you have that now, don't you? Implants that allow disabled people to move machines with their thoughts."

"I guess," Dani mumbled, though she didn't know much about such things.

"It also diminishes pain. It blocks pain receptors in the brain. Not entirely, of course. Without pain, we wouldn't know when to pull our hand out of the fire. But it reduces the intensity."

"Seriously? Then why are you carrying on so much over a little flesh wound?"

"The implant doesn't function here. It's off the grid. I find it very disconcerting being so out of touch with information. And I've never felt this kind of pain in my life. I can't believe you live with this."

"Maybe we get used to it."

"Maybe. That's probably right. You learn biofeedback techniques to cope."

"Let's get back to the implant. Does that have anything to do with the little gadgets everybody wears over their ears?"

"They're related. The little gadget is a computer. We call it iJinn. It does basically everything your smartphone does. Communication, clock, calculator, maps, access to the World Wide Web. It's hands-free, though. The iJinn gets its instructions directly from the implant in your brain."

Dani remembered Dr. Swenson telling her what time it was without consulting a clock. "That's freaky."

"You think so? Add up everything you have right now in this time and you already have all the technology. Most of it is even already applied in some field. In my time, it's gone to the masses."

"What does any of that have to do with what you said, that people can't commit murder?"

"If the implant detects brain chemistry related to extreme aggression, it blocks the neurotransmitters that send signals to the body's motor functions. Essentially, it creates a state of temporary paralysis."

"Wow," Dani said. "That's gotta make police work some kind of different!"

Darius nodded. "That's why there was no way Swenson could kill me. Even if she could overcome the effects of her implant, killing someone and getting away with it would never happen in the middle of a modern, networked city. There are too many eyes on everything. Too many audit trails."

"But you killed Bryan. And he tried to kill you."

"Remember, the implant gets no signal here in your time. That's why it was such a good plan they came up with. Pamela knew that the past was the only place she could get rid of me. When I didn't return, it would have been simple for Bryan to tell a story about how I was lost on the mission. I got hit by a car or fell off a building or something. There would be no way to disprove his story, nor would anybody think to question it. Nobody would suspect a crime."

When Darius broke into another coughing fit, Dani roused herself and filled a glass of water, bringing it to him. She held it to his lips and helped him take a few sips, then she stood over him, observing his miserable, fragile-looking body.

"I don't know what to believe anymore," she said.

"I wish there was some way I could prove to you I'm telling the truth. If you can't trust me, take the beans and return with them yourself. Don't give them to Swenson, that's all I ask. I'll give you the name and address of my associate, Dr. Cortazzi. If you get the beans to him, he'll know what to do."

"But you'll die here."

"I will. But if Cortazzi gets the beans, countless lives will be saved and everything I've worked for will be achieved." Darius closed his eyes and rested his head on the pillow. Within a few minutes, he appeared to be asleep.

Dani began to worry that she'd shot the good guy. She wished there was some way to know for sure that he was telling the truth. Swenson had warned her not to let him get inside her head. *Just buying a little time*, she told herself. *Time to think*.

She remembered the envelope he had handed her. She retrieved it from the table and opened it to find a piece of paper inside, a yellowed page from a magazine. She read through it quickly. It was technical, mostly beyond Dani's understanding, but she got the idea. The article described the medicinal effects of the black beetle bean against certain viral infections in humans. The author was Gail Littleton. The date in the page header was thirteen months into the future. Even if this artifact were authentic, it didn't prove Darius was telling the truth. It didn't prove he wanted to save the beans rather than destroy them. Still, regarding truth and lies, she had heard her share of the latter from Swenson too.

Dani phoned Gail Littleton, who answered immediately. "Dani, it's so nice to hear from you. Is everything all right? Is your girlfriend safe?"

Dani had completely forgotten how she'd flown out of Gail's house this afternoon. "Yes, she's safe. But I need your help. I know you don't practice medicine, but you do have a medical degree, don't you? You're a medical doctor?"

"Yes. Why? Are you hurt?"

"I'm fine, but I have a situation. Could you come over and bring a medical bag? With some strong painkiller, if you can. I'm really in a bind. Please don't ask any questions on the phone and don't talk to anyone. When you get here, I'll explain everything. Can you come?"

"Yes. Where are you?"

Dani gave her careful directions, then hung up, hoping Gail could help explain what was going on here.

She retrieved the transporter beacon from the floor and stood with it in her palm. An easy twist and she would be thrown two hundred years into the future. Maybe. If that wasn't a lie too. She remembered being unable to find her own device earlier. She searched through all the compartments of her duty belt, then searched all of her clothing. *I can't lose that thing*, she reminded herself, trying to remain calm. She began a systematic search of the rooms, under furniture and in drawers. There wasn't much to search, as she had so few belongings. But the beacon was nowhere to be found.

Dani was tired, sweaty and hungry. Though there was nothing she could do about her hunger right now, she could freshen up. She showered quickly, leaving the door open to the main room in case Gail arrived, and put on the outfit she'd intended to wear on her second date with Gemma. When she came out of the bathroom, she heard Darius mumbling. He was still sleeping, dreaming.

About fifty minutes after her call, Gail showed up wearing a long overcoat and carrying a black bag. She looked relieved when Dani opened the door. "I was afraid I'd gotten the address wrong," she said. "This place is a little…seedy. Sorry, but…this isn't where you live, is it?"

Dani shut the door behind her. "Not normally. Thank you for coming."

Gail moved toward the bed as she sloughed her coat off her shoulders. "It's him!" She spun around to face Dani.

"Yes. I shot him. I was hoping you could patch him up and give him something for the pain."

Gail took a few tentative steps toward Darius, who did not stir. Apparently realizing she was safe, the doctor removed Dani's makeshift bandage to visually examine the shoulder. "Why didn't you take him to a hospital?"

"Gail, that's such a long story," Dani replied, feeling exhausted. "Let's talk about that later. Right now, can you do something for him?"

Gail pulled on a pair of gloves and set to work cleaning and disinfecting Darius's wound. "Doesn't look bad. I'll sew it up and he should be okay."

Dani returned to her chair and fell into it.

"Where are the beans?" Gail asked.

"They're right here. Safe and sound. He said he wanted to preserve them, not destroy them. He said he isn't the one who blew up Genepac."

"Then who did?"

"Agent Bryan. So he says. The man he killed."

"But then why have you got him cuffed to the bed."

"I haven't decided if he's telling the truth."

Gail worked unhurriedly while Darius remained in a state of semi-consciousness. Dani felt herself nodding off too and had to jerk herself back into wakefulness more than once.

"Can you get me a glass of water?" Gail asked.

Rousing herself, Dani went to the kitchen. When she returned with the water, Darius's eyes were half open. Gail took the mug, then held a pill up in front of his eyes. "I want you to swallow this," she said. "It will help with the pain."

He opened his mouth and she put the pill on his tongue, then poured the water slowly after it. After he had swallowed the pill, she dipped a cloth in the water and wiped it across his forehead, cleaning off beads of perspiration.

"This man seems very ill," she noted. "Not related to the bullet wound. There's something else going on with him."

"He's ill, yes. But it's nothing you can treat, believe me."

"Why do I get the feeling something very strange is going on here?"

"Maybe you've got good instincts. By the way, do you have any aspirin in that bag? I've got a bitch of a headache."

Gail handed her a bottle of aspirin. "You can keep that." She put her tools in the bag and snapped it shut. "Dani, you know I'm supposed to report this."

"I know. But before you do that, have a seat and let me show you something."

Gail sat in the easy chair and Dani handed her the page from the magazine.

She scanned it rapidly. "One of my articles?"

"That's what I want you to tell me."

Gail read the article, pausing more than once to look up at Dani in disbelief. When she had finished, she placed the page in her lap. "I didn't write this."

"You're sure?"

She looked uncertain. "I'd remember if I had, wouldn't I? Besides, I've never seen beetle beans before this week. This was to be my first look at them. I haven't done any work with them, nor has anybody else."

"But you don't seem convinced you didn't write it."

"The thing is, it sounds like me. It's my writing style. It's exactly what I would write if I had made such a finding."

"Putting aside the validity of the byline for a moment, what do you think of the facts? Does it make sense?"

"Without seeing any data, all I can say is that it could be sound. The MRV virus mentioned in this study is not used very often as a test case. In fact, I think I'm one of the few researchers who uses it. It doesn't interest people that much because it's nearly harmless. You would never go about looking for a cure for it. But it's a tough little critter. It's hard to kill. That's why I use it. If I find something that works on this bug, it has possibilities for other applications that are more practical. But according to the article, whoever wrote this didn't find any other real-world application for the beetle bean anti-viral agent."

"Then why publish these results at all?"

"Because you can't test a substance on everything, so you rely on the work of everybody else. You publish everything because the information could be of use to somebody, somewhere."

"Some time," Dani added.

"Yes. You just never know."

"Is it possible that this virus could mutate in the future and become more deadly?"

"Of course. It happens all the time."

"And if it did happen, if it became a serious threat to human life, your...I mean, the information in that article would become very valuable?"

"Yes. And that's exactly why Genepac and companies like it preserve plant biodiversity. We don't know what might someday yield miracles, so we can't afford to lose anything." Gail looked troubled. "I just don't understand this. Why would somebody publish something under my name?"

"Look at the date at the top of the page."

She did so, then looked up with her mouth open. "That's next year. I don't understand. Is this some kind of mock-up for a future issue? But it doesn't make sense. Nothing about this article makes sense."

Dani sat on the end of the bed, careful not to disturb Darius. She recalled Gemma's reaction when she'd tried to explain how she'd been to the future. There was no reason to think Gail, a scientist, would be any easier to convince. But she did at least have a tangible piece of evidence in her hand.

"Now I'm going to explain to you why I didn't take Darius to a hospital. And if you think I'm nuts..." Dani threw up her hands. "Hell, I think I'm nuts most of the time the last few days. I just don't know what to do at this point. I don't know whether to give you the beans or give them to him. If I give them to you, next year you'll write that article, which might have the potential to save millions of lives in the future. If I give them to him, he'll take them into the future and possibly destroy them and you'll never write that article because you'll never have done the experiments. But it's already happened because the article exists in the future. And that's where I lose track." She sighed heavily.

Gail looked askance. "Dani, why don't you start at the beginning and I'll do my best not to think you're nuts because up until a minute ago, I thought you were an incredibly cool-headed and rational person."

CHAPTER TWENTY-ONE

"You were really hungry, weren't you?" Gail observed, watching Dani scarf up her cheeseburger and fries.

Dani nodded, her mouth full, then glanced at Darius. He was lying in bed, no longer handcuffed to it, awake but silent. He had eaten only half a piece of bread and some water. He'd had nothing else all day, but he said if he tried to eat more, it wouldn't stay down. Relishing her burger, Dani couldn't help thinking about next week when she might look like him and be unable to eat solid food. *All the more reason to enjoy this*, she decided.

"Thanks for getting it," she said, squeezing the rest of the ketchup packet onto her fries.

Gail sat in the easy chair, her long legs crossed at the knee. *What a strange little dinner party*, Dani thought. "You believe me, don't you?" she asked.

"I've never been one to judge too quickly. A good scientist doesn't prejudge; she waits for the proof."

"I don't really have any proof."

"No, you don't. But neither can I disprove your story. You know, Dani, a lot of scientists really, really want many of the incredibly improbable science fictions to be fact. I don't know anything about temporal mechanics." She glanced at Darius. "But time travel is just too cool not to believe in. I hope it's true." She picked up her bag. "I'm sorry Gemma doesn't believe you."

"She's got a more personal investment. And apparently she's dated a lot of psychos, so I can understand why she thinks I'm just another one."

"What are you going to do now?"

"Give him the beans and then we both go back to the future." She wiped her mouth with a napkin. "I sure hope they have cheeseburgers there." She glanced at Darius, who gave a slight shake of his head. "Apparently I'm going to be a vegetarian after all. Gemma would love the irony of that if only she were in on the joke."

"I know you aren't thrilled with leaving," said Gail, "but I envy you so much. I wish I could go in your place. Unlike you, I don't have the interpersonal connections here. I have my work, and I think it would be fabulous to see what changes, inventions and discoveries have been made in my field two hundred years from now."

"Don't despair, Doctor," Darius chimed in. "I'm acquainted with your biographical data, and I believe you will be more than happy with how your life unfolds in the next several years. If I come back a decade from now and offer to take you into the future, believe me, you won't want to go."

Gail's face broke into a wide and genuine smile.

Dani finished her fries and collected the take-out boxes, dumping them into the trash. She returned to the front room and said, "Gail, thank you for coming. And thank you for helping me decide about him." She jerked her chin toward the bed. "I think it's time for us to say good-bye."

Darius propped himself up on an elbow. "Dr. Littleton, thank you for tending to my shoulder. Despite my little ruse this morning, I'm actually a great admirer of your work. And of course we're all indebted to you for the beetle beans."

"You're welcome. If any of this is actually happening, then I'm a great admirer of your work too, Dr. Darius." She stepped over and shook his hand. Then she moved toward Dani, pulling on her coat. "Good luck. I hope you have a magnificent life in the future. Are you sure I can't watch?"

Dani shook her head. "My guess is that I've violated protocol a bunch of times already."

Gail nodded. "I understand." She leaned in to kiss Dani tenderly on the cheek. Then she smiled wistfully at each of them in turn before leaving.

"What was that about protocol?" Darius asked. "We don't have any time travel protocol yet. We're still writing that book."

"I just said that to make her leave." Dani picked up the transporter beacon and the bag of beans from the table where she'd left them. "I don't want her around for the next stage."

"What next stage? We disappear, poof. That's it."

Dani approached the bed and tucked the beans and beacon into his right palm. "I won't be coming with you. I've lost my beacon."

"Oh, dear," he said, looking at the items in his hand. "That's bad. You'll have only another week or so before…"

"I know. It's okay. I don't have a life in the future anyway. Everything that matters to me is here."

"It's suicide to stay. One of us has to take these back. It could be you."

Dani shook her head. "Obviously, it should be you. You're clearly a brilliant scientist, a top man in the field of temporal mechanics and in charge of a super-important project. I'd be completely useless in your world."

"That's very generous of you."

She shrugged. "My beacon might turn up. If not, at least I'll be home at the end. If I make it long enough, I'll go to my sister's wedding. I was supposed to be maid of honor. Now I'll just be an anonymous person in the back with tears streaming down her cheeks." Dani never thought she would be sorry to miss out on that role, but now she really was. "The only thing I regret about dying is that nobody's going to mourn me. Not my family, not even Gemma."

"I'll mourn you, Officer Barsetti. I'll make a legend of you. You will be the woman who saved the world."

"That's very kind, but whatever happens two hundred years from now won't be of much comfort to me here."

"I was hoping to cheer you up. I'm really sorry you've lost your beacon. If you had it, I might be able to help you return to your time permanently."

Dani perked up. "What do you mean?"

"It's purely hypothetical, because I've never had anyone from the past to try it out on. But I've been experimenting with the concept that if you transport someone back to their own time at a very precise moment, they might resync with their original timeline. The precision is important. You have to know the exact second when they left their time."

"I wouldn't know that, not to the exact second."

"No, no, but it was recorded when you came through the transporter. It's in the logs. If I removed the temporal signature for the future, which would take some reconfiguring of the equipment, and then you were sent back to that precise moment, you might be able to resume your life as if none of this had ever happened."

"Swenson didn't tell me about that."

"No, she wouldn't because she doesn't know about it. This is my idea, all theoretical. It's untested. It might not even work. But I'll tell you, I would love to test it out."

"So would I, but the darn thing just isn't here. I've looked everywhere. It must have fallen out somewhere around town. I don't suppose you could beam me another one when you get back?"

He smiled faintly. "I wish I could. The device has to travel with a person or it will be rendered inert. The same thing holds true if somebody tries to bring two of them through. Only one will be operative." He shook his head dejectedly. "I'm very sorry your life has been stolen from you."

"If the plague is cured, it's not in vain, right? Logic clearly dictates that the needs of the many outweigh the needs of the few."

A light switched on in his eyes. "*Star Trek*, right? *The Wrath of Khan.*"

Dani laughed. "I can't believe you know that."

"Oh, yes. The *Star Trek* legacy is alive and well, part of the human collective consciousness. Chaucer, Shakespeare, the Beatles, *Star Trek*." He smiled to himself, then his smile faded. He looked at Dani with a pained expression, then he made a move to get out of bed. Dani took hold of his arm and helped him. He stood shakily, his injured arm motionless at his side.

"You will recover from the temporal…what's it?" she asked.

"Asynchrony. I'll recover. The degradation stops immediately after transport. Then it's just a matter of natural healing."

"What about Hale and Swenson? Will you be in danger when you return?"

"No. I'll be able to deal with them. Don't worry."

"Okay." She nodded. "Then I guess this is it."

Darius held the silver tube in his hand. "Thank you for believing me. All of us in the twenty-third century are indebted to you, all six billion of us."

Six billion? Did she hear that right? There were almost seven and a half billion now. But she wouldn't have a chance to ask about it because Darius had already twisted the top of the tube. The three blue lights lit up.

"Good-bye, Dr. Darius."

Smiling sympathetically, he placed his thumb over the top of the tube. Immediately, there was a bright flash of light. Dani turned her head and shielded her eyes until it was over. When she looked back, Darius was gone. So was the page from the magazine that had been lying on the table. Because Darius had taken the beans, Gail Littleton would never get her hands on them and would never write that article. Now it had never existed.

"I hope he made it," she whispered, glancing around the empty room. "But I'll never know."

CHAPTER TWENTY-TWO

Gemma picked up the throw rugs in her bedroom, then ran a dust mop around the floor, resorting to housework to put herself in a calmer frame of mind. It sometimes worked. But she was skeptical this time. Though she had sat still for the previous hour staring at the TV, she had no memory of the show. It had passed before her eyes without seeping anywhere near her brain. Dani and her preposterous story had taken up all the space in her thoughts.

She was angry, really angry, because she had liked Dani so much. Their courtship had been short, but oh, so sweet. She wondered if the police would catch up to her and put her away. She felt sorry for going to the cops, but it was the right thing to do, to stop Dani from going on with her delusion. It had taken an hour and a half to file that report and give them a detailed description of "the suspect." She had hated doing it and felt horribly guilty.

Dani had seemed so sincere, telling her story about being zapped into the future and then back again. Dani really believed it. She seemed genuinely alarmed that she couldn't find her communicator or whatever the thing was that was supposed to zap her back to the future again. If she did get arrested, maybe she'd get treatment like Miko thought. That was certainly more humane than leaving her wandering around suffering from her delusions.

As Gemma reached under the bed, the mop hit something that skittered across the floor and into the baseboard on the other side of the room. She went to see what it was and picked up a silver metallic object about the size of a lipstick tube. It wasn't hers. She'd never seen it before. It had a seam around the middle and a bluish window under that. She was about to twist it open when she remembered Dani looking for her lost device. Was this what she had been looking for?

Maybe it had fallen out of her clothes Tuesday night. They hadn't been particularly careful during the removal of clothing. Gemma decided not to open it. There was a small lingering doubt in her mind, the nearly impossible chance that Dani was telling the truth. According to the bizarre story, Dani had picked up one of these things and been flung into the future, erasing herself from the present.

What would that be like? Gemma wondered. *What if none of your friends or even your family members had ever known you? What if your wife had never known you? That would be unbearably sad.*

She sat on the edge of her bed, tears forming in her eyes, and stared at the device in her hand. It blurred as her tears fell. Even if Dani had hallucinated the entire scenario, in her mind, she believed it all. She believed nobody knew her, even her most beloved person, even her dog. What a miserable hell to inhabit.

She rolled the tube between her thumb and forefinger. The phone ringing caused her to jump. "Hello," she said, wiping the tears off her cheek.

"Gemma Mettler?" asked a female voice.

"Yes."

"This is Sergeant Rhonda Tyler from the SFPD. You filed a report about Daniella Barsetti yesterday."

"Yes. Have you found her?"

"No, not yet. This case is of special interest to me. I was wondering if you could come in and answer a few more questions."

Gemma changed her clothes and went down to the station, not at all happy to be spending her Saturday selling out Dani yet again. She wondered if she'd be put in one of those interrogation rooms with a two-way mirror and a recording device. She wondered why she had gotten herself into this. She had to wait in the lobby for ten minutes before a young uniformed officer escorted her through a security door and into Sergeant Tyler's office.

"Thank you for coming in, Ms. Mettler," Tyler greeted her, standing and extending her hand. She was a thin, outdoorsy sort with straight blond hair, freckled cheeks and fine wrinkles across her upper lip.

Gemma shook her hand while the police officer left, closing the door behind him.

"Sit down," Tyler said, indicating the chair across the desk from her.

Gemma sat, holding her purse in her lap with both hands. The sergeant smiled reassuringly, then opened a folder on her desk and picked up an ink pen.

"Are you nervous?"

Gemma nodded.

"There's no need. You're not in any trouble. When I heard about your encounter with Daniella Barsetti, I was really excited, I have to tell you. So far, we've had no luck finding her."

"Have you been looking for her?"

"Yes."

Gemma leaned forward. "So you *do* know her?"

"I've met her a couple of times. She showed up at the Genepac building two days in a row. You've heard of that incident?"

"Yes. Dani told me about it. She said a man named Leo Darius planted the bomb."

"That's what we were told."

"You mean there really is a Leo Darius?"

Tyler looked at her quizzically. "Why would you question that?"

Because Dani said he's from the future, Gemma thought. But she decided to keep that to herself, at least for now. "I thought she made it all up. I thought she was pretending to be a police officer. So she's not pretending? She really is with the SFPD and she really is on this case?"

"No, she's not." Tyler spoke tersely.

Gemma's momentary hope fizzled.

"What else did Barsetti tell you about the bombing?"

"Not much. She said Darius was extremely dangerous, that she had to find him and stop him."

"Stop him from what?"

"Further acts of violence, I assume."

"How and when did you meet her?" Tyler asked.

Gemma told the sergeant the circumstances of their meeting at Stormy's while Tyler made notes.

"Your friend, Miko, she can ID her as well?"

"Yes."

"Can you give me her address and phone number?"

Gemma hated to drag Miko into it, but she gave the sergeant the information.

"Did you see her again after that evening when she walked you home?" Tyler asked.

Gemma felt her face flush. "The next night. We went out to dinner and dancing."

Tyler looked up from her page with interest. "I see. So this was a romantic liaison? You were on a date?"

Gemma nodded.

Tyler leaned back in her chair. "How do you feel about Dani Barsetti, Ms. Mettler?"

"I liked her at first, but when I found out she lied to me about being a police officer, I sent her away. I was angry. Now..."

"Yes?"

"Now I just want her to get help."

"What makes you think she needs help?"

"Because of impersonating a cop, for one thing."

"And what else?"

Gemma was reluctant to talk about Dani's wild story. "Look, can you tell me why you're trying to find her? What has she done other than impersonating a police officer?"

Tyler sucked her teeth before leaning forward and planting her arms on the table. "We're not sure. That's what we're trying to find out. Barsetti, or whatever her name is, showed up at a crime scene, asked a lot of questions, chased a man she claimed was Darius and shot at him."

"Shot at him?" Gemma straightened up.

"She missed. We have only her word for it that he was Darius. How could she have known that? It's possible he's a red herring. We haven't been able to locate him since. Was she trying to throw us off the trail? Maybe *her* trail? Is she Darius? It would explain a lot about her behavior at that site."

"Oh, no, that can't be true! She believes she's a cop. She thoroughly believes it, and she's sincerely trying to stop Darius, whoever he is."

"Suppose you tell me everything, Gemma? Tell me what Barsetti believes."

"Dani needs help. She's not evil. She's just sick."

"Then tell me what you know so we can find her and get her the help she needs."

Gemma went over the details she knew about Dani, which were actually very few when you threw out the stuff about time travel. There was no guarantee that anything Dani had said about herself was true.

"Did you observe any tattoos, scars or birthmarks?"

"Yes, she has a tattoo of a bird, a tropical-looking bird with long tail feathers, about six inches long."

"Where?"

"Um, on her side," Gemma said uncomfortably, "on the side of her right breast, and then down on the rib cage. The bird sort of curves around..." Gemma stopped talking, her right hand indicating her own breast, as she recalled cupping a portion of that bird in her hand.

Tyler had raised her gaze from her notepad, waiting for Gemma to finish her sentence, seemingly indifferent to the idea of Gemma's intimacy with Dani's body.

"Could you draw it for us?" she asked.

"I think so."

"How many dates did you say you had?"

Gemma squirmed in her chair. "One."

Tyler tapped the top of the pen on the pad, clicking it on and off. "You didn't happen to visit her place at any time?"

"No."

"Did anything come up in conversation about where she lives? What kind of place? Apartment? House? Neighborhood?"

"She said Potrero Hill. That's all. No specifics." Gemma hated this. It felt like a betrayal, even though she knew it was for Dani's own good. "You know, Sergeant, I barely know her. There was just the one evening."

"I understand, but she spent the night with you, right, and you were together for several hours? You could have potentially learned a great deal about her. Who her family is, where she went to school, any number of things."

"We weren't talking all that time."

Tyler's upper lip curled slightly while she struggled not to smile.

"I do have a phone number. I gave that to the officer I talked to yesterday."

"Yes, it turns out to be a burner phone. Anonymous. We tried it. She didn't answer. Not too surprising." The sergeant sat back in her chair. "But she might answer you." Tyler looked like she had an idea. "She likes you, right? The date went well?"

Gemma felt her face grow hot. "She likes me. But the last time I talked to her, I told her I never wanted to see her again."

"Doesn't mean *she* wouldn't want to. What do you think? If you called her and invited her over, would she come?"

"I...I..." Gemma stuttered uncomfortably. "Yes, I think she would, but..."

Tyler nodded and smiled. "Yes, I think she would too."

CHAPTER TWENTY-THREE

Dani knelt on the floor of the bathroom, gripping the toilet with both hands and heaving into the bowl. Her nose and eyes ran and her stomach emptied itself. So much for Joe's Scramble at the corner café, she thought.

She hung over the bowl, panting, willing her body to calm itself. Finally, it felt like the wave of nausea had passed. She sat on the floor and ripped off a length of toilet paper to wipe her eyes, her nose and her sour mouth.

Temporal asynchrony, she thought. *It's like stomach flu.* She wished she could call her mom and tell her she was sick. But even if she could tell her mom, there was nothing her mom could do about this. There was nothing anybody could do.

During the loud and all-consuming heaving process, she thought she heard ringing, like a phone, but it could have been her ears ringing. She blew her nose, flushed the toilet, then got up and rinsed out her mouth. She went into the other room and picked up her phone. She was excited to see a message from Gemma but was even more excited when she read it. "Found your device in my apartment. Can you come by and get it?"

She found it! Dani forgot her nauseated stomach. Her entire body trembled with relief. She had searched her car and her apartment so many times she was intimately acquainted with every crumb on the floor of both. She hadn't thought that she might have lost it at Gemma's. Thank God! She wasn't going to die after all!

Dani texted a reply. "Yes, I can pick it up. Need to have it soonest. Today? Thanks."

She put the phone on the bedside table and lay on the bed. She felt tired and weak, but was ecstatic with Gemma's news. Despite the brave speech she had given Darius, she was terrified of the anonymous death she would face here.

She turned on her side and within minutes was asleep.

When Dani awoke, she felt groggy. It was afternoon. After brushing her teeth and washing her face, she remembered the message from Gemma. She checked her phone for a reply.

"Yes," she'd written. "Come at four thirty."

Not mad at me anymore? Dani thought. Maybe she'd get to say good-bye after all. It would be sweet to end their time together on a cordial note.

At four thirty on the dot, she found a parking space on a side street and walked to the corner. Everything looked peaceful in front of the apartment. One of Gemma's cats, the one named Bear, was on the porch railing grooming himself. Nobody was on the street. Dani walked up to the door and rang the bell. She wore the outfit she'd bought for their second date. Why not? She hoped Gemma would ask her in, treat this like a social occasion and not just a business transaction. This could be the last time they ever saw one another. That was a hard fact to grasp. But, above all, Dani wanted her transporter beacon back. Maybe she should just take it and go and not try to make some big, emotional thing out of this.

The door opened and Gemma stood before her, a friendly but unnatural smile on her lips.

"Hi," Dani said, feeling overjoyed to be looking into Gemma's precious face.

"Hi. Come in." Gemma stood aside and Dani passed her, stepping into the hallway. Closing the door, Gemma said, "Come into the kitchen. Do you want a beer or water or something?"

Dani followed her, noticing how strained her speech was. She was acting casual and breezy, "acting" being the crucial word. So apparently she wasn't over being mad. No affectionate good-bye after all, Dani realized sadly. But she wouldn't push it. She'd done her best with Gemma and it hadn't worked out. She'd let her off easy this time and just walk away.

"I'm really glad you found my beacon," said Dani. "I'd feel a lot better if I could get my hands on it."

"Oh, sure. No beer, then?" Gemma turned to face her, her back to the kitchen counter, her demeanor oddly nervous.

"Maybe after." Dani watched as Gemma's eyes moved slightly to the left to focus on something behind Dani. The creaking of a floorboard caused her to spring into action. She spun around and leapt back, grabbing Gemma around the waist and flinging her in front of her body like a shield.

Gemma screamed, then put both hands up in front of her face as if she could block the gunfire threatened by the two cops who stood in the hallway with their weapons drawn. *They won't shoot her,* Dani told herself, and she was confident of that.

But Gemma, terrified, yelled, "Don't shoot! Don't shoot!"

Both cops were frozen in place. One of them was Palmer, and she knew he was beating himself up that he had let this happen. It should have been easy. Dani was unprepared, unarmed. Their job was to get the suspect inside the house with the door closed, then grab her. But they should have put themselves between Gemma and herself. Stupid mistake.

Dani repositioned her arms so she held Gemma more securely, then stepped backward toward the door, dragging Gemma with her.

"Let her go," said Palmer. "Nobody needs to get hurt here. Sergeant Tyler would like to talk to you, Officer Barsetti. You just come along peacefully and everything will be fine."

Dani was determined not to spend the last week of her life in a jail cell. She knew what would happen if she went with them. Tyler would grill her and she'd have no way to answer.

She wouldn't even be able to give her a name that would satisfy her. She'd be charged with impersonating an officer, failure to identify herself and who knows what else. Tyler would show her no pity. She'd put her on ice until she felt like talking, and that would be the end of her story.

"I'm going out the back door," she whispered into Gemma's ear. "I'll let you go outside. If you get away from me before then, they're going to shoot me. I don't think you want that."

Gemma shook her head.

"Let her go," Palmer said again, "and put up your hands. Don't make things worse for yourself. You're not in serious trouble right now, but if you kidnap this woman, you can be sure you're going to be locked up."

Dani reached behind herself with one arm to turn the doorknob, gripping Gemma like a vise with her other arm. She eased open the door, then positioned herself and Gemma in the doorway. There were two concrete steps from the small back porch down to the patchy grass of the yard. Dani backed toward the steps, clearing the doorway.

"Please let me go," Gemma whimpered. She was scared, near tears, and it sliced through Dani's heart to be causing her so much anguish. "Please don't hurt me."

"I would never…" There's no point in trying to talk to her, she realized, and no time. "Look, Gemma, where's the device? Give it to me!"

Gemma was now sobbing. "I don't have it," she cried.

"Oh, God!" Dani exclaimed, realizing that Gemma had lied to lure her here. "Gem, how could you!"

"I'm sorry," Gemma gulped.

The two cops, Dani saw, had taken steps toward the doorway. Any minute they would rush her. She had to go now if there was any chance of getting away. In her head, she planned her route precisely. Then she kicked the door shut in the faces of the cops and let Gemma loose. She'd bought herself maybe a four- or five-second lead.

She took off running to the back of the property, going up and over the fence with the aid of an upturned wine barrel planter. She knew the neighborhood, the layout of the lots, who had dogs, and where her car was parked, all information her pursuers did not have. She ran through the Carltons' yard, then scaled their back fence into the Yees' flower garden. Coming down the other side of the fence, her hand encountered an exposed nail, ripping the skin open. She suppressed her cry, holding her hand up for inspection. Blood oozed out of a jagged tear. She ran across the Yees' yard, her shoes sinking in the muddy earth of a colorful primrose patch. In order to skirt the dogs in the Werners' yard, she had to take a circuitous route to her car. The dogs were already barking, hearing her nearby. She scaled another fence using an upside-down wheelbarrow. She dropped down into Old Man Reimer's yard where he was standing, stooped over in his tomato patch, a running hose in hand. He looked up at her, startled.

She ran past him, through his side yard and out his gate to the street. She knew that one of the cops, probably not Palmer, had followed her over the first fence and may have been blocked from going farther by the Werners' dogs, who were still fiercely barking. Palmer would have radioed for help and already be out on the street looking for her. Her plan was to be out of here long before backup could arrive. She dashed the hundred feet down the street, hopped in her car, and made a U-turn, her heart pounding hard from adrenaline. She could avoid Gemma's street altogether and, hopefully, escape without being seen. Even if somebody got her car's license number, they couldn't trace it to her. She hadn't registered the car. The teenaged girl who had sold it to her would only be able to give them a name and description, which they already had.

Feeling relieved, she turned another corner and knew she'd made it out. She drove down to Bay Street and headed east, feeling much calmer. She held her bloody left hand in her lap and drove with her right. The cut was painful, but the bleeding had slowed. The blood that had run down her fingers was sticky and drying. It was nothing. Just a scratch.

Only now did she have a chance to think about what had just happened. It was so hard not to think of Gemma as an ally. It had never occurred to Dani that she was walking into a trap.

But it wouldn't happen twice. She couldn't trust Gemma and she wouldn't see her again. That thought made her heart ache.

Gemma would be okay. She'd eventually find someone who would inspire her to quit her dead-end job and strike out on her own. To be courageous and fly. Like Bloody Betty.

She smiled to herself. She'd forgotten about Bloody Betty, Gemma's fearless alter ego. Maybe the blood on her hand had reminded her. Bloody Betty was derived from an unlikely place, a sex education film Gemma had seen in sixth grade. It was to teach girls that menstruation wasn't a curse, that you could go about your regular life while on your period. The way Gemma had told the story was funny. The girl in the film, Betty, was shown running hurdles, playing tennis, ice skating, dancing with boys, going to movies with a large convoy of girlfriends, working as a volunteer at a hospital, paddling a kayak and hiking in Yosemite. Menstruation, it seemed, turned a girl into a superhero with scads of friends and a rewarding job, capable of doing anything. She was a phenomenon! Gemma had made a private joke out of the idea, naming the heroine of the film Bloody Betty. So whenever Gemma felt timid, she would invoke Bloody Betty, the part of herself that was confident, talented and fearless. Bloody Betty was the woman who had quit her job at the FDA and started her own business. Gemma was capable of more than she knew. She had reserves of strength. She simply had to bring them to the fore.

As Dani drove, the sun dipped below the taller hotels and apartment houses, and another unwelcome bit of reality seeped into her mind. It was all over now. Briefly, she had thought she was saved. But it had been a trick. The beacon was still lost. She had no way to get to safety after all. Her fate was sealed. She had been here almost one week. She had just one more left. She recalled Darius after his week and a half being in the past. He was still getting around, but wouldn't have been much longer. *If there's anything I need to do here*, she told herself, *I'd better do it soon.*

CHAPTER TWENTY-FOUR

When Gemma got home on Monday, she picked up Smokey and walked to the kitchen, retrieving a can of cat food from the cupboard. She put Smokey down and popped the lid. Bear came running in, sending up a chorus of demanding meows. Both of them crowded close to the food dish where Gemma dumped the contents of the can. Tossing the can in the trash, she saw the blinking light on the phone. Land line messages were usually telemarketers, but they were occasionally friends or the always-dreaded calls from the nursing home. She punched the play button.

"Hello, Gem. It's Dani."

Gemma froze.

"I just want to say that I understand why you did what you did. I hope you don't feel guilty. There's no harm done, really. It actually took a lot of guts to do it. I wonder if you dredged up old Bloody Betty for the job." She chuckled. "Anyway, I have no hard feelings. I'm fine and everything will be fine. I wish you nothing but the best life has to offer. I'm glad we got to know one another, at least a little bit, and I hope you remember me with a little fondness, despite all the weirdness. Don't worry. I won't bother you anymore. Take good care of yourself and be happy. I love you."

The message clicked off. Gemma stood motionless for a long time. Eventually, the shiver running down her spine caused her to move. She pressed a button on the phone to replay the message. Dani's voice, clear and calm, held no irony or bitterness. She seemed to be sincere. But Dani's message of goodwill was not the reason Gemma listened so carefully to each word. There it was again, the second time. Dani had said "Bloody Betty." When the message concluded, Gemma slid into a kitchen chair, stunned and confused. She had never told a soul about Bloody Betty. Nobody knew about her. Nobody. But Dani knew. She not only knew the name, but she knew what it meant.

She sat staring at the wall, unseeing, for a long time, until Bear rubbed against her leg, rousing her.

Then she called Miko. "I need to talk. Can I come over? Something's very wrong."

As soon as Gemma was inside Miko's apartment, she sank into the sofa and burst into tears. Miko sat next to her, patting her knee.

"What happened?" she asked impatiently, then shoved a box of tissues toward her.

Gemma took one and dried her eyes, then blew her nose, trying hard to get control of herself. After a few minutes, she finally felt capable of talking.

"Miko, I'm so confused." She crumpled the tissue in her palm.

"This is about Dani again, isn't it?" Miko sighed melodramatically.

Oreo came up and put his nose against Gemma's knee sympathetically. She reached down to pat him on the head.

"Is she still on the loose?" Miko asked.

"Apparently. She left me a voice mail today."

"Are you afraid she's going to come back? You can stay here for a while if you're afraid."

"Thanks. But I'm not afraid. I don't think she'll be back. Oh, Miko, you should have seen the look in her eyes Saturday. She felt so betrayed, so bewildered, like she could never have imagined I would do something like that to her. It broke my heart. It scares me to death to think I could have gotten her killed."

Miko patted her arm. "Gem, you did the right thing. You can't have lunatics running around the city with guns. You did the right thing cooperating with the police."

"I don't know. I'm beginning to think I shouldn't have done it."

"Why not? What should you have done instead?"

Gemma shook her head. "I don't know. I'm telling you, I'm confused." Gemma rubbed her hand across her wet eyes. "She thinks I'm her wife. She thinks she's in love with me, that we had a life together. And then…I betrayed her."

"Oh, don't start crying again, Gem. Whatever she thinks, it's not your doing. I hope they find her and get her the help she needs. That's the best thing. What did she say in the voice mail anyway?"

"She said she forgave me for setting her up with the cops. She said she loves me and…well, it sounded like a good-bye." Gemma dabbed the wadded tissue into the corner of her eye. "I just don't know what to do. If she dies while I have the means to save her, I may as well have killed her myself."

"What are you talking about, if she dies?"

Gemma put her hand in her pocket and wrapped it around the metallic tube there, bringing it out to display in her palm. "This is the thing she came for Saturday, the reason she came over."

They both stared at it before Miko said, "But you didn't give it to her?"

"I had no chance. The way things happened, there was no way. For one thing, I thought they were going to arrest her, so I thought it would be better if I kept it for her. I didn't tell the police about it. I hid it in my room. I actually didn't think it mattered. When I asked her to come over, it was just the excuse, and I thought this was just a piece of junk, some kid's toy."

"And now you think differently?"

Gemma shrugged. "I don't know what to think. I didn't think there was a chance in hell she was telling the truth until…" Gemma closed her hand over the device.

"Until what?" Miko leaned in, her eyes narrowing.

"She mentioned something from my past that I've never told anybody. It was my secret, a name I gave my alter ego. An invisible friend type of thing. That name has only ever existed in my own mind."

"Really? And Dani knows it?"

Gemma nodded.

"Could you have said it in your sleep?" Miko lifted Oreo into her lap.

"I doubt it. I haven't even thought of it in a long time. And she didn't just know the name. She knew what it meant to me. So for the first time I'm wondering if her story could be true. That in some reality she and I are together, have been together for years and I've told her things like that."

"Okay, you're freaking me out now. What is that thing anyway?"

Gemma opened her palm to reveal the device. "She says she needs it to go back to the future."

"Seriously?" Miko put Oreo on the floor again and took the tube from Gemma's hand. "Looks like a lipstick tube. Did you open it? Maybe it's my shade." She pulled on one end, trying to pull it apart.

Gemma snatched it back. "I don't think you should mess with it. It could be dangerous. Sergeant Tyler seems to think Dani could be involved in last week's bombing on the Peninsula."

Miko jumped back to the far end of the couch. "Really? That could be a bomb and you just let me try to pull it apart?"

"Well, Dani said…"

"Really, Gem? Do we believe what Dani said? That if she misplaced her bomb in your apartment, she'd tell you she was looking for a bomb? If there's any chance that thing can blow up, you need to get it to the police ASAP. If they arrest her and find out you've been hanging onto that, even if it doesn't explode, you're going to be in a shitload of trouble."

Gemma remembered how Sergeant Tyler had seemed unconvinced that Gemma was telling everything she knew. And she'd been right. Gemma had told them nothing about Dani's fantastical time travel story. Tyler could tell she was holding back and might suspect her of deeper involvement, perhaps even in a crime. "I guess you're right."

"Damn right, I'm right!" Miko sprang off the couch and walked purposefully to the door. "Now get that thing out of here before you blow up my place, girl!"

CHAPTER TWENTY-FIVE

Dani sat on the low wall at the edge of Union Square, people watching. It was a chilly, clear evening, and her clothes were insufficient for the weather. She didn't have a coat and didn't see much point in buying one. Her uniform would have kept her much warmer, but she hadn't worn it since last week. She couldn't wear it now that she was a "person of interest." That's how the news referred to her. They had a sketch, which was fairly accurate, but no photo. As long as she didn't wear the uniform and didn't tell anybody her name, she figured she could move around the city more or less openly. She wondered if Gemma had been the one to talk to the sketch artist. Maybe it had been Tyler herself. Of course they had no photo, she realized. There were no photos of her anywhere, not a single one. There were no baby pictures, no school photos, no picture of her graduating from the academy, no wedding photos, none of the dozens of goofy selfies she and Gemma had taken together. She could remember them vividly, but they no longer existed.

She pulled out her phone and held it at arm's length, smiled, then snapped a photo of herself with a red tour bus in the background. With bitter amusement, she realized this was the only photo of her that would ever exist.

She watched the elevator ride up the side of the St. Francis Hotel toward a gray sky. Across the street, several floors of Macy's presented their displays to downtown. Looking at Macy's windows made her think of the holidays. Macy's windows at Christmastime, it was a big deal. Here in Union Square, the big tree would go up around Thanksgiving and the absurd little ice rink would beckon incompetent California skaters who'd never been on ice before. She and Gemma always came to watch them. She hugged her arms closer, thinking about how she wouldn't be a part of that world—or any other—by then.

The holidays reminded her of gifts, and that reminded her that her sister was getting married in three days, on Saturday. The church would be full of people Dani knew. She was still debating about whether or not to go. She wasn't sure if she'd be able to go, if she would still be well enough to get around. Even if she didn't attend in person, she thought, she could still send flowers. Why not?

She consulted her phone to look up the nearest flower shop. It wouldn't connect to the Internet. She tried again. Nothing. *This damn burner*, she thought. *It was a lemon from the beginning. What does it matter?* She stood up and tossed the phone in a nearby trash can. There was nobody to call and nobody who would call her, other than maybe Sergeant Tyler thinking she was stupid enough to answer.

She remembered a florist not far away on O'Farrell St. It would be an easy walk. Walking was a good idea anyway to shake off some of the cold. She left the park and walked down Geary Street past the art galleries and an Asian import store. Everything was familiar. There were memories for her everywhere she went in this city. She'd been walking for a couple of days, going to places she knew, places she wanted to revisit, and sifting through all those memories, most of them good. She was saying good-bye. She'd keep on walking until she didn't have the strength to continue.

She crossed Mason amid a crowd of tourists and shoppers and stopped in front of the Pinecrest Café. On this corner, as usual, Sally Kirkland held out her hand to passersby. This was her corner, hard won and lucrative. The mostly well-off theater patrons had to pass this spot on their way to the Geary or Curran theaters. Sally, with her stooped, frail body and lined, sad face raked it in. She made enough to afford a small apartment not far away, which she shared with her sister. Enough for rent and food and basic cable. She had her problems, but she did okay.

Dani went down Mason toward the florist. Along the way, she passed a homeless man she knew. He didn't do as well as Sally because he was younger, around forty, and looked able-bodied. But he was far from employable. His problems were many, both physical and mental. He held a black and white cat gently in his lap. The cat didn't seem the least bit bothered by the heavy stream of foot traffic. Dani fished a bill from her pocket and tucked it into Jerry's cup.

"Bless you," he said, looking up to meet her eyes. She nodded and walked on. At the next corner, she stopped to get her bearings, trying to remember which direction the flower shop was. Hearing a man hollering, she turned to see Jerry, his cat tucked under his arm with all four legs dangling, hobbling quickly toward her, a determined look on his face.

"Lady!" he called frantically. "Lady!"

Moving through the crowd like a runaway rumble cart, Jerry managed to get the attention of the entire block. The pedestrians parted for him like the Red Sea. He did not move fast, as he was lame, but he moved large and erratically. Dani faced him and waited for his arrival. He pulled up to her and stopped, out of breath. He held up her contribution and said, "Lady, this is a hundred-dollar bill!"

Dani smiled. "I know. You'd better put it away before somebody rolls you for it."

"But a hundred-dollar bill," he said again, as if he had been unable to make her understand.

"It's okay, Jerry. Why don't you go into Macy's and buy yourself a pair of pants or a new shirt?"

He carefully folded the money. "Oh, I might buy a new shirt, yeah, but not at Macy's. I'll go to the thrift store!"

"Very smart."

He peered into her face. "Do I know you?"

"Once upon a time," she replied, then patted his shoulder and turned to cross the street.

"Thank you!" he called after her.

After she ordered the flowers, she stopped into a grocery store to get some supplies. She wouldn't need much, just a few days' worth of food, some bread, cans of soup, something easy on the stomach. Feeling tired, she decided she had done enough for today and set off toward her sad little apartment.

By Thursday, Dani felt truly lousy. She was too sick to eat anything and stayed in her room all day, venturing out the door only once, to visit her neighbor, Mr. Molson, who by now she knew to be a disabled vet of the war in Iraq. She gave him the pink slip and car keys to her Jetta. "What's the catch?" he asked.

"No catch. I'm leaving town and I don't need it. I don't have time to sell it and I don't know anybody else to give it to. It runs okay. If you don't need a car, you can sell it. It's not worth much, but you might get a couple thousand for it. It's in the garage across the street. Stall 433, which is paid up for the rest of the month."

He looked puzzled, then chuckled. "It's not stolen, is it?"

She smiled and shook her head. "I just bought it. Didn't even get it registered, so you can put it in your name."

"Thanks!" Molson looked at her more intently, into her eyes. "Are you okay? You look kinda beat up."

"I'm feeling lousy, actually. Food poisoning. That's what I get for eating at cheap dives."

The answer seemed to satisfy him.

Tying up loose ends, that's what she was doing. She couldn't do much for Sergeant Tyler about the mystery of her identity. When they found her body, along with the uniform, police badge, her driver's license and her credit cards, all in the name of Daniella Barsetti, they'd be left without answers. She knew how that would eat at Tyler for years.

There was one more thing, the money. She'd given out a few hundreds to the homeless, but she still had around ten thousand dollars. She'd been trying to think of something she could do with it, something that would really help somebody. She didn't want to leave it here for the police to confiscate. She didn't have much more time to mull it over, but she was confident that something would come to her.

On Saturday, though she was not at all up to it, Dani decided to go to Rachel's wedding. It was her last chance to see her family and she couldn't resist the opportunity. She started the day off by eating an unbuttered piece of toast, then throwing it up. She followed that with a slowly sipped half a ginger ale, which had thankfully stayed down. She took a taxi to St. Paul's Catholic Church in Noe Valley. It was a beautiful and magnificent cathedral, not the church her family normally attended for mass, but only for special occasions. When you wanted pomp and circumstance, this place delivered much better than their neighborhood church. She tried to be unobtrusive by coming in close to the time for the beginning of the ceremony when everybody else was more or less seated and by sitting near the back. She didn't want to run into her mother for a number of reasons, but mainly because Aunt Kathy and Uncle Marcello might be in the building, and how could she explain that she wasn't their daughter after all? If her mother asked them about their police officer daughter, she'd learn that Dani was an imposter. But Dani didn't expect any of these questions to come up until the reception, which she did not plan to attend. The mystery of Daniella Barsetti would never be solved, not for Sergeant Tyler and not for Nora Barsetti. She tucked herself into a rear pew against the wall.

She could see her mother in the front pew along with other near relatives, but she didn't see her brother Nick. On the other side were the parents and siblings of Rachel's groom. A piano stood in readiness for the beginning of the ceremony and flowers were strategically arranged, including the ones she had sent, an ostentatious spray of white, yellow and orange. She hoped the ceremony would go quickly, as she did not feel well and didn't know how long she could stay awake.

She noticed a young man in the pew in front of her, a family friend the same age as Nick. He'd been a neighbor of their family when they were kids. He sat with his head bowed, absorbed by his phone.

"Hey, Troy," she said, sliding over behind him.

He looked up, then turned around to face her, his expression one of perplexity. She'd completely forgotten that he wouldn't know her.

"I…" he began, then opted for the wedding stand-by question. "Groom or bride?"

"Bride," she answered. "We met ages ago when you were a kid when I was visiting Rachel's family. I'm a distant cousin. My name's Dani."

He nodded. "Yeah, sorry, I don't remember."

"No reason you should. But you're a friend of Nick's, right?"

He nodded again. "I used to be. When we were kids."

"I haven't seen him here today. Have you?"

Troy jerked his head oddly. He was clearly surprised at the question. "You're a really distant cousin, aren't you?"

"I guess. It's been a long time since I've seen this side of the family."

He looked embarrassed. "Well, it's not a secret. Everybody knows. I mean, everybody around here knows."

"Knows what?"

Even though "it" wasn't a secret, Troy whispered. "Nick's in prison. He's been there almost two years already."

Dani reeled back in the pew. "Prison?"

"Yeah. He went down for breaking and entering and aggravated assault. He broke into some dude's house and the dude tried to hit him with a baseball bat. Nick took it away from him and beat him with it."

Dani gasped, her hand instinctively going to her mouth.

"He didn't kill him, but it was ugly. It wasn't the first time, burglary, I mean. He did it to support his habit. They got him for possession too and a couple of other drug-related charges."

"Oh, God!" Dani said. "How horrible. I had no idea."

Troy shrugged. "Yeah, it's too bad. He was really smart, had so much potential. Until he went off track. People tried to help him. It just didn't do any good."

After Troy went back to his phone, Dani sat back in her pew, stunned and saddened. This was all her fault, she thought. Because she wasn't here. In her timeline, Nick was a model student at Cal Poly. His brief detour during high school into drug use had never gotten a strong hold on him. The bad guys he'd started to get involved with had found themselves up against a strong deterrent—Dani. They didn't want to be around a guy whose sister was a cop, especially after she came down on them. And Nick. She came down on him too. She watched him constantly and kept him straight until he was on solid footing again. Their parents never even recognized the signs. They didn't know he was in trouble until Dani told them. In this timeline, there was nobody there to tell them. No wonder her mother had looked so stricken when she had thought of her son.

God, what have I done? Dani put her face in her hands in despair just as the piano began to play.

CHAPTER TWENTY-SIX

It hadn't been hard to find the wedding announcement for Rachel Barsetti. Gemma was counting on Dani showing up for the wedding. If she didn't, there wasn't much chance Gemma would ever find her. Her cell phone number no longer worked. It just rang and never went to voice mail. She had gone back to Stormy's to ask if Dani had come in again, but Stormy reported that she hadn't seen her. Recalling what Dani had said about running, she had gone to Crissy Field and sat for three hours watching people flying kites and skateboarding, hoping Dani would jog by. She had even called several hospitals on the chance that Dani had checked herself in because the sickness she believed was coming. She knew that was a long shot. Dani was wanted by the police, thanks to Gemma, so she couldn't very well check herself into a hospital, at least not under that name. She didn't know where else to look. So she desperately hoped this last chance would pay off.

She took the street car to Noe Valley, to a part of the city foreign to her. Gemma still didn't know how to believe Dani's story, but part of her did believe it. And she wanted Dani to know that, that Gemma had reconsidered and hadn't abandoned her. She felt through the material of her zippered pocket to be sure Dani's gadget was still there.

The street car was slower than she had hoped and the route to the church was complicated. She had to get off and wait for another car to take her the last stretch, and then the car didn't stop on 28th as she had anticipated. She consulted her map app and realized she had missed her stop. She got off the street car at the next stop and backtracked on foot, worried that she'd be too late. She rapidly walked the last couple of blocks to the church, an imposing building of gray stone with Gothic-style stained glass windows and soaring spires. The front of the building was dominated by a round stained glass window over three arches. Behind the arches, double doors were open. A couple of young men in suits were under the arches talking. Maybe the ceremony was over.

As she approached the building, people rushed out of the doors and took up places on the steps in an air of excitement, their cameras drawn. A professional photographer was among them. Gemma chose a spot on the sidewalk where she could get a good view and scanned all the faces. The crowd grew larger as everyone from inside poured outside until finally the bride and groom emerged from the church, all smiles, the bride in traditional white and the groom in a black tux. They posed for photos while Gemma continued to look for Dani. The bride, she noticed, had features that resembled Dani's. Maybe this was her sister after all. And these people were her friends and family members. Maybe Dani was here with the people who loved her and cared about her and everything was fine. Gemma began to have second thoughts about coming, falling back on her original assessment that Dani suffered from delusions. If Dani was back with her family, maybe Gemma's presence would merely cause trouble.

But she had to follow through, she told herself, just in case.

She waited until the newlyweds had been whisked away in the limousine before venturing closer. Some of the guests were leaving and others lingered around the entrance to the church. Others might have gone back inside, she realized, so she walked up the steps and into the magnificent interior. The space was massive. The walls soared high above to a dome-shaped ceiling. There were at least thirty rows of pews leading to the altar area, making for a long aisle for a bride to walk. *What a place to get married!* Gemma thought, her head bent back to take in the stained glass.

Small clusters of people were gathered inside talking. She glanced from person to person, searching for Dani. Toward the back of the church, not far from where she had entered, one woman sat near the left wall, her body slumped forward. From her angle, Gemma couldn't see her face, but from the shape of her body and the style of her hair, she was almost certain it was Dani. She felt a surge of joy and triumph.

She entered the pew, making her way to the wall where the woman sat. Dani looked up and recognized her. A smile instantly broke out on her face. *She's happy to see me*, Gemma thought, sliding onto the bench next to her. She did look happy, but she didn't look well. There were dark circles under her eyes and her face was pale and gaunt, cheekbones more sharply defined than ever. Gemma sat close.

"I'm so glad I found you!" she said quietly.

"What are you doing here?"

"I came to see you, of course. I guessed you'd be here, at your sister's wedding." Dani's eyes were full of tenderness and love. What a look!

"You missed the whole thing," Dani said with a small chuckle.

"How was it?"

"Beautiful. Very traditional. This is a great place to get hitched. It was good to see everybody again. That man up there, the one in the blue shirt, that's my grandfather Antonio. And the woman in the yellow hat, that's my mother. Next to her, looking exceptionally handsome today, is my father." Dani snorted a laugh. "I'd introduce you, but it's all way too weird. I'm passing myself off as a distant cousin. Nobody asked any questions. They're all in a good mood and they haven't even started on the champagne yet. It turned out this was the perfect occasion to see them all for the last time, everyone all together and happy."

"Where's your brother? You said you had a younger brother."

Dani nodded, her smile fading. "Nick, yes. I just found out he's in prison. He's been there almost two years and won't be out for a long time."

"Oh, I'm sorry. What do you mean, you just found out? If he's been there two years…"

"He never went to prison in my timeline. He never got seriously into drugs. It's like Oreo was never Miko's dog, and you…" Dani stared deeper into Gemma's eyes. "You had your own consulting company. Some things are the same and some things are different. This is the worst thing, that Nick never straightened up and never went to college and probably never will."

"Because you weren't here?"

Dani nodded dejectedly.

Gemma searched between them for Dani's right hand and clasped it. "I'm so sorry I called the cops on you."

Dani gripped her hand tighter. "No hard feelings. I don't blame you. Of course you think I'm a lunatic. It's what I would have expected of you, but I was hoping for something else."

A little boy in a tiny tux trotted past them and out the front door. The adults followed more slowly, talking and passing their pew without noticing either of them on their way out.

"Did we get married here?" Gemma asked.

Dani looked at her warmly. "No. It wasn't nearly this grand. And besides—Catholic church." She shrugged.

"Oh, right."

"We got married at a historic Gold Rush hotel in the mountains. My parents and brother and sister came. Your mother and a few friends. It was small. That's the way you wanted it."

"I wish I could remember."

Dani opened the bag she carried and took a gold ring from it. "This is my wedding ring, the one you put on my finger, the same as the one you wore. I can tell you, Gem, I'd do it again in a heartbeat. The last four years were the best of my life. You made me a better person. I'd like to think I did the same for you, that you were really happy…except for the sloppiness. I should have tried harder with that." Dani lifted Gemma's hand and slid the ring on her finger. "You can keep this."

"Thank you." Gemma held her hand up to admire the ring. "I have something for you too. Is there someplace private we can go?"

"There's a little room over there. It's probably empty."

They made their way out of the pew. Gemma watched Dani move, noting that she was weak and clearly in pain. She seemed frail and smaller than before, so changed from the vigorous woman she had first met. They went through a side door to a small room that looked like a combination office and storeroom. It contained four chairs, a desk and a low table, and there wasn't room for anything else. Dani shut the door. "You believe me now?" she asked, pushing her bangs away from her eyes and looking beseechingly into Gemma's.

"I do." She put her hand in her pocket and pulled out the device. "But I'm confused about why you didn't come back for this, if it's really so essential, if it can save your life."

Dani's mouth fell open. "Oh, my God! You *do* have it."

"I told you I did."

"I thought…when I asked you that day to give it to me, you said you didn't have it."

"I meant I didn't have it on me. It was in my bedroom, and under the circumstances there was no way to get it."

"I thought it was part of the trap, just something you said to lure me there."

Gemma shook her head, holding the silver tube in the flat palm of her hand. "Take it."

Dani's hand shook as she picked up the device. Then she wrapped her hand around it tightly and swallowed hard. "Gemma, you've saved my life! Now I can go back." Dani's eyes shone with gratitude. She looked like she was about to cry.

"That little thing can really send you through time?"

"That's the idea. It reactivates the worm hole I came through and holds it open for the return trip. Something like that. They

tried to give me a crash course on temporal mechanics, but..."
She shook her head. "Maybe Miko can explain it to you."

"Is there a special place you have to be to use it? Some kind
of star gate or time portal or something?"

"No. I can do it right here." Dani flung her arms around
Gemma and hugged her close. It felt good to be in her arms.
After a moment of just holding one another, Dani kissed her,
flooding Gemma's body with warmth. It felt so right to be here
with her, their bodies pressed up against one another, their lips
touching. Gemma was sorry when Dani pulled away.

"What's the future like?" she asked.

"I didn't see much of it. I think it's probably a lot like here,
just with more fancy gadgets."

"I wish I could go with you."

"Me too." A look of sadness passed over her face. "I should
go."

"Do you have to go right now? Can't you stay a while?"

"I'm actually feeling pretty lousy. Things aren't working too
well inside my body. Besides, why drag it out? This is so tough
already. I'm going to miss you so much."

"Okay," Gemma said reluctantly. She felt that they had only
just been reunited. She wanted to get to know Dani and hear all
about the life they had shared. "What happens now?"

"I turn this thing on, then I disappear. There'll be a bright
flash of light, so you'll need to shield your eyes. And that's it.
You'll walk out of here and go on with your life. There is one
thing I want to say to you, Gem." Dani placed her hand on
Gemma's cheek and gazed into her eyes. "You can do anything
you set your mind to. You should pursue your dreams. Believe
me, you have it in you to succeed. It's already happened in the
other timeline, so go for it, okay?"

"Can I do it without you?"

"I'm sure you can. You just needed somebody to believe in
you so you could believe in yourself." Dani kissed her briefly on
the lips. "I believe in you."

Overcome with emotion, Gemma fell into one of the chairs.
Her heart was breaking. She was about to lose something
wonderful without ever having had the chance to know it.

"I always hate to see you cry," Dani said, stroking her hair. "Remember me and have a good life." Dani held the silver tube between her thumb and forefinger. "I love you, Gem, through all of time and space."

"I love you too, Dani," Gemma sobbed.

Dani twisted the top of the tube, causing three blue lights to illuminate. Gemma was afraid, afraid that nothing would happen and also afraid that something would happen. Dani smiled encouragingly at her, then placed her thumb on the top of the tube. Gemma gasped when a burst of white light filled the room. She closed her eyes and turned away until the light faded outside her closed eyelids. When she opened them, Dani was gone. She sat unmoving with her mouth open. So it was true, after all.

A flash of gold caught her eye. She looked down to see the ring on her finger.

CHAPTER TWENTY-SEVEN

Dani woke with the worst headache she'd ever had. She was lying on her back, feeling like she'd fallen off a three-story building. Maybe she had. She couldn't remember what had happened. She opened her eyes and looked around the eggshell-colored room. It had no windows and not much furniture. There was light but no light fixtures, no lamps. It looked familiar. She heard no sound except her own breathing. She moved her legs, then her arms. Nothing seemed broken or paralyzed, but she felt weak and nauseated.

Gradually, lying still and staring at the ceiling, she began to remember. This was the same room she'd awakened in before, the one she had mistaken for a hospital room.

She'd been in the church with Gemma. She'd used the beacon and transported back to the future. Apparently it had worked. But this time she was still wearing her own clothes, the outfit she'd worn to Rachel's wedding.

As she swung her legs over the side of the bed and sat up, her head felt like it would crack open.

"Oh, shit!" she said, waiting for the nausea to subside.

The door opened and Lara entered, looking just as she had before, right down to the clothes she was wearing. There was the same practiced smile on her face. If Lara was here, did that mean that Swenson and Hale were also here? Had they been here when Darius returned? Dani began to worry that Darius had failed. If he was out of the picture, that meant nobody could or would send her back to her own time. Considering how she had helped Darius, she knew she couldn't expect a lot of sympathy from Swenson. *It could get really ugly here*, she realized.

"Good afternoon," said Lara, handing her a glass of what looked like club soda. "Drink this. You'll feel better."

Dani looked at the glass, then smelled the liquid, the tiny bubbles tickling her nose. "How long have I been asleep?"

"One hour. We have been treating you for temporal asynchrony, but no solid food yet."

As if! Dani thought, her stomach clenching at the thought. "Is Dr. Darius here?" she asked.

"Yes. Dr. Darius is here and is waiting for you to wake up."

Relieved, Dani drank the liquid, noting that it tasted like club soda. Maybe it was. Not everything had to change over the course of two hundred years.

"You are particularly sensitive to the negative physical effects of transporting."

"Yeah, I was always the one who got car sick."

"Car sick," repeated Lara carefully.

"Motion sickness."

"Yes, I understand."

Dani handed Lara the glass, then she stood, grabbing the edge of the bedframe as a wave of dizziness struck.

"I can bring you a motorized chair," Lara offered.

Dani released the bed and stood to her full height. "I can walk."

She followed Lara shakily past the conference room where she had met with the others the first time and down a long, curving hallway to a pair of double doors. A sign next to them said, "Laboratory – Authorized Personnel Only." Under that was a panel with buttons and a screen. She had been here before, she remembered, the first time she'd transported back to her own time. This laboratory housed the time machine.

Lara stood in front of the panel and pushed a button. A light scanned her face, then the door opened.

Inside was a large, bright room with several counters, instrument panels, giant video screens, and a high ceiling pouring down light. The room was dominated by a twelve-foot-high circular chamber of metal and glass, the time machine. Leo Darius appeared from behind it and approached. He smiled, looking a lot better than he had when she'd last seen him. There was more color in his cheeks, more vigor in his body and his face was freshly shaved. He wore brown slacks and a white coat of shimmery material like satin, and over his ear he wore one of those iJinn devices.

"Welcome back, Dani," he said enthusiastically. "I'm overjoyed you found your beacon in time. How are you feeling?"

"I'll survive."

"Yes, you will. Without any permanent damage, I believe."

"What about you?" Dani asked. "Are you okay? I mean…" she glanced at Lara, careful to say nothing specific. "Did it go okay?"

"Yes, yes! No problem. Lara, thank you. You can go."

Lara left the lab and the two of them were alone.

"Can you trust her?" Dani asked.

"Of course," Darius laughed. "I programmed her."

Dani stared at the door that Lara had exited through, quickly revising her previous impressions of her. She turned back to Darius. "Are the beans safe?"

"Yes, yes. I've already started them." He led her to a table holding a glass box connected to plastic tubes cloudy with condensation. Inside the box were two black beans that had nearly doubled in size and sprouted tendrils of white roots. "I decided to try only two at first, in case something goes wrong. Then we'll have another chance. But we won't have too many chances with only ten beans. I'm optimistic though." He breathed deeply. "Those two little beans offer so much hope. It's hard for me to look at them without getting emotional."

"How's your shoulder?" Dani asked.

"Healing. And since I've been home, the pain has been minimal."

That was one feature of the iJinn Dani could live with, she decided. "What happened with Swenson and her boys?"

Darius waved a hand dismissively. "Taken care of. So, Dani, do you still want to return to your own time?"

"Yes, absolutely."

"Good. I'm anxious to see if it works." He rubbed his hands together. "As soon as you arrived this afternoon, I started working on the calculations. There'll be an extra step this time, removing the temporal signature imprinted on you. I believe it's possible because it was artificially applied and not an innate part of you. I think we've got a good chance. But remember, if I don't get the timing right, you'll be right back where you were. Out of phase."

"And nobody will know me. I'll have no past."

"That's right. And you'll be stuck. This time, you'll go back without a beacon. I can't give you one for a number of reasons. One, I can't let that technology exist in your time. And, two, if we are successful, you won't remember any of this and you'll have this odd-looking device in hand. You'll probably activate it out of curiosity, starting the whole thing over again. It's a one-shot deal. If you don't resync with your own time after I send you back, considering your already deteriorated condition, you'll only have a few days before…"

"I die."

He nodded grimly.

"It's worth the risk," Dani said with certainty. "I belong back there. I want to go back to my own life and have Sunday dinner at my parents' house with my wife and my sister and her new husband."

"I understand. I'd probably make the same choice. To tell you the truth, Dani, my time and your time are not so very different. We work, play, love, get old and die. Human experience doesn't change much. Only the trappings change. What really matters are the relationships we forge with other people. And you clearly have some meaningful ones."

"Were you able to pinpoint my arrival here?"

"Yes, no problem. Everything was recorded." He turned to a digital console. "It was October 3 at one thirty-seven forty-one in the afternoon. All we have to do is feed that time into the time machine's destination chronometer." He tapped a screen to his left.

Dani leaned in to see that the information on the screen currently read "0500, April 18, 1906." She looked up questioningly to meet his eyes. "Isn't that the day the great San Francisco earthquake took place?"

He appeared momentarily startled, then chuckled lightheartedly. "Yes, it is."

"You aren't planning on going there, are you?"

"No, no. Just spinning the dial, thinking about significant dates in history. And like I said before, we do experiment with inanimate objects. I was toying with the idea of sending them a bucket of water." He laughed unreservedly, then said, "Just kidding."

Darius seemed much more jolly than Dani remembered him. Of course, he had been sick and worried, then hunted and shot, so why wouldn't he be more jolly now that he was home and safe?

"If you're up to it," he said, "I'd like to send you back tomorrow morning."

"I'm up to it right now."

He smiled appreciatively. "You aren't, actually. I'm anxious to try it too, but you'll be stronger by morning. The medicine Lara's giving you will not only speed up your recovery, but it will help reduce the negative impact of your trip back. You can try some solid food this evening, and make sure you drink a lot of water."

"Do you think I could see outside?" she asked. "Just get a glimpse of what it's like here so I know what I'm turning down."

He smiled benignly. "Sure, why not?" He walked to the long wall opposite the door and waved his hand in front of it. Two of the curved panels slid apart, revealing a huge window like a viewing deck on a cruise ship. Dani walked over and looked out.

She was up above the city in a high-rise building. She could see a piece of the San Francisco Bay glittering in the slant sunlight of early evening. On the far left was a beautifully familiar sight, the Golden Gate Bridge, looking the same as ever except that there were other structures near it, transparent, tube-like structures spanning the Bay. She looked in the other direction and saw the same type of enclosed bridges. No sign of the Bay Bridge. The city itself was a mixture of many different styles of architecture, some familiar and some not familiar. There were large domes here and there and some of the newer-looking buildings were curving structures instead of rectangular. She thought about the building she was in, how the hallways curved. She looked for Coit Tower, another cylindrical building, and found it, dwarfed by other buildings, barely visible on Telegraph Hill. She found the Transamerica Pyramid, standing like an old friend amid other unfamiliar buildings. Many of the new buildings were made of a dark, shiny material that glinted like glass but did not look transparent. She looked down to the street below. It was busy with people walking and hundreds of moving vehicles that looked like giant eggs, all identical. People got in and out of them at corners, but they didn't park. While she watched, one of the eggs sprouted wings and shot straight up into the air, then zipped by the building, a red light flashing on top. Looking out at the horizon, she saw a few other of these flying eggs.

"What do you think?" Darius asked, drawing her attention from the view.

"It's incredible. Are those flying cars?"

"Yes. But not all of them fly. The airways wouldn't be able to cope with all the traffic, but emergency vehicles drive or fly, depending on the need. The ones you see in the air, most of those are ambulances. The earthbound vehicles aren't what you're used to either. They drive themselves and are solar powered. And they aren't privately owned. They're more like pods, part of a large public transportation system. You might travel to work in one of them and back home at the end of the day in another."

"Not so much fun to drive now, then, is it?"

"Fun?" He laughed. "No, not so much fun, but a lot safer. To us, your method where everybody drives around however they please, at whatever speed they please, crashing into each other, seems completely ludicrous. I can tell you now that I was terrified riding on your streets. That's not a reflection on your driving, by the way. I understand driving cars is very popular in virtual reality games, and we do have actual vehicles like yours for sport. You can rent one and go out on the open road, and some serious hobbyists own them, but they aren't used for everyday transportation anymore."

While they stood watching out the window, a blue and white machine flew up and hovered outside. It was about the size of a beach ball, had blinking red and blue lights, two spinning rotors, one on top and one behind, and two lenses that looked remarkably eye-like. On the side of the vehicle were the letters "SFPD."

Darius gave a friendly wave at the thing, then it turned and zipped away.

"What was that?" asked Dani.

"Police patrol drone."

"Robocop," Dani said.

"We're lucky it didn't scan you."

"Why?"

"It wouldn't be able to identify you. You're in no database. You also have no implant. It would tag you as a rogue and somebody would be here in no time to ask questions. We definitely want to avoid that sort of complication. If you see another one, duck."

Dani studied his face, a mixture of amusement and concern. She decided he was serious about ducking. "If I stayed here, would I have to get one of those brain implants?"

"Oh, yes, unless you wanted to live off the grid."

"Off the grid?"

"In the wilderness. Isolated. People do. It's a much harder life."

"Like survivalists."

"Yes. Not many people choose it."

Dani turned her attention back to the scene through the window. Dusk was beginning to cast a pink-tinted glow over the city. "Where are you with space travel? Have we walked on Mars?"

He put his hand on her shoulder. "Mars, yes, humans have set foot on Mars. Dani, we could talk for hours about what's happened in the last two hundred years in that field and many others, and how the Giants are doing these days and what passes for modern music. But I do have important work to do if we're going to be ready for your trip in the morning."

"Sorry. This is all so fascinating. I could ask you a million questions. Like about the vegetarian situation. Have you ever had a steak?"

He shook his head, looking slightly amused. "You're very fond of beef, aren't you?"

"Yeah. But I like fish too. Well, you know, San Francisco! How could I not? Living here, you must have had shellfish. Cioppino? What about abalone? God, that stuff's fabulous, but I've only had it a couple times. It's so damned expensive."

"Sadly, abalone has been extinct for a long time. Quite a few fish have gone extinct since your time. And land animals too, like the black rhino. Hunted to extinction by humans. So many other plants and animals have gone extinct from the destruction of their habitats."

"That's too bad. I was hoping we could have turned that around."

Darius frowned. "Too little too late. For every one shopper who brings her own bags to the store, a thousand others take home plastic bags."

"You don't still…"

He shook his head. "Oh, no, no, we don't use plastic bags, but *you* did. That's the problem. And your children did. No matter how much humans said they wanted to save the planet, with ten billion of them living on it, all selfishly choosing opulence and convenience, that was impossible."

"Ten billion?"

"Ten billion. All of them polluting the land, air and water and eating up all the plants and animals like a scourge of locusts across the face of the earth."

Darius's jolly demeanor had disappeared, replaced by downright anger that turned his face red. Dani instinctively took a step back from him.

"Once humans evolved on this planet," he continued, "it was doomed. No other species has ravaged its environment so completely as humans. It's indefensible, especially from a species that has declared itself *intelligent*." He spat out the final word.

"But you said six billion."

He looked confused. "What?"

"When you left me last week. You said there were six billion people."

"Ah, yes. There are six billion *now*. The population reached ten billion in 2071. It isn't unlikely that you will live to see that obscene milestone."

She did a rapid calculation in her head and realized he was right.

"If population growth was so out of control in the twenty-first century, what happened between then and now? Why the huge and rapid decline?"

"I would like to say that we wised up. But that isn't it. It's the plague. Remember what I told you. A deadly virus." He waved his hand to shut the window, then walked to the tiny greenhouse that contained the precious sprouting black beetle beans. "And these are the only known cure. Without them, it is possible that in time the plague could wipe out the entire human race." He spoke without emotion, staring at the glass box, and for a moment seemed to have forgotten Dani. At last he turned toward her, his demeanor cheerful again. "Have a restful evening, Dani. If you need anything, Lara will be available to you. I'll see you in the morning and then we'll send you back where you belong."

CHAPTER TWENTY-EIGHT

Dani couldn't sleep. She could see how the automatically adjusting temperature and firmness of the bed could provide a remarkably comfortable sleeping experience, but the strangeness of her surroundings and the anxiety over tomorrow weighed heavily on her thoughts, preventing her from relaxing. Also, she was hungry. The dinner she'd been given had been inadequate. She must be healing quickly, she realized, because she could think of nothing but cutting into a juicy rib eye steak. Not that she'd have that chance here. They were all vegetarians. Maybe that's why some people decided to live off the grid, so they could eat meat.

As soon as her feet touched the floor, light flooded into the room. She put on her clothes and slipped into her shoes. She stepped over to the door and it automatically opened for her. Her first step into the hallway brought Lara immediately to her side.

"Can I help you?" she asked with her odd smile.

Now that Dani knew she was a machine, she made no attempt to soften her opinion that Lara was really creepy.

"I'm hungry," Dani replied. "Can you bring me something to eat? That white stuff from dinner was edible, but none of that crunchy stuff, okay?"

"It is not time for eating now. It is time for sleeping."

"Maybe so, but I want something to eat. And I'd like to look outside while I'm eating. Is there a room with a view around here that I can use?"

"The lounge has a viewing window."

"Can I go there?"

"I have not been told otherwise. I will show you the way and bring you a meal."

"Thank you."

After walking a couple of minutes down a curving hallway, Lara left her in a room with tables and chairs and a huge window open to the city at night. Vehicles flew past, lit with red and white lights, and the entire city shone with the light from thousands of buildings. All the bridges were lit, looking like massive glow tubes. The scene was beautiful, and Dani had a hard time turning away from it when Lara reentered the room carrying a tray. After putting it on one of the tables, she left the room. Dani guessed that she hadn't gone far. She had the feeling she was being kept under close scrutiny. She could understand Darius being nervous about her. The best thing for him and for his top-secret facility was to get her out of here and back where she belonged as fast as possible.

She arranged her chair so she could look out the window while she ate. Lara had brought some of the white stuff as she had requested and something new, an orange, spongy square. Cube-shaped food seemed to be popular here. Dani tasted it cautiously. It was a little sweet, actually pretty good and reminded her of roasted carrots, something Gemma made a lot in the winter months. The white stuff needed salt, but she hadn't seen anything yet in the way of condiments or spices. *A bottle of Tabasco would go really far here*, she thought.

The scene out the window was mesmerizing, such a disquieting mixture of old and new. She finished the orange square and took a drink of water. A blue and white beach ball zipped past the window but didn't pause to look in. *What did they do with rogues?* she wondered before deciding she didn't want to find out firsthand.

She got up from the table and approached the window, scanning the horizon, locating familiar places illuminated by innumerable white lights. There was so much light that no stars were visible. Her gaze traveled in the direction of the Marina District and Cow Hollow. She tried to pick out Greenwich Street but wasn't sure she could see any of it. There were a lot of buildings in the way. She felt a hollow ache in her chest, knowing that Gemma Mettler no longer lived there, hadn't been living there for over a hundred years. If she had to stay here, how would she cope with that reality? Her parents, her brother, her sister were all long gone. Were there some descendants of theirs, her own great-nephews and nieces, still living here in San Francisco? If so, would she want to know about them?

She was startled from her thoughts by muffled noises from the other side of the left-hand wall. Possibly the sound of furniture moving. She got up and stood close to the wall to listen. Someone was in the room next to her. She could hear his voice, faintly and indistinctly, but well enough to know it wasn't Darius. She pressed her ear to the wall, then heard a woman's voice. It was familiar. It had to be Pamela Swenson, she decided.

Were they still here, then? Darius had said they had been taken care of. She had assumed they had been removed, arrested for trying to kill him. But she knew nothing about the penal system of the future. Maybe they didn't even have jails anymore. Maybe criminals could get instantly rehabilitated, like reprogramming a computer. They zapped your brain and you were all sweet and harmless again.

She listened more intently, but couldn't make out any actual words.

I'd like to give them a piece of my mind, she thought. *Maybe even a piece of my fist.* She turned from the wall and strode to the door, which immediately opened for her. Lara was in the hallway as if standing guard.

"Who's in the room next to this one?" she asked.

"You will have to ask Dr. Darius that question. He is asleep."

"Maybe I'll just take a look."

Dani swept past creepy Lara, but before she reached the door to the next room, Lara had run ahead of her and inserted herself between Dani and the doorway.

"You are not authorized for this area," Lara pronounced.

"Why not?"

"You will have to ask Dr. Darius that question. He is asleep."

"Why don't you go ask him for me?"

"I must stay with you."

"I'm beginning to get that." Dani approached the door, pushing Lara gently aside. The door did not open. It must be locked. There was a control panel beside it like the one at the entrance to the laboratory and the one at the exit door that had trapped her earlier. She vividly remembered the feeling of total helplessness. She didn't want that to happen again.

"Please go back to your room," Lara said.

Dani pounded on the door with her fist. "Who's in there?" she hollered.

Scuffling sounds from within suggested people moving around. Then she heard Swenson's voice on the other side of the door. "Hello?"

"Hello," Dani replied. "Is that Dr. Swenson?"

"Yes! Who are you?" There was a tinge of desperation in her voice.

Lara stood directly beside Dani and repeated her request. "Please go back to your room."

Ignoring Lara, Dani spoke to Swenson through the door. "It's Dani Barsetti. Open this door."

"We can't open it. We're locked in."

Dani stepped back from the door, confused. Lara took hold of her arm, her grip alarmingly strong, especially in contrast to her diminutive size. Her facial expression remained unchanged, the odd little smile even more odd under the circumstances. It was unnerving.

"Come with me," she said, pulling Dani by the arm.

Dani could tell that Lara could easily overpower her if she didn't cooperate. "Okay," she said. "No need to get rough. I'll go to my room."

Lara released her arm. Someone pounded on the other side of the door, then she heard Swenson ask, "Are you there?"

"Before I go to my room," Dani said to Lara, "can I get the rest of my meal? I haven't finished eating. I'll take it back to my own room."

Lara nodded and followed Dani back to the lounge, leaving Swenson pounding on the interior of the locked door.

"Did you enjoy your meal?" Lara asked, as if they had not just had a threatening confrontation.

"Yes, I did. I wouldn't say I could get entirely used to this type of food, but I wouldn't starve either." Dani picked up the tray, then deliberately dropped it to the floor. Food and utensils went flying. "Oops!" she said.

Lara leaned over to clean up just as Dani had hoped. She picked up a chair and smashed it over Lara's back, knocking her to the floor. She swung the chair again as hard as she could, aiming for the head. There was an audible crack when it connected. Dani wasn't sure if it came from the chair or Lara. She stood with the chair over her head, prepared to deliver another blow, but Lara lay unmoving, face down. Dani prodded her with her foot. There was no response. She put the chair down and turned Lara over. Her eyes were open and her expression was placid, but the eyes didn't blink, and Dani took that to mean that Lara was immobilized. She hoped she didn't have the ability to reboot herself.

Dani lifted the robot to her feet, then flung her over her shoulder. Though she was powerful, she was no heavier than a woman of her size. Dani returned to the room next door.

"What's happening?" Swenson shouted from within.

"I'm coming in," Dani called through the door.

She stood Lara in front of herself, then pressed the Open button on the control panel. When the scanner activated, she held Lara's head so the retina scan would pass over her face. When the white light went off, the door opened and Dani released Lara, who remained standing and motionless in the doorway.

Inside the room, Swenson and Hale stood staring in wonderment.

"What's going on here?" Dani demanded.

Her question seemed to stir Swenson to action. She rushed over to Lara and opened a panel on the back of her neck. "I'm making sure she stays off," she explained. "How did you do this?"

Dani shrugged. "Just hit her a couple times with a chair."

Swenson looked at her in astonishment. "Violence?" She turned toward Hale with an air of triumph. "I told you she was capable of it."

"Look," said Dani, "tell me what's going on? Are you prisoners?"

"Yes. Darius has taken control of the entire facility. He's locked us out of the system, so we can't communicate with anybody or leave." Dani noticed that neither of them wore an iJinn device.

"He's imprisoned you because you tried to kill him. Who could blame him?"

Swenson shook her head. "No. That isn't it. We don't have time to explain. We have to get to him before he realizes he's vulnerable. You, you can stop him. Like you did with her." She pointed at Lara. "Come on!"

"Wait." Dani took hold of Swenson's arm firmly. "You lied to me before, and I'm not about to help you, not without an explanation. So let's all sit down and talk."

Swenson frowned. "We don't have time to talk. You have to take care of Darius now." She pulled against Dani's grip, but Dani merely held on tighter.

"Whoa! We're not going anywhere and I'm certainly not going to bash anybody's head in just because you tell me to. You can understand that I might have trust issues, right?"

Swenson tried to yank her arm away again, her teeth set firmly in a determined grimace. "Release me!"

"I'm in charge now, okay?" Dani stared her down, her grip unyielding.

Swenson quit struggling, a look of resignation on her face. Dani released her and the three of them went inside where they sat around a table. Lara stood eerily in the open doorway, eyes open as if watching them.

"We couldn't tell you everything before," Swenson said. "We couldn't let you know who Darius really was. It would have created too many complications, too many difficult questions. It didn't seem like you needed to know everything, just that a dangerous man had to be stopped. We thought it would be easier for all of us, you included, if you had a simplified version of the truth. It all seemed so straightforward. You would find him, shoot him, and everything would be okay. But you failed."

"I didn't exactly fail. I had him, but I chose to let him go."

"What?" Hale stared unbelievingly at her. "Why would you do that?" He looked helplessly at Swenson, who turned her own questioning look back on Dani.

"He's obviously not what you told me he was. You lied to me. I'm only glad I found out before I killed an innocent man."

"Innocent? Leo Darius is a mass murderer. He's responsible for millions, even billions of deaths."

"Billions?"

"There's a virus," Swenson explained. "It's virulent and deadly."

"MRV," Dani said.

"You've heard of it?"

"Darius said it's your plague."

"That's true."

"That's why he wanted the seeds. He's growing them right now, to harvest and make the cure. I saw them myself in the lab. He's trying to save people from the plague."

Hale shook his head emphatically. "No. That's what he wants you to believe. That was our original plan. All of us agreed to it. That's what Bryan was sent back to do. His mission was to bring back the beans."

"Bryan? But he blew up the Genepac supply."

"No," Swenson said sharply. "Don't you see? You've been tricked. I told you he was clever. I told you not to listen to him. Darius followed Frank into your time to stop him from bringing the beans back. He blew up Genepac just like Frank told you he did. And then he tricked you into giving him the only remaining beans in the world. My God, Daniella, do you know what you've done?"

Dani's mind was spinning. "I don't understand. Why? How has Darius murdered billions of people?"

Dr. Hale looked deadly serious, leaning forward into the table. "He went back in time." he said quietly. "He went back to the year 2100 with a mutated version of MRV, a version he engineered himself to be deadly to humans. We've known ever since your time that MRV was a tough bug to kill, which is why he chose it."

"Dr. Littleton told me that's why she liked to use it in her tests."

"Darius turned a harmless virus into a deadly one. With the mutation he created, he had a very effective biological weapon at his disposal. During his trip to 2100, he released the virus into the population. From that date forward, it has been killing off what Darius believes is a contagion on the planet—humans."

Dani felt a chill run up her spine, recalling the angry words Darius had spoken to her earlier.

"If Darius has his way," Swenson added, "he will do everything he can to make sure humans are completely eradicated. The reason he wants the beetle beans is that he's experimenting with a new version of MRV, one that has no cure. He wants to be sure his new virus is resistant to the beetle bean agent, so he's growing the beans to test it. Even though he can now destroy all of the beetle beans in existence, he's obsessed with making sure nobody ever finds a way to defeat his virus."

"If this is true, why don't you tell the police or the FBI or whoever you need to tell to get him locked up?"

"We can't prove that he did it," Hale said. "He'll deny it. Just like he did with you."

"He's erased the records of his trip to 2100," Swenson added. "The logs show nothing and nobody witnessed the trip."

"Then how do *you* know he did it? He told me himself that the virus mutated, that the world population topped out at ten billion and then began falling because of the virus."

"Actually the world population stabilized at ten billion *before* the virus came into the picture. There were some very effective attempts to curb population growth. I believe that we would have been able to control it naturally, that the problem was on the verge of being solved. Darius and I had this argument many times. He didn't think it was possible to stop population growth without a radical intervention like a global environmental catastrophe or a helpful little microbe that infected only humans."

"What's the evidence that Darius created the helpful little microbe?"

"It's a matter of deduction," Hale replied. "There is no doubt he's been working with MRV. He even admits that. The only reason we know this at all is that I saw the log entry before he erased it. It was there one morning, an unplanned transport to April 15, 2100, Beijing, China. I asked him about it. He said it was just a probe he had sent to collect air samples. I don't think it was collecting air samples. I think it was releasing the virus. From there, the virus would take care of the rest and it would appear to have occurred naturally. Because if it was just a harmless probe, why did he erase the evidence?"

Swenson intervened. "The first confirmed case of a death caused by MRV was in Beijing on April 24, 2100, nine days after the so-called probe sent by Darius. We have no proof he's responsible. But we know he did it. Look, he's locked us up here because we know it. He's going to keep us here until he's created a version of MRV that's resistant to the beetle beans. Then it won't matter what he does or what we do. The virus will be on the loose and there won't be any way to stop it."

"Won't somebody notice you didn't come home? You do have homes, don't you? Kids? Spouses?"

"I live alone," Hale said with a shrug. "Except for my cat Pharoah."

"Right. The cat from ancient Egypt." Dani turned her gaze to Swenson.

"Frank Bryan was my husband," she said. "There's nobody else at home."

Taken aback, Dani met her eyes with remorse, remembering how she had delivered the news of Bryan's death. "I'm sorry."

"By the time someone notices we're missing it will be too late. Darius will have his superbug."

"Have you tried to go back to 2100 yourselves to stop him before he released the virus?"

Hale shook his head. "Over a hundred years of history has happened since that time. If we could do what you're suggesting, we would completely rewrite history, *our* history. Things might even be worse. Anything could happen. All of the billions of people who have died from the plague would never have died from it. Our world would be unrecognizable in billions of unpredictable ways. We can't do that. It's already happened and this is now our reality. We can live with that. But we can't let him continue the annihilation of humanity, and we can't let him control the world's supply of black beetle beans. He must be stopped now!"

"And you can't kill him because…?"

The two of them exchanged looks with one another before Swenson said, "There's a microchip in our…"

"Oh, right," Dani said, slapping the table with her palm. "The chip. Sends a little shock wave to shut down your brain if you lift a hand against your fellow man."

"Something like that."

"So a man can kill billions of people, but he can't kill one bad guy? Seems like there's a flaw in this technology."

"We can't just sit here chatting all night." Swenson stood. "We need to get those beans."

Dani also stood, blocking Swenson's way to the door. "I didn't say I believe you."

"What is wrong with you?" she asked angrily. "You already let him get away once."

"You said yourself you have no evidence that he's responsible for the plague. It's conjecture. You also have no evidence he isn't working on the cure. The beans are growing in the lab. You're telling me he's making an indestructible virus. He's telling me he's making a cure. Why should I believe you when I know you've already lied to me?"

Dr. Swenson shrank back from Dani, looking frustrated.

"You two can stay locked up in here for now while I talk to Darius. I'll get to the bottom of this."

"No!" Hale screamed. "You can't do this!" He lunged for her, his arms outstretched as if he intended to strangle her.

She jumped back and watched his body go rigid, shudder and fall to the floor with a thud. He lay motionless on his side, eyes open, looking mystified. *Okay*, she thought appreciatively, *so that's how it works.*

Swenson knelt beside him, rolling him onto his back into a more natural position.

"How long is he going to be like that?" Dani asked.

"About fifteen minutes."

Dani stepped around Lara to get out of the room.

"You're making a big mistake," Swenson warned. "He tricked you once. He can do it again."

"We'll see. But you can understand why I can't just take your word for it?"

"I'm sorry I couldn't tell you the entire truth, Daniella. Mr. Moon wouldn't allow it."

Dani paused, looking back over Lara's shoulder. "Speaking of old Filbert, where is he, by the way? Locked up somewhere else?"

Swenson shook her head forlornly. "No. He resisted. He tried to escape and contact his superiors. Despite lack of hard evidence, he thought he could buy us some time by convening an investigative panel. He wasn't able to escape. Lara saw to that. Then Darius punished him."

"Punished him how?"

"He sent him back in time without a transporter. He threatened to do the same to us if we resisted. Moon is doomed to die of temporal asynchrony among strangers. If he survives the earthquake and fires, that is."

"Earthquake?" Dani's nerves went taut.

"Darius sent him to San Francisco, April 18, 1906, a few minutes before the earthquake would hit."

An image of the time machine chronometer flashed through Dani's mind. 0500, April 18, 1906. Swenson didn't know Dani had seen that. And Darius had not explained it, had laughed it off, but there had to be some reason the time machine had been set to that date.

"Jesus!" Dani squeezed her eyes shut, a sinking feeling in her gut. *Everybody was such a damned good liar in the future!* When she opened her eyes, she met the pleading look of Pamela Swenson head on. "Okay," she relented. "How do we take him down?"

"We still have no evidence against him that would stand up in any court. That's our problem. We can't do anything here. We have to do the same thing to him that he did to Moon, imprison him in the past."

"Where he'll die a painful death?" Dani shook her head.

"Daniella," Swenson said soberly, "you've never seen someone die of the MRV virus. It's horrific. And not only is it a horrible death, but it's a lonely one. Nobody wants to be anywhere near someone who's infected. Patients are quarantined and their fearful relatives stay away."

A full understanding of the gravity of Darius's crimes began to gel for Dani. The human population of the planet had already been decimated by what he had done and he wasn't finished yet. She nodded slowly. "Send him back with me to my time."

"You? You can't go back. That's suicide."

"Not necessarily. Darius said I might be able to go back. If you send me back to the precise moment I left, I might resync with my own timeline. He was going to send me back tomorrow morning. Is it possible?"

"I suppose it's possible. Gavin is more qualified to answer that than I am. We'll have to subdue Darius somehow. Can you knock him over the head a couple times with a chair?"

Dani couldn't help but smile at the hopeful look on Swenson's face. "There's probably a simpler way."

"Yes, sorry. I can prepare a sedative and you can inject him with it. Then we'll need to find a way to get into the lab. We've been locked out."

"We've got her," Dani said, jerking her head toward Lara.

A smile spread across Swenson's face.

Dani picked up Lara and slung her over her shoulder. "Okay. It's a plan."

CHAPTER TWENTY-NINE

Darius sat slumped in a chair while Dr. Hale worked on the time machine, preparing to send them back to the twenty-first century. Most of the preparatory work had already been done by Darius. All Hale had to do was set the chronometer and activate the machine.

"I've found the log entry," he said over his shoulder. "You came through on Monday, October 3, at one thirty-seven in the afternoon. We can send you back to a couple of seconds before you zapped out."

"Will a couple of seconds be close enough?" Dani asked.

"It has to be. If I put you back at the exact moment, the moment you activated the beacon, you'll come right back here. There will be no chance to change anything. We have to catch you before you activate it. We also have to be sure Darius doesn't get his hands on Bryan's beacon."

"How do we do that?" asked Dani. "If I resync with my own timeline, I won't know what's going on. I won't know what the beacon is or that Darius needs to be kept from it."

"That's why I'm coming with you," Swenson said. "I'm going to take the beacon away from you myself, then use it to come back here. That will leave you and Darius in the past with no means of returning. If this doesn't work, you won't have another chance. You'll both be trapped in the past and will die."

"At least we won't die alone then." Dani swallowed hard, her mind returning to the scene outside the window earlier in the evening. She might like it here. At least she was guaranteed a natural life. But then she thought of Gemma and how lonely the passing years here would be without her. She also thought of her brother Nick. If she didn't go back, his life would be destroyed. Between Gemma and Nick, it was definitely worth the risk to try. "Am I going to pass out like the other times?"

"You shouldn't," Swenson said. "We gave you a double dose of phenethylamine this time so you can cope better with the physical shock. There will still be some disorientation, but it should be brief."

Dani nodded. "I'm ready."

Darius groaned and rolled his head to the side. The sedative was wearing off.

"Hurry up," Swenson shot at Hale.

"Okay. Almost there. Get him into the machine. I just need a couple more minutes."

Dani and Swenson each took hold of one of Darius's arms and lifted him to his feet. He opened his eyes and looked at Dani without seeming to see her. They half dragged, half walked him into the time machine where they held him up between them.

"What exactly is going to happen?" Dani asked Swenson.

"We'll travel together back to the moment you left your time. As soon as we materialize there, one of two scenarios will take place. The first possibility is that we will look at one another and realize we failed, which will be obvious because of how you're dressed."

Dani glanced down at her shirt and black jeans. "Huh?"

"You were wearing your uniform when you left your timeline. The second possibility is that we will succeed. You will resync with your time and immediately forget everything that happened since you left it. At that point, you will have Bryan's transport beacon in your hand and it will be activated. I'll have only a second or so to take it from you before you transport here like you did the first time. Once I take the beacon from you, I'll disappear and you'll have your life back."

"This is so confusing. If we succeed and everything that's happened since I picked up that beacon never happened, what about Darius and the beans? Did that happen?"

"It's only your timeline that will change. Events will be altered for you and those whose lives you interact with, but not for us. We will simply go on from here. We'll have the beans. Dr. Littleton will never see them. But it was never an important discovery in your time, so the loss is inconsequential."

"Will you try to go back again to fix some of the things that went wrong this time? Like stopping Darius from killing Agent...I mean your husband?"

A wave of sadness passed across Swenson's face. "No. It's too dangerous. We have to be satisfied with getting the beans. That's the main thing. If this experience has proven anything, it's shown how unpredictable a trip into the past can be. After our first actual mission, two people have already lost their lives, Frank and Mr. Moon. Depending on the outcome of the trip we're about to take, the count will be either three or four." She inclined her head toward Darius, who was mumbling almost inaudibly, his eyes closed. "Truly, this has been a disaster. I'd be surprised if this project was allowed to continue at all. Even if it is, without Darius..." She glanced toward Hale, who was not facing them, but was obviously listening. "Let's just say, we have a significant learning curve ahead of us."

Darius stirred, looking from one to the other of them with bewilderment.

"Let's go," Swenson said firmly.

"What's this?" Darius demanded, tugging his arm against Dani's grip. She held on more tightly.

"Good luck!" Hale called to them. "I hope to see you soon, Pamela." He pressed a button and the chamber began to rotate. Dani's heart pounded fast.

"Stop!" Darius hollered, trying to pull away from the women holding him. But he was weakened by the sedative and they were both able to maintain their grip.

The chamber began to hum. The humming got louder and Dani felt dizzy. She closed her eyes, but even with them closed, she saw a bright flash of light through her eyelids. Her stomach lurched. Then everything spun out of control.

CHAPTER THIRTY

Gemma tossed a manila folder carelessly on her desk. It slid into her pencil cup and knocked it over, sending pens and pencils skittering across the floor. She breathed out a shoulder-slumping sigh.

Lois removed her earbuds and looked up expectantly. "Didn't Sylvester like your report?" she asked.

John Sylvestri was their boss, but Lois always called him Sylvester. One small way she wrested a bit of perceived power from a powerless situation. But, in reality, she had no power and no influence, and neither did Gemma. They were mere functionaries.

"He didn't like it or not like it," she said. "We never got that far." She knelt to scoop up the items on the floor. "He gave me the wrong set of stats from the Midwest, so the whole thing's a bust."

"You mean you have to do it over?"

Gemma fell into her desk chair without answering.

"But I thought it was due this morning."

"It was. So now I'm sure Sylvestri is marching down to the director's office to tell him I screwed up and it's going to be late."

"Bastard," muttered Lois.

Gemma logged into her computer.

"Aren't you going to eat lunch? It's nearly one thirty."

"I guess so, yeah. The report's already way late, after all. What's another half hour, right?"

"You don't sound angry," observed Lois.

"No, I'm over being angry. Except maybe at myself."

"Why?"

"I have to ask myself, why am I here? It's not really Sylvestri's fault that I'm spending my days on Excel spreadsheets instead of doing something more challenging." She thought of what Dani had told her, about how she had her own business in the other timeline. She'd been thinking about that a lot.

"What do you want to do instead?" asked Lois.

Gemma fished a ramen noodle cup from her bag. She ripped the plastic off and peeled back the top cover. "I'm a nutritionist. I should be working with people directly to improve their eating habits, their health and their lives."

Lois laughed, which perplexed Gemma. She turned to face her. "Look what you're eating for lunch. You should start with yourself."

Gemma shrugged. "I know, but it's just so easy and I didn't feel like doing anything this morning." She filled her hot water pot and turned it on. It immediately began to gurgle.

Lois had a ham sandwich on white bread. Neither of them would make much of a poster child for the agency today.

A moment of silence passed while Lois ate and Gemma plotted another line of dots on her graph as she waited for the noodles to soften. When they were ready, she faced the wall, her back to Lois, and twirled the noodles onto a plastic fork, relishing the hot, slurpy saltiness of her forbidden meal. After a couple of bites, she stopped eating and sat back in her chair, remembering what Dani had told her about who she was in the other timeline. She had drive and passion. She had achieved something important. She couldn't just keep dreaming and complaining day after day. She had to actually do something.

She turned to Lois. "You're right. Why am I eating this? Starting tomorrow, I'll make some effort to bring a better lunch. And then I'm going to start planning for a new career."

"Doing what?"

"Improving the food served in hospitals and nursing homes. What we always talk about."

Lois nodded appreciatively. "More power to you, girl!"

Gemma swiveled in her chair to look out the window. From this office on Harbor View Parkway, she had a view of the park across the street with its tranquil fountains and walking paths. Most of the trees were evergreens, but here and there was a maple, adding autumn color to the view. Maybe she would never see Dani again, nor would she ever know what it was like to be her life partner, but she did know that with Dani she would have been a better person. She would have faced life's challenges with more resolve. She would have had more confidence and more optimism. She knew all of those attributes had to be within her even without Dani. Maybe Dani could replace Bloody Betty and be her new secret cheerleader, the voice she called on in times of need. She remembered Dani saying "I believe in you" and "I love you." She would always remember and cherish those words. She felt for the gold chain around her neck and pulled the wedding ring into view, clasping it in her palm. She hoped Dani would be happy living in the future.

The scene out the window swam before her eyes, blurring into a mottled backdrop of green with dots of yellow and orange. She turned back to her desk and wiped a tear from her cheek. She reached for a Kleenex, but the box wasn't where it always was. A wave of dizziness overcame her and she felt that her chair was tipping over. She grabbed the edge of her desk to keep herself upright. The disorientation was almost immediately over and everything was solid and certain again. Nothing seemed disturbed. The wall clock, showing the time as one thirty-eight, was still on the wall, as were her pictures and bookshelves. She glanced out the window at the busy street and the Burger King across the way. People were going about their business. Nobody seemed panicked.

"Shelley!" she called through the open door.

In two seconds, Shelley was in the room, an alarmed expression on her face, her short ruffled skirt looking as absurd as ever. "What is it?"

"Did we just have an earthquake?"

"I didn't feel anything. Are you okay?"

Gemma nodded. "Yes. Everything's fine. It must have been small, at least here. But why don't you check on it anyway, in case it hit hard somewhere else?"

Shelley nodded and was about to leave, but then paused in the doorway. "I almost forgot to ask. How did it go this morning in San Raphael?"

Gemma felt a rush of triumph, remembering her morning. "I'm sure I've got the contract. I've been dying for you to get back from lunch so I could tell you."

"Congratulations! That's super. You're heading for the big time, Ms. Mettler."

"Thanks. I can't wait to tell Dani. She's never surprised. She always just says, 'Told you so,' but she'll be thrilled anyway. I think I'll take the rest of the afternoon off and swing by to see my mother before going home. Earthquakes always make me a little anxious."

"I know what you mean. Let me check on that before you go." Shelley returned to her office, and Gemma packed some folders into her briefcase, checked her email one more time, then logged out of the computer.

Shelley stuck her head back in. "No earthquakes reported in the Bay Area today, Gemma."

"Hmmm. Okay. That's good. I guess it was just me, then. A bit of vertigo."

"You're not pregnant, are you?" Shelley grinned.

"Not yet." Gemma felt satisfaction at Shelley's surprised gape. She hadn't shared with Shelley her intentions of starting a family. She hadn't told anybody, but the idea was growing more and more real in her mind, so it was time everybody started getting used to it.

* * *

Dani's knees buckled and she nearly went down, assailed by dizziness and disorientation. For a split second, she didn't know where she was or what was happening. She felt someone's fingers pry her right hand open and wrench something from her grasp. She tried hard to focus on the person beside her. It was a woman with auburn hair and piercing brown eyes. In her hand was a small silver tube with glowing blue lights, the same object Dani had just picked up from the roof. The woman knelt beside Agent Bryan's body and touched two fingers tenderly to his lips.

"Who are you?" Dani asked. "Where did you come from?"

The woman stood and faced her. She appeared to smile, then she nodded at Dani conspiratorially before disappearing in a burst of blinding white light. Dani instinctively shut her eyes. When she opened them, she was alone on the roof with Agent Bryan's body.

Perkins burst from the stairwell and jogged to her side, his attention riveted on Bryan. "Is he..."

"He's dead."

"Darius?"

Dani nodded. Both of them scanned the roof for the suspect. "I already checked behind the HVAC units. He's gotten off this roof somehow. I don't know if he went down the fire escape or..."

"There he is!" Perkins yelled, pulling his weapon.

Dani followed his aim to see a man in brown pants on the neighboring rooftop. He was staring at them, standing motionless in full view. His hands were empty. No weapon. He looked directly into Dani's eyes, and she thought she could read ambivalence there. Was he going to give himself up?

"Stop!" Perkins commanded. "Put your hands in the air!"

"Dani," hollered Darius across the gap between them. "Look at your clothes! Look at your clothes! It worked!" A triumphant smile broke out on his face and he clapped his hands together gleefully.

"What the hell is with this guy?" Perkins muttered. Then to Darius, he ordered, "Hands on your head, now!"

Dani glanced down at her uniform, confused. There was nothing to see, nothing out of the ordinary.

Instead of putting up his hands, Darius took off running, his body lurching like he was drunk. Perkins fired a shot and missed him, but the gunfire caused the suspect to turn and look their way, still running. He tripped over something and went flying. Dani gasped and watched as Darius landed on the lip of the roof and flipped over it, his body launching itself into the air. She and Perkins sprinted to the edge of their building and looked over. Several stories beneath them, in the alley below, the man lay on the pavement, his limbs crumpled into unnatural angles. Dani saw his leg jerk once, then he lay motionless. Within seconds, several police officers convened on the spot, but there was no sense of urgency below. Darius was obviously dead.

CHAPTER THIRTY-ONE

After swinging by Palm Terrace to reassure herself that her mother was okay, Gemma drove home. She didn't know why she felt disoriented, especially if there had been no earthquake. Maybe it was just the stress of the big meeting this morning. She'd been preparing for it for weeks and it had taken a lot out of her. She parked in her driveway and waved at her neighbor Joanne watering her flower boxes.

She walked up to the steps and put the key in the lock, marveling again at how smoothly the new deadbolt slid back. It was nice to have a handy person around, especially with an old house like this. From inside the apartment, she could hear Tucker barking in joyful anticipation of her arrival. She opened the door to greet him. He ran up and put his front paws on her leg, begging for attention. She scooped him into her arms and went into the bedroom to take off her shoes. Dani's pajamas were on the floor by the bathroom where she had taken them off before her shower.

Gemma put Tucker down and picked up the pajamas with a sigh. "I'm not even going to try anymore," she said. "She just can't put anything where it belongs." She looked at the dresser. One side belonged to her, the other to Dani. On the Gemma side, a few bottles, decorative boxes and a tray for her phone and money were carefully placed. On the other side, a chaotic jumble of coins, electronics cords and chargers, papers, photos, rubber bands, plastic bags, credit cards and a couple of magazines clearly told the story of their personalities. Gemma smiled to herself. "For better or worse," she mumbled.

After changing into her house shoes, she went to the kitchen to wash the dishes from the morning. She remembered their argument and felt sorry. She'd been worried about her mother, about what would happen if she got kicked out of another nursing home. And she'd been tense because of her upcoming interview. She'd taken it out on Dani. But, really, Dani had done nothing wrong. She'd make it up to her tonight. They'd have a nice dinner out to celebrate her victory, then go to bed early. Gemma smiled to herself.

A half hour later Dani leaned over her shoulder in the kitchen and kissed her on the neck. When Gemma turned around, she saw that Dani was holding an African violet in a colorful little pot. The flowers were an intriguing shade of orange.

"Sorry for this morning," she said, smiling repentantly.

Gemma took the plant. "It's forgotten. Thank you for this. I love it. It's a very unusual color." She placed the pot next to the others on the windowsill, then turned around and kissed Dani, savoring her mouth deeply before stepping back. Tucker hopped around Dani's legs expectantly. She leaned over and scratched behind his ears. "You miss me, boy?" she asked, laughing at his joyful expression.

When she stood up, she said, "So how did the interview go today?"

"Terrific!"

Dani grabbed her and swung her around in a circle, then set her down and kissed her. "I knew it."

"I think they loved me."

"Who wouldn't love you? I'm so happy for you. For us. And so proud of you."

"Thanks." Gemma retrieved her glass of iced tea from the counter. "Do you want one of these?"

Dani nodded and sat at the kitchen table, stretching her arms above her head. "Tell me all about it."

"I intend to." Gemma filled a glass with ice. "I thought we could go out to dinner and I'll talk your ear off, telling you how incredible I was."

Dani chuckled.

"You're home earlier than I thought you'd be. Did Rachel get her dress?"

"Oh, I called her and asked if we could do it tomorrow. I just couldn't get away early today."

When Gemma placed the glass of iced tea on the table, she noticed Dani rubbing her temple.

"What's wrong? Aren't you feeling well?"

"It's nothing. Just a headache."

"Do you want some aspirin?"

"No, thanks. I took some down at the station before I left. It's better already."

Gemma leaned against the counter, facing Dani. "How was your day?"

"It wasn't great. We lost a man today."

"Oh! Not again!"

"Not one of ours. An FBI agent. The one I told you about, the one who was after this Darius guy. That's who shot him, actually."

"Did you get him?"

"We did. He's dead too. He fell off a building."

"Oh, dear. I hope you didn't see that."

"I did actually."

Gemma approached her and gave her a hug. "I'm so sorry."

"It's okay. At least he didn't get away. It was a weird day. There were a couple of minutes there where...I don't know what happened. Maybe I blacked out. I thought I saw a woman who leaned over Agent Bryan's body, then disappeared in a flash of light." Dani shook her head. "If I didn't know better, I'd think I saw an angel."

Gemma circled her arm around Dani's shoulders. "Are you sure you're okay?"

"I'll be fine."

Gemma cradled Dani's head in her hands, then stroked her gently. "I'm so glad you're safe. God, Dani, I don't know what I'd do if I lost you. My life would be nothing, so empty and meaningless."

Dani put her hand over Gemma's. "Don't worry. I'm still here. I wasn't hurt. It's just a headache."

"Did the FBI agent have a family?"

"I don't know. Nobody knows much about him. It's a real mystery, actually. He may not even be an FBI agent. The FBI says they've never heard of him. We're running his prints, but it's obvious he was working under an assumed name. It's the same with Darius. I have a feeling we'll never get the real story about those two."

Dani drained half the glass of tea in one swallow while Gemma returned to the sink to let out the dishwater.

"There was another mystery down at the station today," said Dani. "You remember the collection we've got going on for that little girl with leukemia, Lydia?"

"Sure. The girl who wants to go to London."

"Right. Yesterday we were almost to a thousand dollars."

"Not very impressive after all this time."

"Exactly, but today Riley starts screaming from the break room and everybody comes running, thinking he's shot his leg off or something. Turns out he was just collecting the donations. Somebody put ten thousand dollars in the box."

Gemma spun around to stare. "Did you say ten *thousand*?"

Dani nodded. "A big wad of hundreds."

"Who did it?"

"Nobody fessed up. Nobody knows. I guess they want to be anonymous. Maybe it's some sort of atonement. There doesn't seem to be anything funny about the money. We ran a couple of the serial numbers just to be sure. It's legit."

"That's incredible."

"I know. It's enough. We can send the kid and her whole family to England to watch the changing of the guards at

Buckingham Palace or whatever it is she wants to do." Dani stood and slipped her arms around Gemma's waist. "I'm so glad I have you to come home to, Gem. You and Tucker. I'm a lucky woman." She kissed Gemma on the mouth, then said, "I'll go shower, then we can go paint the town red. Maybe even a little dancing?" Dani grinned and peeled off her sweater.

"That would be fun."

Dani produced a folded piece of paper from her sweater pocket. "By the way, I was talking to one of the guys today at the station. He and his wife have been trying to get pregnant for a while. They finally did." Dani looked uncharacteristically sheepish as she handed the paper to Gemma. "That's the name of their doctor. He said she's really easy to work with. Very accessible. And they've seen lesbian couples there, so..." Dani averted her eyes, looking uncomfortable.

Gemma glanced at the name on the paper, then wrapped her arms around Dani and kissed her on her reddening cheek.

Dani gave her a knowing nod before heading out of the kitchen, Tucker trotting along at her heels.

Gemma hollered after her. "And don't leave your underwear on the bathroom floor. There's a place for that, you know?"

She heard a grunt from the hallway, Dani's usual non-committal response.

"I love you too, babe," she said quietly to herself. She placed the doctor's name under a magnet on the refrigerator, then went back to putting away dishes, grateful for her wonderful wife and her wonderful life.

EPILOGUE

After cleaning up a traffic accident at Haight and Divisidero, Dani and Perkins returned to their patrol car. It was Tuesday afternoon. So far, their day had been quiet. Dani was more than thankful for that after yesterday's craziness. Perkins hitched up his pants before punching the key fob to unlock the car doors.

Coming around to the passenger side, Dani noticed they'd parked next to a familiar historic landmark. "Have you ever seen this?" she asked, waving Perkins over. She pointed to a bronze plaque embedded in a concrete marker. He stepped closer to read it, and she read it for the hundredth time silently to herself.

"During the great earthquake of 1906, on this spot, Filbert Moon, a drifter of unknown origin, pushed Mrs. Violet Baumbach and her daughter Eliza out of the way of a falling building, sacrificing his life to save theirs. As he lay dying under a pile of rubble, Mrs. Baumbach thanked him and expressed her sorrow that he would not survive. 'No need to worry, madam,' he said. 'I have lived well in my time.'"

After reading the plaque, Perkins shot Dani a questioning look. "Yeah, nice bit of San Francisco trivia," he said. "What about it?"

"The girl, Eliza Baumbach, was my great-great-grandmother."

Perkins glanced back at the plaque with greater appreciation. "Wow. So if this Moon guy hadn't pushed them out of the way, you'd never have been born."

"Exactly. This is one of our favorite family stories. The only problem is that we've never been able to figure out who this Filbert Moon was. With a unique name like that, you'd think it would be easy, but a lot of family members have researched it with no results. Filbert Moon remains a mystery."

"Well, maybe his sole recordable achievement in his life was this one selfless act."

Dani shrugged. "Maybe so."

They returned to the patrol car and resumed their normal beat. Perkins drove while Dani sat in the passenger seat watching out the window. She was still thinking about Leo Darius lying on the street where he had fallen to his death. She realized Perkins was also preoccupied with Darius when he said, "What did he mean by 'It worked'?"

Dani shook her head. "No idea. I don't know how he knew my name either."

"Ah, the guy was unhinged. You can't make sense out of somebody like that."

They passed by the panhandle of Golden Gate Park. Gus was in the process of lifting a little girl onto the pony cart. She was about six years old and grinning ear to ear. Her mother waited until she was seated before climbing on board herself. Comet looked bored, her eyes half shut.

Perkins turned down Hyde and they rode between apartment houses while Dani ticked off familiar landmarks in her mind. Ahead was a glimpse of the bay with Alcatraz in the foreground and the smooth hills of Angel Island behind that. A cable car loaded with passengers came toward them, bringing with it the familiar clang of the bell and the laughter of vacationers. When they passed Lombard Street, the crookedest street in the world, Dani couldn't help looking down at its kinky twists. A solid line of cars drove slowly down it, tourists checking off one of the items on their list of must-dos. Beyond and below, a solid block of white buildings spread out to the edge of the bay. Coit Tower rose up from a clump of greenery above them all. The sky was clear and the water calm and blue, dotted with a few white sails. It was a magnificent city, she thought. People were always predicting it would fall into the ocean when the next big earthquake ripped through the San Andreas Fault, but Dani had a feeling it would always be here, the shining city by the bay, shining into the future for a long, long time to come.

Bella Books, Inc.

Women. Books. Even Better Together.

P.O. Box 10543
Tallahassee, FL 32302

Phone: 800-729-4992
www.bellabooks.com